D0734893

what we knew

also by
barbara stewart

the in-between

what we knew

barbara stewart

st. martin's griffin ⚞ new york

This is a work of fiction. All of the characters, organizations, and events portrayed in this novel or either products of the author's imagination or are used fictitiously.

WHAT WE KNEW. Copyright © 2015 by Barbara Stewart. All rights reserved. Printed in the United States of America. For information, address St. Martin's Press, 175 Fifth Avenue, New York, N.Y. 10010.

www.stmartins.com

Designed by Anna Gorovoy

The Library of Congress Cataloging-in-Publication Data is available upon request.

ISBN 978-1-250-05139-4 (trade paperback)
ISBN 978-1-4668-6714-7 (e-book)

St. Martin's Griffin books may be purchased for educational, business, or promotional use. For information on bulk purchases, please contact the Macmillan Corporate and Premium Sales Department at 1-800-221-7945, extension 5442, or write to specialmarkets@macmillan.com.

First Edition: July 2015

10 9 8 7 6 5 4 3 2 1

for kelly

acknowledgments

Special thanks to my agent, Amy Tipton, and my editor, Vicki Lame. I'm honored to work with you both.

Thanks to my team at St. Martin's Press: Elizabeth Curione, Marie Estrada, Joy Gannon, Anna Gorovoy, Bridget Hartzle, Karen Masnica, Lisa Marie Pompilio, and NaNá Stoelzle.

Thanks to my family: Mom and Dad, Kelly, Fred, Mary, Sarah, Fred, and Sue. You guys are the best!

And finally, a big thank-you to Dave—for everything.

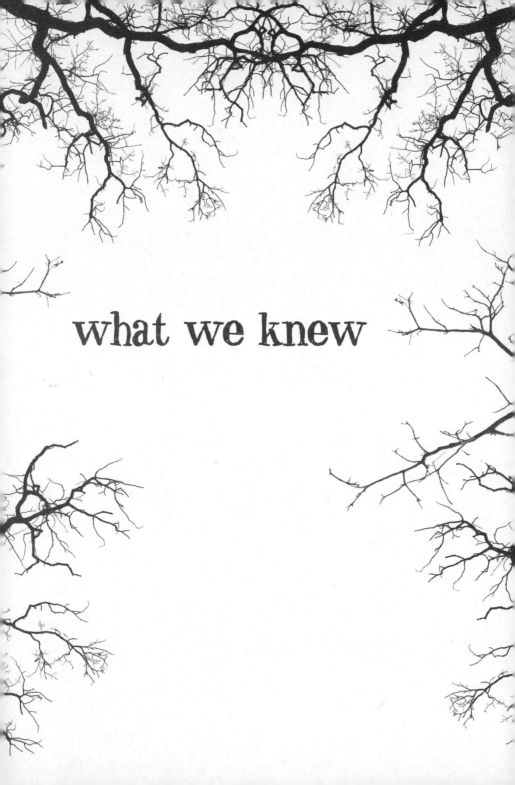

what we knew

one

To: splendidhavoc@horizon.net
From: blackolcun@horizon.net
Subject: SOS

You remember Banana Man, right? That urban legend
when we were kids? The reason we always took the long
way home? All through middle school, it was either down
Bradley, past the hospital and up McClellan, or it was
over the hill and through the park. Not you. Lisa and me.
I don't know if you ever cut through the woods. Maybe
you weren't afraid. Maybe you didn't have anything to fear.
After all, it was the girls he wanted. Banana Man. What a
stupid name. When I was little, I imagined a monster: stilt
legs and long teeth, oily black eyes. God, I had so many

nightmares about those woods. Did you know that? How I used to dream of running and running until I found a shack and thought I was safe? But in the end, the shack was always his home, and he was waiting inside, waiting to shred me with his jagged fingernails. It all changed when Lisa told me about flashers: *No, silly. You know, he shows girls his **banana**.* Then I pictured some drooling perv in a belted raincoat, with a comb-over and thick, thick glasses. But that's not how he looks. Looked. No. He looked like somebody's dad. I thought he was just something somebody's parents made up to keep us out of the woods. Mom says the story's been around forever. But he's real. And now he's dead. He's dead, Scott. And I killed him.

two

i felt it in the air, a dangerous energy pulsing. I've always been sensitive to other people's moods—Lisa's, especially—and this was going to be monumental, explosive. It was in my bones, my gut, this tingling nervousness that made me wish I'd stayed home or gone somewhere alone with Adam. We were in Trent's bedroom on the third floor, drinking achingly sweet wine coolers, smoking, blasting Trent's expensive speakers. Exactly what we'd done four nights in a row since summer started.

But tonight was different.

There was the kind of stifling attic heat that bakes your brain. Everything reeked of boy: socks and dirty sheets and god-knows-what. The window was open, but there was no breeze to take the edge off. The balance had shifted. It was supposed to be me and Adam, and Lisa and Gabe, and Trent and Rachel. But Gabe had to work. And then Rachel got pissed at

Trent—something stupid—and stormed out. Her squealing tires made us laugh.

Was their fight the match that lit the fuse? Or maybe it started long before that night, building and building, gathering strength like a storm. An act of nature. Something none of us had the power to control.

"Where are my keys?" Trent asked, looking at his desk. "Who moved my keys?"

I finished my wine cooler—warm and syrupy—and held it in my mouth. I swear I could feel my teeth corroding. Adam picked at the rubber on his sneaker. Behind the drum set, Lisa spun around and crashed a cymbal.

"If one of you guys is screwing with me—" Trent said, overturning a laundry basket on the bed and digging through his clothes.

Adam fell back on his elbow and reached for the bottle on the windowsill. "Maybe Rachel took them," he said. Trent's jaw tightened and Adam backpedaled. "Not on purpose."

"Yes, on purpose," I said, coaxing the bottle from Adam's grip.

Lisa nodded. "Tracy's right. She wants you to chase after her," she said, twirling a drumstick. "Don't do it. Get 'em tomorrow."

"I have to work in the morning." Trent groaned, raking his wild hair. A bead of sweat traveled down his neck. His T-shirt was wet and limp, like he'd pulled it straight from the washer. He snatched up his phone and tapped the screen. We were all silent, waiting to see if Rachel would answer.

"C'mon," Trent said. "Everybody up. We're going for a walk."

Stupid and wasted, the four of us stumbled through the darkened streets, Trent and Lisa in the lead. It was easily still eighty, but after Trent's bedroom it felt cool. I rubbed my arms, and

Adam offered me his white oxford. He had dozens of them, all identical. White oxford, T-shirt, jeans, black Cons. That's what he wore year-round, except for winter when he layered a big black sweater on top.

"Can I keep it?" I asked, lifting the collar to my nose. "It smells like you."

Adam hugged me to his side and slowed his pace, dragging me with him onto someone's front lawn. I hesitated, then sunk into him. His kisses were soft, not rough and hurried like that jerk from Troy High that time that had . . .

"Get a room!" Trent shouted, pulling me out of my thoughts. Lisa waved for us to keep up. Walking and kissing was complicated, so finally we just walked, arms around one another. Under the streetlights, we all looked sinisterly beautiful: Lisa's red lips purpled, her tiny pigtails bronzed. Trent's glasses reflecting the lights, making his eyes seem to disappear. And Adam's hair, black as wet asphalt, shadowed his face. A cell phone chimed. Trent's. Rachel apologizing.

"Yes, I want my keys. No, I'm on my way to you. Fine. See ya." Trent kicked a paper cup into the street. A car raced by, horn honking. "She'll meet us at the middle school."

Hillhurst Middle. Our old school—Lisa's and mine. Trent and Adam had gone to Oneida. We were almost there, but Lisa was hungry so we stopped at a gas station. I didn't have any money, so Adam bought me a box of sour balls. Lisa got some cigar-shaped Mexican thing from the heat-lamp island. Marching up Bradley, she waved it like a conductor's baton, waiting for it to cool. At the top of the hill, she took a bite and made a yuck face. "You want it?"

I squinted. "What is it?" It looked like a petrified finger.

"Taquito," Lisa said.

"Beef or chicken?" I asked, poking it.

Lisa shrugged.

"Yeah," I said. "I'll pass."

The taquito landed in the street. A siren whooped. Blue lights flashed. A cop car pulled to the curb with its window down. My heart started pounding. I thought of my mom and Scott, and the time she had to bail him out of jail for resisting arrest at a sit-in. I checked my breath and popped another sour ball.

"What did you toss back there?" The cop was obviously talking to Lisa, but she pointed to herself innocently and looked around. "Me? A taquito?"

"Pick it up," the cop ordered. "Or I'll write you a ticket for littering."

Lisa hesitated. "It's biodegradable."

"Probably not," Trent said.

Lisa shot him a look and then turned to the cop. "Seriously?"

Lisa, please, I thought. *Don't start.* Adam reached for my hand and squeezed. The radio squawked. The cop checked something on his dashboard. "Pick it up," he said flatly. We all watched as Lisa tromped through the headlights, arms swinging. Huffing, she pinched the taquito between her fingers and held it out in front of her like it was venomous. "Happy?" she said.

The cop smiled and waved. "Have a good night."

After the cruiser made the turn for the hospital, Trent burst out laughing. "He was screwing with you," he said.

"Well, screw him," Lisa shot back, cocking her arm like a pitcher.

"Don't," I said, afraid the cop might circle back. "There's a Dumpster at the school."

"Can you hold it for me?"

Dodging her reach, I sprinted uphill, but Lisa gave chase

brandishing the taquito, waggling it obscenely behind me. Giggling, we collided in the shadow of the school, waiting until the guys caught up. The empty playground was eerie. Deeper than it looked during the day when it was filled with screeching kids. The light over the east entrance reached only so far. Everything beyond the basketball hoop dissolved into darkness. The chain-link fence cast a black net over the four of us as we sat on the curb, checking our phones. Eventually, Rachel's hatchback sputtered up the hill. I think she was pissed that Trent wasn't alone, because Lisa waved and Rachel hit the gas, swerving like she meant to hit us. Everyone scrambled back. Trent's keys flew out the window.

"You suck!" he shouted at the black exhaust.

I tugged Lisa's pigtail to get her attention. "I've got to go," I said quietly.

"It's early," Lisa said. "It's not even ten."

Cupping my mouth, I whispered, "To the bathroom."

"Go behind the school," she said.

I looked up at the black windows and looked away.

Lisa heaved an exaggerated sigh. "Just go."

Judging from the smell, I wasn't the first person to go behind Hillhurst. Probably not even the first person that night. I moved deeper into the shadows and prayed the stupid cop didn't patrol the alley. Or worse, that some homeless drunk wouldn't come stumbling around the corner.

"Lisa?" I whisper-shouted. "Watch for weirdoes."

Her voice echoed off the bricks: "I'm watching! Go!"

Unbuttoning my shorts, I thought, *Watch for Banana Man*, and shivered. I hadn't thought about that lame legend in forever. I'm too old to be afraid of boogeymen, but I tensed anyway as a long shadow oozed across the asphalt. I froze, until I heard laughing and running. Lisa, Trent, and Adam advancing. "We can hear you peeing!" Lisa sang around the corner.

I hiked my shorts and raced for the cone of light where Trent and Adam were smoking. Adam offered me a drag, but Lisa was waving her hand and fake coughing, so I passed. Trent pushed his glasses up his nose. "You guys want to see something creepy?" he asked. An evil grin split his face.

"No," Lisa said, bored. "Why?"

"You guys ever hear a story about some psycho who lives in the woods?" he asked.

My neck tingled at the weirdness of his timing. "You're kidding, right?" I said. "I was just thinking about Banana Man."

"That's what we called him, too," Adam said, flicking his cigarette at the SMOKE-FREE ZONE sign.

"He was a flasher," I said.

Trent moved closer to Lisa. "I heard he did way sicker stuff than showing his junk."

Lisa folded her arms. "He's not real," she said.

"Oh, he's real," Trent insisted. "I found out where he lives. His house or whatever."

I pictured the shack from my nightmares. My heart beat harder. The buzz from drinking was gone. In its place throbbed childish fear.

But there is no Banana Man . . .

"C'mon," he said, leading us around front, past the main entrance. At the corner, with the school at our backs, we stared at the woods hesitantly. A siren wailed in the distance. Adam stilled my shaking hand.

"We don't have to do this," Trent said, teetering on the edge of the curb. "I can show you tomorrow when it's light."

"No, let's do it," I said, more confidently than I felt. "But hurry. It's ten after. I've got to be home soon." From the other side of the street, I glanced back at the school. This was as far as I'd ever been and only on a dare. Suddenly, I was nine again: *I'm not going! You go! Did you hear something? I think I heard something! Run!*

I shivered.

Adam rolled his eyes as Trent turned on his key-chain flashlight. Holding it under his chin, he laughed like a mad scientist, the yellow beam distorting his features.

"If this is some lame joke . . ." Lisa said.

"No joke," Trent said. "You'll see."

Trent went first, pushing through the wall of brush. Lisa was next and then Adam. I don't know why we followed. I guess we didn't believe him. I waded into the tangle of vines and branches, clearing a path with my arms. I hate the woods. I'm not an outdoorsy kind of girl. I hate getting slapped by twigs, having my legs scratched. And as we trekked deeper into the darkness, I worried less about Banana Man and more about breaking an ankle or losing an eye. The ground felt soft and spongy. Adam told me to watch my step, but I couldn't see my feet. I went down hard.

"Trent!" Adam shouted. "Wait!"

The tiny light quit bouncing. I brushed dirt from my stinging knees and kicked the stupid log.

"Lisa?" I called.

"I'm right here," she said.

I looked back. Her voice seemed to come from behind, but behind me was nothing—just the blackness of closed eyelids. My internal compass was off. I tried to keep myself calm, believing if I walked left, I'd end up in the hospital overflow lot. Right, the park. Panic soured my stomach. The absolute quiet was worse than the darkness. It was a deafening silence. All the familiar static—the noises that remind you of your place in the world, that you aren't alone—had faded. The only sound was our breathing. I bit my lip and followed Trent's light.

"We're almost there," Trent said as Lisa hooked her finger through his belt loop. "This is the tricky part." He aimed the beam at his feet, but there was nothing there. The ground just stopped, slipping away into blackness. We were eye level with the tops of the trees.

"Forget it," I said. "I'm going back."

"No. Wait," Trent said. "Look." He stepped off and didn't plummet to his death. Stairs. In the middle of the woods. A wooden staircase like the one that goes down to the river behind my father's apartment building.

If he still lived there—I hadn't seen him in months.

"They're rotten," Trent said, taking Lisa's hand. "So step where I step."

"Gabe will never speak to you again if you get his girlfriend killed," I said.

Lisa's laugh—high and tight—betrayed her nerves. She slowly lowered one foot and then the other, sighing with relief when the groaning structure didn't collapse. Gripping the splintered rail, the four of us descended silently. The stairs seemed to go on forever. The decaying wood smelled of mushrooms. The sweet, powdery smell of Lisa's deodorant hit my nose. I was damp with sweat. The cold, sickly kind that comes from fear. I wanted to be home. I *needed* to be home. The alarm clock outside my mother's bedroom was set for my curfew. If I was one second late, I'd be grounded. When we reached the bottom, I checked my phone. It didn't seem possible. I asked Adam how long he thought we'd been in the woods.

"I don't know. A while," he said. "Why?"

"My phone says it's still ten after ten."

I looked up. No trees blocked the view straight above, but the sky was flat black. No stars. No moon. Not even the constant orange glow of light pollution. Unless there's a blackout, there's always light. It's never truly dark. You can see it from outer space. It was as if someone had unplugged the universe.

I checked my phone again. No signal. I left it on. It was brighter than Trent's stupid flashlight.

"It's just over there," Trent said. "See?"

"See what?" Adam said.

"I can't see shit," Lisa said.

My vision snapped into focus. A rambling maze of black tarp shelters. More lean-to than tent, but with four sides instead of three. Just like Scott used to put up in our backyard when he was a scout. But bigger. Much, much bigger.

"It's probably some homeless guy," I said.

Trent warned us against the ropes zigzagging between the trees. Anyone not paying attention would get clotheslined. We ducked beneath the webs and followed Trent around a rocky outcrop. A path lined with carpet scraps led to a makeshift porch. Trent pulled back a flap and stuck his head in.

"Hey!" he shouted. "Anybody home?"

Lisa punched his arm. Adam whipped his head around like he'd heard something. "This is stupid," he said. "Really stupid. What if he's got a gun?"

"Nobody's here," Trent said casually. "Trust me."

"Wait," I said, hooking his sleeve. "How is this any different from breaking into a house on Bradley or Parkwood?"

Trent shook me off. "Because it's not an actual house," he said. "And this is public property."

"If I hear a chainsaw . . ." Lisa whispered, clutching my waist.

In my nightmares, Banana Man lived in an empty shack. But this wasn't a shack. And it wasn't empty. Trent swept the room with his flashlight. A shiver ran up my back. I don't know what I'd expected to find. Maybe some crates and nasty bedding, with hypodermic needles scattered about. Certainly not a fully furnished living room. I spun around, taking it all in: sofa, armchair, coffee table, rocking chair. A bookcase without books. Picture frames without pictures. An upright piano. The fact that everything was so ordinary only made it creepier.

"How did he get all this here?" I whispered.

"People have been using the woods as a dump for years," Trent said. "I swear that's my grandmother's old couch. I remember the stain."

Adam scratched our initials into the piano with a key and then we moved on, following the carpet scraps to a kitchen. The glow from my phone skimmed over something that looked like an ancient washing machine. Lisa tripped over a step stool. We shuffled along in the near-dark, bumping into tables and chairs, the black walls sucking up the light, until Adam found a battery-powered lantern. He flicked the switch, flooding the next room—the bedroom—with harsh brightness. I counted four sleeping bags on a musty mattress. A cardboard dresser sagged in the corner and the carpet squished underfoot—the bedroom leaked.

"Maybe it's a family," I said sadly, thinking of that kid Lisa's sister was friends with, the one who lived in a minivan with his dad and two sisters because the bank took their house.

"Think he's got any booze?" Lisa asked.

"Already checked," came Trent's voice from the next room over, and then the sound of water. Lisa went to investigate.

"Nice, Trent," she said.

"Are you peeing on the floor?" I asked, shining my phone at his backside. Sometimes I hated Trent. I thought of my brother and how different he was from my friends. Scott would've emptied his pockets for this guy, giving what little he had for someone who had less.

"There's no toilet," Trent smirked, zipping his fly.

Adam shook his head and moved on. In the kitchen, Lisa poked through boxes of crackers and oatmeal and pancake mix. "Maybe he's got some cash stashed in one of these," she said, dumping a jar of instant coffee in the dishpan. "Help me look, Trace. See what's in that cooler."

I couldn't shake the feeling that someone was watching. What if the place was booby-trapped? I wasn't about to get my face blown off for a couple of bucks. I nudged the red chest with my toe and listened. Just water sloshing, so I carefully lifted the lid. My hand flew to my nose as if I'd been punched. A bulging milk jug, rancid hot dogs, a black peach, all floating in a gray slurry. I kicked the cooler and the lid slapped closed.

"Maybe he's dead," I said. "Maybe whoever was living here died."

I still felt uncomfortable, but it wasn't fear. More like pity, a gnawing sadness. I felt like a witness to something tragic. No one lived here, not anymore. It was in the air—the stench of hopelessness, loss. I know it sounds strange, but you can smell sorrow. The year before my parents divorced, scorched dinners and cologne and burning rubber permeated our house. I wanted out before the misery of the place took root, like an infection in my bones.

"Can we please go?" I asked Lisa. "This place is a downer."

"In a minute," she said, shining her phone inside a sugar bowl. "Check the bedroom again."

I could hear Adam in the living room, banging on the piano. I put my phone on the dresser and pulled the top drawer, but the handles came off in my hands. The whole thing was waterlogged, the cardboard disintegrating into a mildewy pulp. I tore the front off and shone the light inside. Nothing. No letters, no photos, no newspaper clippings. I checked under the bed and then checked the bathroom. A bucket for a sink and a bar of white soap. A grimy towel on a crate. There was nothing personal anywhere. I felt suddenly trapped in a creepy diorama of a home. No story, no history, just stuff, junk. Even the homeless have their keepsakes. Who would care that Trent had peed on the floor? Who would care that Lisa had smashed all the plates? Who would care that Adam had carved up the piano?

Just as the knot in my stomach began to loosen, Trent made us all go into the last room, the one jutting off the back like an afterthought. The whole reason he'd brought us there, he said. Gray plastic barrels lined one wall, bald tires lined the other. The guy must've run out of carpet—the floor was pine needles. My light grazed a large rusty toolbox, a stool, and a workbench cluttered with cigar boxes. Adam picked one up and shook it. It sounded like marbles. He lifted the lid.

"What the f—"

Trent started laughing. "Is this guy a freak, or what?"

"It's like that horror movie!" Lisa screeched. "The one with the brother and sister driving home from college. There's that monster that plucks people's eyes out."

"Banana Man wasn't a monster," Adam said. "He was a child molester."

Lisa shrugged. "Same thing."

"They're glass," I said, rolling a blue one between my thumb and forefinger. "My grandfather had a glass eye." I fished out another one. Green, flecked with gold. "Why would he need so many?" I asked. Trent didn't care about the eyes. He wanted to know what was in the barrels. He tried using a screwdriver, but the lids wouldn't budge. While Trent was off searching the other rooms for something resembling a crowbar, Adam found a six-pack hidden beneath some oily rags.

"Look what Trent missed," he said. "Who's thirsty?"

Lisa raised her hand.

Adam grabbed a can, but then dropped it like he'd burned his palm. As he stumbled back into one of the barrels, his face twisted in fear.

"Are you trying to give me a heart attack?" I whispered, frightened.

But Lisa was frozen, too. No one moved. We all just stood there, staring at the rising tarp wall. The pit of my stomach knew. I knew. A moaning shadow ducked beneath the plastic. Its long arms rose higher and higher, clawing the musty air. My knees buckled. Lisa grabbed my arm and cried out for Trent. The shadow lunged sideways, around the workbench, and then doubled over, howling at Lisa's shrieking. Adam clutched his chest. "Goddamn it, Trent!" He hurled a beer can, but Trent, laughing, escaped between tarps.

Running wasn't possible, not in the dark, with the trees and the rocks and the roots. We chased Trent out the back way, toward Parkwood instead of Bradley, avoiding the stairs. My chest was still swollen with panic. I couldn't get enough air. Tripping, gasping, I clawed at Lisa's heaving shoulders. I couldn't tell if she was laughing or crying. We were moving fast. Too fast. Trent smacked his head on a tree limb. His glasses went flying. We stopped to find them, and that's when Lisa realized she'd lost her necklace, the one from Gabe for their anniversary. She stumbled in circles, cursing and flailing, until something crashed behind us. A residual scream crawled up my throat, and then my phone rang.

"Go! Go! Go!" Adam shouted, pushing forward.

I glanced at the screen: MOM. I had a signal. A connection to reality. My mother waking me from a stupid nightmare. I was instantly safer. The spell was broken. Through the trees—finally, *finally*—blazed the lights from the grocery store where we shopped.

I could breathe again.

"Holy hell!" Lisa screamed, slapping at Trent. "I'm never going anywhere with you ever again! Never! Ever!" She stopped slapping when she noticed his forehead. "You're bleeding," she said. And then to her feet: "Ow." She was missing a flip-flop. "I'm so telling Gabe about this," she said, touching the spot on her collarbone where her necklace used to live.

"You should've seen your faces!" Trent howled. "It was just like the movies!"

Pulling a twig from my hair, I said, "Is this the part where we kill you?"

Adam poked Trent in the chest. "*I'm* gonna kill you."

Trent snorted. He tried lighting a cigarette, but his hands were shaking. Above his eye an impressive bruise was forming. Lisa sacrificed one of her two tank tops to mop the blood streaming down his temple.

While Lisa played nurse, I bummed a smoke off Adam and wandered over to the employee picnic table to call my mother.

"You forgot your key," she said.

I felt my pocket. She was right.

"I'll leave the back door unlocked. Where are you?"

I watched a guy in a Day-Glo vest herd stray shopping carts into a corral, and said, "Trent's."

"Lisa with you?"

Lisa was perched on someone's bumper, examining the sole of her foot.

"Yeah. I'll be home in a few minutes. Don't leave the door unlocked. Put the key where Scott used to hide it."

"Are you okay?"

Lisa jumped on Trent's back. Adam stole her surviving flip-flop and made for the Dumpster. I watched my friends joking, laughing, chasing each other around the parking lot, and said, "Yeah."

But not really. My stomach churned with guilt and fear about what we'd done. You can't just destroy someone's home—even if it's not a real home. There are always consequences. For everything. I was spooked, but nobody else seemed worried. Trent galloped over with Lisa, who stuck her foot in my face. "Kiss my boo-boo," she said.

I flicked her big toe. "C'mon," I said. "We've got to go."

Adam tossed her flip-flop in the air and then fit it on her foot.

"Wait," Lisa said, frowning down at me. "I left my bag at Trent's."

Grunting, Trent hefted her higher. Lisa squealed. "I'd drive you guys, but I'm almost out of gas," Trent said. "I'll loan you some socks, though. To wear home."

Lisa rode Trent back to his house. Adam wanted to give me a ride, too, but I'd had enough excitement for one night. I wanted my feet solidly on the ground. Adam and I waited on the porch while Lisa hobbled upstairs with Trent.

"I'll get to hear about her foot for days," I said.

I smoothed Adam's hair out of his eyes, kissing his forehead.

"How'd we escape unscathed?" I asked, kissing him again.

"Have you seen your knees?" he asked, smiling softly.

I sat on the steps and stuck my legs out straight. Under the porch light—red and raw and streaked with dirt—they looked worse than they felt. Tomorrow, if Lisa and I took Katie swimming, they'd sting like hell. I checked my phone: 10:38. The night seemed endless, like when Lisa and I stayed out until dawn at the diner where her mom waitressed. Getting wasted on candy-flavored drinks, eavesdropping on Trent and Rachel's fight, getting stopped by a cop for the improper disposal of a taquito—it all felt like days ago.

I brought my ugly knees up under my chin. Adam kissed one and then the other. I picked a pine needle from his hair. "You think he's real?" I asked.

"Banana Man?" He shook his head. "I feel like a jerk for what we did back there."

"Me, too."

Then he kissed my cheek and kept going. My eyebrows. My eyes. My nose. I cupped his face and pressed my lips to his until Trent's mom let their cat out, ruining the mood. I compulsively checked my phone. Time was working again. If we hurried, Lisa and I would make it before my mom sent out the search dogs.

"How long does it take to find a pair of socks?" I said.

"In that room?" Adam scoffed. "Days."

"I'll be back." I kissed the top of his head and jogged upstairs. Trent's door was closed. I threw it open. I froze.

Lisa was on Trent's bed.

Under Trent.

In her lacy peach bra.

My face burned. It was that jerk from Troy all over again. Only Lisa wasn't there to save me. *Wait . . . No . . .*

I could practically feel him on top of me again, holding me down. My tongue tripped over the words screaming in my head. *Stop . . . Please . . .*

"Spit it out, Trace," Trent laughed as he rolled off the bed and grabbed his shirt. There was a reason why our drama teacher cast him as the devil in our last production. I grabbed Lisa's tank top, holding it out to her, but Lisa crossed her arms and shook her head.

I looked at the tank top in my hand. It was the wrong one anyway, the one she'd used to wipe Trent's face. I rubbed the stained ribbing—stiff and coppery—and thought: *the blood in our veins runs blue.* Not red, not until it comes in contact with air. How many things are like that, the opposite of what you thought to be true? You spend your whole life thinking things are one way and then something comes along and destroys the illusion. But then you find out that's false, too: the blood in our bodies *is* red. Sometimes it's hard to know what to believe. Lisa needed saving, but not from Trent. She wanted to be there.

You had, too.

Invisible fingers, *his* fingers, tightened around my throat.

"I'll call you tomorrow," Lisa said, nodding her head toward the door pointedly.

I tried to say okay, but my voice failed again. Clinging to the banister, I stumbled down the stairs. Outside, Adam was kicking a soccer ball around the yard.

"Lisa's staying," I nearly cried. Adam looked confused. I shook my head. "My knees hurt."

"I'll walk with you," he said, offering his arm for support.

"No. I'm fine. Can you make sure she gets home?"

The second it left my mouth, I was sorry I'd said it. I didn't trust her that night.

"Maybe you could call her a cab," I said, digging through my pocket for cash I didn't have.

"I've got it," he said. He gave me a quick kiss and tapped my nose. "Go, before you're late."

It was stupid, walking alone so late at night, taking the shortest route instead of the safest. I never go that way. It's too dark. But that night I was too busy being angry, angry with Lisa, angry with Trent. After what my father did to my mother, it hurt to think they might be the same. I was wondering whose betrayal would hurt Gabe worse—his girlfriend or his best friend—when I heard it: the whisper of rubber on concrete, a whirring chain spinning. Too close to outrun. A shadow rose up sharply, swallowing mine. Brakes squealed. A hand clutched my shoulder. My body did it again, just like that day in Troy when my arms and legs seized up instead of lashing out. Frozen, I braced for the black pain of a knife in the ribs until a familiar voice asked, "Why so tense?"

My limbs relaxed, softening, and I turned. It wasn't some jerk in a hoodie. It wasn't the monster from my nightmares. Soft brown curls. Warm brown eyes. My heart took on a different rhythm, beating out *Foley, Foley, Foley*. I never know what to call him—Michael Foley. There needs to be a word for someone who straddles friend and soul mate. He was there for me when my parents split up. Lisa talked to me, but Foley listened. He's one of those rare people who make you feel like you're the most important person in the world. That he cares for no one more than you. And he means it. That's why everyone loves him. And because everyone loves him, I can't. I hate that he makes everyone feel special.

I don't like to share.

"How's it going with Adam?" he said. He hopped off his bike

and ran his fingers through his hair. I could remember the way it felt running my own through it. I used to love his hair, especially when he let it get a little too long. Now I loved Adam's.

"Good! Great! Amazing!" I groaned internally—I sounded shrieky and stupid, but I couldn't stop. "We're so good together! I'm really, really happy!"

"Really, really?!" Foley mimicked. I rolled my eyes. But then in that intense voice of his—the one I secretly wished was reserved for me—he said, "If not, I want to know." After what happened with Jerk Face, Foley started keeping tabs on my boyfriends. He's the only one who knows what really happened. Not even Lisa knows.

"I'm a little stressed right now," I said. "It's been a really weird night."

"I'm supposed to meet Jeff Hollenbeck," he said, shifting his weight. "Come with me and we'll talk on the way."

I checked my phone. The only way I'd make it home now was if I sprinted.

"I can't," I said. "Call me, okay? You never call me anymore."

"I will." He smiled and my insides went soft and fluttery. "Hey, it was really good to see you," he said, flicking my collar—Adam's collar. "Really, really."

Watching him bike away, I kicked myself for not going with him. He looked back before he turned the corner and the wind caught his curls and I imagined twisting a soft lock round and round my finger. Foley's never been my boyfriend, but we've fooled around. The last time was a couple of weeks before I started dating Adam. We were in the cemetery. Creepy, I know. But my mother always says it's not the dead you have to fear, it's the living.

Suddenly the street turned darker and quieter. Everything

stilled. It was the same feeling I'd had in the woods. Someone was watching. I could feel eyes everywhere at once. Leering, lurking. From the rooftops, the storm drains, the alley. Under my skin, inside my thoughts. My stomach twisted as my heart sped up. I started running, my eyes focused on the stoplight— green, yellow, red, green, yellow, red—not wanting to see what was behind me, above me, beside me.

I spent a lot of the summer running from things I didn't want to see.

three

i was still lounging on the couch in my pajamas, working on my second bowl of cereal, when Lisa and her little sister, Katie, came in already dressed for the pool.

"Knock much?" I mumbled through a mouthful of O's. I waved my hand for Lisa to move. She was blocking the TV, and they were about to do The Big Reveal on my favorite home makeover show.

"I've been texting you for an hour," she said crankily, crossing her arms.

I glanced down at the phone next to me and lowered my cereal bowl, trying to hide the blinking light I'd been ignoring all morning.

"Miss Thang wants to go swimming," Lisa said.

"It's hot," Katie whined. "I'm sweating my boobs off."

"You don't have any boobs," Lisa said.

Katie stuck out her chest. "More than you."

"Sad but true," Lisa conceded, gesturing to Katie. "Look, she fits in my old bikini."

"I thought you said bikinis are gross," I asked Katie.

"Ryan's gonna be there," she said, cocking her bony hip.

"Isn't that the kid that lives in a van?" I asked.

Katie ignored me, plunking down in the recliner and staring at the TV.

"You and I need to talk," Lisa said, grabbing my hand. She tossed her sister the remote and then dragged me to the kitchen where my eyes snagged on the list of chores stuck to the fridge, punishment for coming home late. Laundry I could handle, but making me scrub the toilet was just mean. My mom knows touching it—even with gloves—makes me gag.

"What happened last night . . ." Lisa said. "It's not what you think."

"How do you know what I think?"

"I didn't . . . you know." Lisa avoided my eyes, examining her nails. "I left right after you."

"Still," I said, rinsing my bowl. "What were you thinking?"

"Jealous?" Lisa wiggled her eyebrows and then screamed when I squirted her with the sink sprayer.

"I ran into Foley last night," I said, sighing.

"See? You're not perfect either."

"We talked," I said. "I didn't stick my tongue down his throat."

I didn't cheat.

Lisa opened the freezer. "Can I have a waffle?" she asked. "Hey, Katie, you want a waffle?"

While Lisa waited for the toaster, I went to get dressed. I struggled into my bathing suit—still damp from yesterday—and dragged my hair into a ponytail. Adam's oxford—it still smelled like him—frayed cutoffs, flip-flops. I was searching for my sunglasses when Lisa's sister started howling in the living room.

"What are you oh-ing about?" I asked, running into the room.

"This guy on TV! He has a tapeworm in his eye!"

"I'm pretty sure you shouldn't be watching that," I said, turning off the TV. My sunglasses were on the end table. I grabbed them as Lisa tossed her sister a waffle on the way out the door. Katie liked to exaggerate, but she was right—it was stupid hot. I started sweating the minute I stepped outside. "Did Trent slip us something last night?" I asked, locking up. "I think I tripped."

"You weren't tripping," Lisa said, fluttering her fingers in my face. "Last night was freaky."

"So there really was a staircase in the woods?" I said. "I didn't dream that part?"

Nibbling the crispy edge around her waffle, Lisa said, "You didn't dream it."

Katie was halfway down the block already. Jogging was out of the question. My knees were killing me. I bribed her to wait with the promise of gum. Sixth-graders will do anything for gum.

"I know I'm being paranoid," I said. "But I swear someone followed me home."

Lisa cocked her head. "That's funny. Adam said he felt weird, too, like we were being watched."

I stopped. "Adam?"

"He walked with me to Cutler."

I lowered my mirrored glasses and trudged on. I hate sun. It gives me a headache. And Lisa was wearing too much concealer. It made her hard to look at. I told her her face looked orange.

"You're in a mood today," she said. "You're being weird. Bitchy weird. What's wrong?"

The hiss of air brakes made me jump. The Route 5 on its way to the mall. The driver waved. I waved back. Marty. He's one of the good ones. He's always been nice to my mom, not like some of the other guys who gave her a hard time after she got promoted to supervisor. My dad used to work for the bus company, too, as the head of maintenance, until he had his meltdown. The last I heard, he was working as a night security guard in some office building downtown.

"Are we going to Trent's tonight?" I asked.

"Yeah, I guess. Gabe's off at four."

"Did you tell him you lost your necklace?"

We sidestepped a broken bottle and hurried past the sleazy bar with the blackened windows. I hate the blocks between Brandywine and Sumner. It's this pocket of sadness in the middle of our neighborhood. My mom said it's spreading from downtown, that it used to be different. Now even the stores are depressing: payday loans and pit bull breeding and rent-to-own furniture. A couple of girls on bikes went by. Katie waved, but they ignored her. When we reached Parkwood, we crossed the street out of habit. It had been a long time since we'd been this aware of the woods. I shivered despite the heat. The three of us kept our eyes on the sidewalk. No one said anything. Lisa and I were kids again, holding our breath to pass a cemetery. And then a horn honked, breaking the spell. Rachel in her fumy hatchback.

"Where you headed?" she asked.

Lisa pointed to the sign for Hillhurst Park and said, "Pool."

"You and Trent patch things up?" I asked. Not that I cared. I just wanted Lisa to squirm.

Rachel lowered her stereo. "Yeah, we're fine. It was nothing."

"See?" I said, nudging Lisa with my elbow. "I told you it wasn't serious."

Lisa whacked me with her bag, and I wheeled on her. "Bug," she said flatly. "Got it."

"I'll catch you tonight at Trent's," Rachel said.

"Yeah," I said, rubbing my arm. "See you later."

Lisa smiled uneasily. "Later."

All three of us clutched our ears as Rachel peeled away from the curb. Two months and she still hadn't mastered stick shift. Katie lowered her hands to her hips and threw us a suspicious squint.

"Why are you guys fighting?" she asked.

"We're not fighting," I said.

Shrugging, she snapped her gum and marched on.

Lisa's breath on my neck made me shudder. "It was a mistake," she hissed. "Wait till you slip up, Kolcun."

My mom calls the pool at Hillhurst the Polio Pit—whatever that means. It's not like a real pool, with diving boards and slides and ladders for getting in and out. It's more like a pond with a concrete bottom. Chlorinated or not, it's kind of scuzzy and today it was crawling with kids. Lisa and I claimed a spot in the grass, away from the mothers with their screechy voices. Katie whipped off her cover-up immediately. I hate feeling like everyone's watching you undress, even if they're not. Lisa held up a towel to hide me while I stripped, then slathered her sister with triple-digit SPF. I'm all about the tanning butter. I like my ghostly skin, but I also like how I look after a week at the pool, especially my legs.

We watched Katie splash around for a while and then dug through our bags for our phones. Lisa cursed. She'd left hers charging on her desk. I stuck one of my buds in her ear as a peace offering, but she plucked it out and handed it back. It was going to be one of those days, the kind where the two of us are completely out of sync. It's better to ignore each other. I put on the playlist Adam made me and stretched out on a towel, closing my eyes. The first song was all tribal drums and jangly guitars. I fell asleep before it ended. When I woke, the sun had shifted. Lisa was sitting with her chin on her knees and had this angry, faraway look.

"Hey," I said, tickling her back with her bathing suit string. "I'm sorry about the Trent thing."

"It's not you," she grumbled. "Stupid Larry."

Stupid Larry is Lisa's stepdad. Her real father suffers from the same disease as mine: deadbeatitis.

"He totally went off on me last night," Lisa complained. "Said he doesn't care what my mother says—from now on he wants me home by ten. Said I shouldn't be out 'tramping' around. Can you believe him?"

I didn't say anything—didn't even crack a smile—but Lisa swatted me with a magazine.

"I'm going to the Snack Shack," she said. "What do you want?"

"Sour gummies," I said. I ran my tongue over my teeth. "And a toothbrush."

Lisa fished her wallet from her bag. "Keep an eye on Katie," she warned. "She'll try to sneak over to the deep end."

I checked my phone. Adam had sent me a text on his way to work. It was his first day washing dishes in the hospital kitchen. Lisa and I were the only ones without jobs. Actually, Lisa had a job—watching Katie. Their mom works nights and sleeps days and can't afford to send Katie to day camp. Me, I had no excuse.

"Hey, Katie!" I shouted over the pool and the noise. Three separate girls—none of them Lisa's sister—stopped bobbing and stared. I waved them away. "Not you! Katie Grant!"

I knew she'd heard me, but she ducked under the rope of red-and-white floats. The water was up to her neck. I waded in after her, my skinned knees burning from the chlorine, and bumped into a kid spinning in circles, making waves with his arm. A kid doing a handstand kicked me in the face. "You're dead, Katie!" I called, pogoing out to the middle. Katie's blue lips quivered when I grabbed her wrist.

"Noooo!" she pleaded. "I'm looking for Ryan! He said he was going to be here."

Her pruney fingers swiped at the bangs plastered to her forehead. I plucked a blade of grass stuck to her cheek, looking at her sadly. I knew exactly how she felt. Foley was famous for saying he'd be one place and ending up in another. How many times had I searched for him at Fun Nights or parties or football games? Not Adam, though. He was always right where I wanted him, right where he said he'd be.

My knees had quieted, so I splashed around with Katie until I saw Lisa coming through the pines. She'd kill me for leaving our stuff out for anyone to steal. I waded out and toweled off and watched her peel away toward the picnic area. Same bouncy walk, same white-blond pigtails, but it wasn't Lisa. I watched Not Lisa flirt with a shirtless guy kicking around a hacky sack. By the time the real Lisa came back, my bathing suit was dry.

"What took you so long?" I said. "Where's my candy?"

"Forget the candy. I've got something better."

She opened her fist. *Wow, a marble,* I thought. *Big deal.* But then she nudged it with her finger. Blue iris. Pupil black as night. My heart thunked.

"I went to find my necklace," she said lightly.

"Have you lost your mind?" I shrieked. "You could've been attacked!"

Lisa rolled her eyes—I was overreacting. But I wasn't. We'd spent our whole lives avoiding the woods for that exact reason.

"It's not as scary during the day," she said.

I looked to the tree line. "Did you find it? Your necklace?"

She shook her head wearily. "No. He's probably got my flip-flop, too."

"Who's got your flip-flop?" Katie asked, crashing belly up on my towel.

Lisa quickly hid the eye in her bag. "Nobody," she said. "We brought you here to swim. Go."

Katie pretended to shiver. "I'm cold. I want to go home."

"She's bummed because Ryan didn't show," I said.

Lisa packed her sunscreen and sunglasses. "Maybe his house got a flat tire."

I tugged my towel out from under Katie and she rolled across the grass.

"I hate you both," she hissed.

"If you're nice to me," Lisa said, "I'll let you in on a secret."

Katie sat up and folded her arms over her chest. Lisa glanced around like she was up to something illegal. "You know that story about the guy who lives in the woods? Banana Man?"

Katie's eyes bulged. "You guys know about Banana Man?" she asked.

Lisa slung her arm over her sister's shoulder. "You think you and your little friends made him up? He's real, girly-girl. We found his house. You want to see it?"

Katie pulled back. "Are you crazy?"

I ducked a Frisbee headed for my face. "Yes, she is," I said.

Scrunching up her nose, Katie whispered, "He's a prevert."

"It's 'pervert.'" I corrected, walking toward the bike path. "But yeah."

"Did you see him?" Katie whispered.

Just as I was about to shake my head, Lisa nodded.

"He's super creepy looking, with rotten teeth and slits for eyes and an ugly purple birthmark on his forehead," she said with wide eyes.

Katie made a questioning face. "Like Larry's?"

Lisa nodded. "Exactly like Larry's."

When we got back to their house, all the shades were pulled down to keep the sun out because their mom was sleeping. Katie took the phone in the bathroom to call her friends—*My sister saw Banana Man!*—and Lisa and I crept down the hall to her bedroom. My hair was a wreck. Lisa dug the eye out of the bottom of her bag and set it on her nightstand. It rolled toward the edge. Propping it against her alarm clock, she commanded it to stay.

"You're not seriously going to leave that there?" I asked.

Lisa smiled. "It's my . . . what do you call things that protect people?"

"A talisman."

"Yeah. One of those."

I shouldn't have been surprised. Lisa's room was one big collage of "found objects." Orange pylons and pink flamingos, street signs and random letters from marquees. My favorite was the collection of wigs she'd liberated from the theater department. While we were fixing our makeup, an engine hummed past the window. The garage door creaked. The screen door slapped against its frame.

"Lisa!"

Larry was home. Lisa barely tolerated her stepfather, but he was always nice to me. He wasn't a bad guy—just a little strict. Stricter than her mom. Mrs. Grant let Lisa get away with a lot—way more than my mom.

"Hey, Trace." Larry waved from the counter where he was going through the mail. I call Lisa's mom *Mom*, but I never know what to call Lisa's stepfather. After ten years Lisa still calls him *Larry*. Katie calls him *Dad*. My mom needs to find someone new, too, but I hope she never remarries, at least not until I'm old enough to move out.

Larry tossed a magazine to Lisa, then crept up behind Katie and took a huge bite out of her ice cream sandwich. "You guys have fun at the pool?" he asked.

Frowning at her nearly empty wrapper, Katie said, "It was okay."

Larry cocked his head as she headed for the trash. "Is that Lisa's old bathing suit?"

Lisa told Katie to go change and then dug a grape Popsicle from the freezer. I wanted a Popsicle, too, but I just stood there awkwardly. Larry rolled his eyes at me—*My stepdaughter has no manners*—then marched to the fridge and asked me what flavor.

"Last one," Lisa said, squeezing past Larry and the freezer to get to Katie. With the rolled-up magazine, she swatted her sister's backside. "Didn't I tell you to change?" she said. "Do it. Now."

Larry crushed the empty Popsicle box and frowned. "Someone's in a mood," he said.

"Someone doesn't appreciate being called a tramp," Lisa said.

Larry's face reddened.

"What's for dinner?" Katie asked. "Can we have tacos?"

My cue to leave. The last thing I wanted was an invitation,

not with Lisa this way. "I better go," I said. "My mother left me a list. If it's not done, she won't let me out later."

"We're meeting at six," Lisa said. Sucking her Popsicle, she glared at Larry, daring him to contradict her.

"Six," I echoed.

It wasn't always like that—so tense. Only when Larry tried to put the reins on Lisa. On normal days, I preferred being at their place. Friends' families are always better than your own. Better food, better houses, better parents. I should've stayed for tacos. An hour later I was kicking myself for rushing home to clean the bathroom.

"I don't care if the toilet sparkles," my mother said. "You've been out every night this week."

Scowling at the reconstituted onions on my burger, I used a ketchup packet to scrape the bun. Fast food again. My dad always liked the other burger place better. He used to sound like a commercial when he'd talk about the superior taste of flame-broiling. Flame-broiled fake meat is still fake meat. When I was a kid I loved the stuff, especially the chicken nuggets. When my dad had a meeting, my mom would bring home the twenty-piece to split, or else she'd make us fish sticks or potpies. Always something my dad didn't mind missing. It was like a food holiday. Until that last year, when it got to be every day.

"I thought we'd go for ice cream," my mom said cheerily.

"No thanks." I bunched my wrappers, tossed them in the trash, and went to brush my teeth.

Lisa was stupid. I'd take Larry over my mother any day. At least he was consistent. You knew what to expect and what he expected of you. My mother's randomness made me crazy. She had no reason for keeping me home.

I flopped on my bed—anger rising in my chest—and turned

on the TV. Everything was either stupid or half over. I was painting my toes black when my mother poked her head in the door.

"Hey, Trace?" she said. "Adam's here."

I capped the polish and heel-walked out to the living room to find Adam parked on the edge of our couch, checking his phone. He'd come straight from work. He wanted to know if I'd eaten.

"My mother says I can't go out," I said, loud enough for her to hear me in the kitchen.

Adam squeezed my shoulders and half smiled. "We can hang out here."

I glanced around our pathetic living room: sad plaid couch and corduroy recliner. The dinky television I had to squint to see. Every surface covered with pictures of Scott and me. If you spun around fast enough, you could watch us grow up. "That sounds fun," I said flatly. "Hear that, Mom? Adam doesn't mind hanging out here. He hasn't had dinner, though. Can you make him something?"

My mother dropped something heavy and huffed. "Just go," she said wearily. "Please go."

The knot in my chest slackened. I could breathe again. I was glad I hadn't called Lisa. She'd be waiting at the corner with Gabe. I skipped into the kitchen and cautiously kissed my mother's cheek. "I love you," I said. My mother shrugged. I felt like a jerk. Staying home wasn't supposed to be punishment. She wanted to spend time with me. When I told her I'd be home early, she looked vaguely appreciative, so I didn't tell her why: Lisa's new curfew was ten.

I felt even worse when we all stopped for cones.

"You're dripping." Lisa laughed, lapping up half my sprinkles. It was my favorite time of day, with the sun low in the sky and the whole night ahead of us. Adam sucked down a vanilla-chocolate twist and ordered a chili dog. Gabe lumbered to the window for another cheeseburger. There was a dopey-giant quality about him that cracked me up, especially when he chased Adam into the street with the mustard dispenser and then hung his head in shame after the woman running the window yelled at him.

"Who wants to hit the bowling alley on the way to Trent's?" Gabe asked.

The bowling alley wasn't a bowling alley, just an alley behind a row of shops where Gabe likes to smoke a bowl. He's not a pothead, but he usually has something on him. Huddled in the shadows, Lisa and I giggled like a couple of idiots while Adam stood lookout. Gabe offered to trade places but Adam passed. Something about random drug testing at the hospital. After a couple of hits, though, Gabe pocketed his lighter. He wanted to save the rest for Trent's.

"It's good Gabe likes to share," I blurted and then clapped my hand over my mouth.

Lisa's cheeks ballooned before her face exploded in a cloud of smoke. Once she started snorting, she couldn't stop. The two of us danced around the alley, laughing and slapping at each other, until Adam herded us toward Trent's. The house looked bigger than normal. Bluer, too. I giggled up the stairs to his room, imagining us as the Prize Patrol come to present Trent with a million-dollar check.

"Knock-knock," Lisa said, pushing the door with her toe. Rachel was sitting on the bed, fanning herself with a playbill. When we ran into her earlier, her hair was still normal—shoulder length and boring brown. Now it was cut close to her head and plum. "Like it?" she asked.

I did. She looked older. She let me touch it and it felt like feathers.

"You should let me do yours," she said.

I pulled out my ponytail holder. "Do it now."

"No! No! No!" Adam shouted, tackling me to the floor. He was only playing, but I got him in a hold and flipped him. Toppling sideways, he laughed, surprised by my strength. So was I. Where had it been when I really needed it?

"What is it with guys and long hair?" Lisa asked, poking Adam in the ribs.

Trent dragged Rachel onto his lap. "I think she looks hot with it short."

"I'm sure you do," Lisa said, giggling behind her hand.

Trent's eyes narrowed. "Have you guys been smoking?"

Lisa busted up. I pinched the air with my fingers. "Maybe just a little." More laughs and then Gabe broke out his lighter and pipe. Trent pulled a bottle of vodka—courtesy of his older brother—from beneath the bed. Rachel ran downstairs for juice and cups.

It felt like it was shaping up to be one of those nights—one of the really good ones—with Adam spinning music on Trent's turntable and everybody dancing and Trent keeping our cups full.

Then Lisa brought up Banana Man. She wanted to go back for her stupid necklace.

For once, Trent was the voice of reason: "I don't think it's a good idea."

Gabe and Adam agreed. "You're pretty wasted," Gabe said.

Lisa staggered and flopped on the bed. "That freak's got my necklace. I want my necklace."

"He's not real," Trent groaned. "It was a joke. A really bad joke. Get over it."

I dropped down beside Lisa and petted her head. Her face was wheeling, swirling, like one of those spin-art paintings. I lifted my head and tried focusing on Adam, but my eyes drifted toward Gabe, smiling sweetly, towering over everyone except Trent. If Gabe was a jolly giant, Trent was a sci-fi praying mantis. A six-foot creature with razor mandibles, tearing at Rachel's face. I closed my eyes. I shouldn't have smoked before drinking. When I opened them again, everyone had moved, including me.

We were in a circle on the floor, like children playing a game. Lisa had her head on Gabe's shoulder, but her eyes were on Trent. Something sparked between them. Trent saw me looking and flashed a sick smile. The burden of knowing turned my stomach. Black ooze trickled through my brain. That's when the circuit breaker in my head blew and everything went dark. I started crying. Lisa trying to calm me only made it worse. The world was out of control. I was out of control. Adam helped me to Trent's brother's bedroom, but the monster from my dreams was lurking in the corner. Mouth full of blades. Empty pits for eyes. Black blood drained from the sockets. It coated the floor and began to rise. Sticky and warm, it covered my feet, my ankles. My knees stung. Slick tendrils coiled my thighs.

I heard myself whimper, *No*.

"It's okay," Adam sang. "I'm right here."

I put my mouth on his. I needed him to keep me from going under. I rested my hand on his zipper, but he gently moved it to his chest. Chewing his earlobe, I tried again.

"Hey, hey, hey," Adam whispered. "Slow down . . . what's the rush?"

I kept chewing, and Adam groaned. "You're killing me," he said, moving his mouth to mine. "If you don't quit it, you might be sorry."

I smiled and our teeth clicked. "Maybe I want to be sorry."

Adam put his hands on my shoulders and stepped back. "I'm gonna get you some water," he said. I slumped on the bed. The guy I didn't love took what I wasn't ready to give. Now the guy I loved was denying me a chance to erase the ugly shadow darkening my heart. Neither of them cared what I wanted. It was never about me. The room felt suddenly cold. I wrapped a blanket around my shoulders and slid to the floor, waiting for Adam. But he never came back. It was Lisa who brought me water. It was Lisa who helped me to Trent's room to say good night. It was Lisa who took me home.

So much for Adam being right where I wanted him.

four

To: splendidhavoc@horizon.net
From: blackolcun@horizon.net
Subject: SOS

And now he's dead. I killed him.

Everything is so messed up. Sex is so messed up. That's
why we did what we did. Because some creep couldn't
keep it in his pants. I can't imagine wanting anything so
badly that I'd hurt someone to get it. How can something
that's supposed to be a basic human need destroy
people? It makes us do the craziest things. Look at Dad. I
saw his girlfriend. I can't believe he gave up Mom for *that*.
What were you picturing? High heels? A syrupy laugh?

Someone who made our father feel manly? Me, too. But she's a troll.

Did I ever tell you about the time in third grade when Mrs. Lochman did a unit on the human body? Lisa ended up in the office because she had a meltdown when the film showed a cartoon boy and girl naked, side by side. I guess it was no big deal to me—growing up with a brother and all—but Lisa started crying. She was *that* shocked or embarrassed or whatever. But that's my point: it's supposed to be natural—sex—but it's not. I mean it can be, I guess, but most of the time it's so out of balance. Like with me and Adam. At first it was sweet the way he acted like he was controlling himself, just barely. Then there was this night in Trent's brother's bedroom. Adam didn't want to fool around because I was wasted. I get it. But a few days later, when the time seemed really right, he was pushing me away again. It's like our roles got reversed. It's supposed to be the girl fighting off the guy, but every time we were alone, Adam got all . . . I don't know. Is there a word for guys who are skittish about sex? (We all know the word for what I was being.) How can I feel like a prude one day and a slut the next? Maybe I'm both. Or maybe I'm just really messed up. I didn't used to be. I'm not trying to be vague, but something happened. There was this jerk from Troy, and I think that's what sent me over the edge tonight. I didn't mean for the man in the woods to die. I just wanted to put the fear of darkness in him.

five

there's something very trash-glam about hanging out in a diner all night. The one where Lisa's mom waitresses hasn't been remodeled since the eighties. Picture mauve booths and pendant lights, tropical fish tanks, enormous rotating dessert cases, and mirrors. Lots and lots of mirrors. I examined my new hair from every angle. Rachel kept the length for Adam, but razored in layers and added a blue streak. Super-shine lip gloss. Black T-shirt with silver studs. Cargo skate shorts.

"Stop!" Lisa said, threatening me with a butter knife. "Stop looking at yourself!"

"I can't help it," I said. "There's something about these lights. Check out my tan."

"It makes the food look better," she said.

I forked a chunk of cheesecake and crammed it in my mouth.

Lisa opened her day planner and drew a tiny heart next to the date. It was code: she'd been with Gabe. She used her calendar like a diary, but instead of words she used symbols. Hearts and suns and frowny faces and stars. A record of her life in hieroglyphics.

"Is there something wrong with me?" I asked. "Do I give off an offensive odor?"

Lisa looked up. "Sometimes you smell like beef stroganoff." I chucked an ice cube at her.

"No! No!" She laughed, shielding her head. "I think it's sexy!"

"It's just that . . . Adam." My mouth went dry. I drank some water. "We haven't . . . you know."

Lisa shrugged. "Maybe he's . . . religious."

I rolled my eyes. "He drinks and smokes. He's not religious. I don't think he's anything."

Lisa pulled out a bottle of sparkly blue polish. She ate a bite of her pie, and then spread her fingers on the table. "Seriously," she said. "You should be happy. You guys are so cute. Rachel calls you The Perfect Couple."

Painting Lisa's nails, I asked if she agreed with Rachel.

"Duh. You two were made for each other. Don't ruin it. Not that sex ruins it, but it's not all that."

When Lisa went to the restroom to run her fingers under the dryer, I checked her planner for the date I'd found her with Trent. No heart. Just a skull and crossbones. Her symbol for an exceptionally sucky day. Good. She regretted it. I put it back before she returned with a pot of coffee. I held my hand over my cup. I had to watch it. During finals, I drank so much I got the shakes and threw up.

"You're going to stunt your growth!" Lisa's mom shouted from the counter. After she finished filling sugar dispensers, she scooted in beside me with a tray of silverware and a stack of napkins. Bev, the other waitress, was loading coffee filters for the one-thirty rush. It didn't matter that it was midweek. Once the bars closed, the place would be packed. Saturdays were the worst. When Lisa and I pulled all-nighters, cramming for tests, we usually had to give up our booth and move to the counter.

"Smoke break?" Bev asked Lisa's mom.

"We'll do this," Lisa said, dragging the tray across the table. "Go smoke your cigarette. Before the crazies descend."

Rolling silverware, we talked about everything and everyone. My brother's abrupt departure back in May. Katie's crush on Homeless Ryan. The Amazing Disappearing Foley and how he needed a tracking chip. The only thing we didn't talk about for the first time in days was Banana Man. Maybe Lisa had finally lost interest. Bev came and collected the tray just as Lisa's mom dropped off a plate of cheese fries. A song we both loved came on, and Lisa sang it in the vibrato that could have landed her the lead in our last musical—if she hadn't chickened out at the audition. She stopped, though, when Reggie from the kitchen came out to listen. I was always trying to get Lisa to sing more. It sounds corny, but sometimes I'd get a lump in my throat—her voice is that beautiful.

"You're ridiculous," I said, blowing on a fry. "If I had your voice, I'd never stop singing."

A tap at the window made us both jump. Gabe pressed his nose to the glass. He smiled his goofy smile and then took off around the building. As much as I liked him, his intrusion instantly ruined my mood.

"Hey," he said, sliding in beside Lisa. "I won't stay. I just wanted to give you this." He handed her a gold box. Lisa just stared for a moment before peeking under the lid. A new necklace. Exactly like the one she'd lost in the woods. I was about to text Adam to join us, but remembered he was already in bed. His brother was flying in from California the next day, so Adam had requested an early shift.

While Gabe and Lisa were kissing, I snapped a bunch of pictures of myself and then watched the first drunks trickle in until a familiar face caught my eye. I waved, but he didn't see me. "Foley's here," I said. Lisa detached herself from Gabe and asked, "Who's the woman?" Long, straight hair. Sleeveless dress. Gladiator sandals. Definitely older. Older than us. Older than Foley. "I don't know," I said. I'd never seen her before.

Lisa's lip curled. "What is she, like, twenty?"

I waited until they found a booth in Bev's section before going over.

"Hey, stranger," I said, ruffling Foley's curls.

Foley's face lit up. "Trace!" His eyes bulged as he took in my hair. "I like it!" The woman across from him was unimpressed. She buried her hands in her enormous leather bag and started texting. "Sit," Foley said, getting out to let me in.

I hesitated. I didn't want to be trapped. "If you guys want to be . . . you know." Bev dropped off some menus. I bounced over the seat, accidentally kicking the woman under the table.

"Tracy, this is Jeanine. Jeanine, Tracy."

Foley said they volunteered together at the Social Justice Center. They'd spent the night stuffing envelopes. Something about a big fund-raiser coming up.

"My brother used to do stuff with you guys," I told Jeanine.

"Who's your brother?"

"Scott," I said. "Scott Kolcun."

Jeanine squirted her hand with antibacterial gel. She offered some to Foley, but none to me. "Never heard of him," she said.

When Bev came back to take our orders, we had to shout over

all the noise. It was like someone had opened a hydrant, flooding the place with drunks. All I wanted was a soda. Foley got a steak sandwich with extra peppers. I've always wondered who orders a salad plate in a diner. Jeanine requested fat-free dressing on the side. I collected the menus and passed them to Bev.

"So," Jeanine said, shaking a sugar packet. "Michael and I—"

Brakes screeched in my head. Michael? Nobody calls Foley *Michael*. I missed Jeanine's question. Something about my opinion on the conflict in some country I didn't know existed. I've never been good at geography. She was trying to make me look stupid in front of Foley. I'm sure Scott was somewhere ripping his hair out. It's not that I don't care about human rights, it's just that I'm more concerned with the injustices happening right here, right now, before my eyes. Like the man sleeping in the doorway across the street, or the crack-skinny girl in the next booth over giving all her cash to a guy with a mouth grille. Or the one that's always behind my eyes, the one that sneaks up on me in the strangest places. I wanted to tell Jeanine to go stuff some more envelopes. Instead, I told Foley to let me out.

"That was quick," Lisa said. "Who's the chick?"

"One of those social justice snobs," I said, trying to calm the riot in my chest. "You know the type: super-expensive college. Home slumming it for the summer."

"What's Foley doing with her?"

I shrugged. "There must be something wrong with her. Maybe she has *issues*."

I was suddenly starving, but Gabe scarfed the last fry and my soda was with Foley and Jeanine. I tried to see around the corner, but even with all the mirrors, their booth was in a blind spot. I played with the studs on my shirt, and then played with my phone. Dodging monkeys through crumbling ruins, I tried to ignore Gabe and Lisa saying good night. After I beat my score, I looked up. He was gone.

"Are Adam and I that sickening?" I asked.

"Way more." Lisa flipped her place mat and drew a hangman's scaffold. One word. Nine letters.

"Banana Man is two words," I said.

Lisa huffed and scribbled out the spaces. Four letters this time. I started with vowels. The second letter was E. Lisa was so transparent. "Jerk?" I guessed.

"Get out of my head," Lisa whined, crumpling the game.

I tried keeping an eye on the register for Foley, but the craziness was peaking. It wasn't until around three that the diner emptied. Lisa's mom started trucking loads of dishes to the kitchen while Lisa wiped down some tables. I wandered the diner with my phone, pretending I'd lost my reception.

"Looking for your friend?" Bev asked. "He just left."

I ran to the front window: Foley. With Jeanine. Arm in arm, waiting at the light. My heart kicked. I sat down sadly.

"You want a pancake?" Bev asked. I shook my head. I wasn't hungry.

The sky was just starting to pink when Lisa's mom took a break and drove us home. I made Lisa hide her eyeball before we crashed to the sound of water running in the bathroom, coffee brewing in the kitchen—Larry getting ready for work. I love the feeling of going to bed when everybody else is waking up. When you know the next day will be a total waste. And it was. We sat around in our pajamas eating frozen pizzas and playing video games. At least we didn't have to entertain Katie—she'd gone to a friend's for the day. Lisa was giving me a facial when Adam called. Did I want to meet his brother? Tonight?

I could hear Chris in the background, *Don't make me wait! You're all Adam talks about!*

I think I expected Chris to be an older version of Adam—physically, at least. Personality was anybody's guess. They didn't grow up together. When their parents split, Adam stayed here with their dad, and Chris moved to California with their mom. Looking at them you'd never think they were brothers. The guy behind the wheel had short, sandy hair and blue eyes and one of those perma-tans you only see on celebrities and people living near the ocean. Next to Chris, Adam looked like he'd been locked in a basement his whole life.

"So what do you crazy kids do for fun?" Chris asked. What we did for fun—sit around Trent's bedroom most nights—sounded pretty lame. I shrugged. "I'm pretty awesome at mini golf." That wasn't true—I hadn't played in years. "I don't know if Adam told you, but some really big colleges are competing for me. I'm talking full ride. All expenses paid."

Chris smiled at me in the rearview mirror. "That's sounds like a challenge."

I shrugged again. "If you're okay with losing."

My heart sank when we drove to the place where my dad used to take Scott and me. The parking lot was overgrown with weeds. A faded FOR LEASE sign hung from a chain. The storybook characters we used to climb on had shrunk and crumbled. It all looked so sad, with Rapunzel and Goldilocks and Red Riding Hood missing hunks of plaster, their chicken-wire skeletons exposed.

"Sorry," I said.

"You're not getting off that easy," Chris said. Adam agreed. He told his brother how to get to another one, a better one, with a T. rex and a moated castle and a giant octopus named Timmy.

Scott would love it. I'd make him take me when he came home. I'd even let him have his lucky color ball, which was my lucky color, too: orange. Adam's was black. Chris, yellow.

While we waited to play the first hole, Chris ran to get a drink from the vending machine. Adam penciled our initials on the scorecard. I sat on the wall beside him and watched some kids tromp through the moat.

"Having fun?" Adam asked.

"Yeah," I said, bumping him with my shoulder.

"My brother thinks you're cool."

"Ya think?" I pressed my lips to his, infusing his face with color.

Chris poked Adam with his club. "No fraternizing with the enemy," he said. "She's trying to wreck your concentration." When the group ahead of us finished, Chris bowed. "Ladies first."

I put my ball on the rubber mat and positioned myself: feet hip-width apart, shoulders squared, elbows straight but loose. "Don't choke," Chris said. Adam coughed loudly. I sighted down the fairway and swung. The ball glided straight down the green toward the windmill, missing the moving paddle and continuing through the passageway. Adam ran to see where it went.

"No way!" he shouted. "You sunk it!"

My mouth fell open. Scott was the champion in our family. I was the reason mini golf had a six-stroke limit. I ran to see if Adam was lying.

"How did I not know this about you?" he said, tickling my sides. "What other talents are you hiding?"

"She's a nuclear physicist," Chris said.

"And a spy." I laughed.

Somehow I managed to live up to my phony reputation. Adam did pretty well, too. He won the free ice cream on the eighteenth hole. I think it was something about Chris. He's one of those people who brings out the best in you, like when you take a photo and tweak the saturation, making the colors pop. Everything that night seemed a little funnier or smarter or cooler with him around.

"I need caffeine," Chris said, taking a bite out of Adam's cone. "What's your favorite place?"

I'd watched the sun come up that morning with Lisa. Now the sky was pink again, the edges bruised deep purple. A longing ache filled my chest. I wanted the day to last forever. I told Adam and Chris about how my mom and dad, back when they were in high school, used to drive to New York City for a cup of coffee.

"Let's do it," Chris said.

"Really?" I said. "New York City? My brother's there, you know. I've got to tell my mom I'm staying somewhere."

"Tell her Rachel's having a party," Adam said. "Tell her she wants you to stay over."

I didn't think it would fly, but it did—under one condition: I was to come straight home in the morning and clean the house. My mother said she had a friend coming over and she didn't want a mess. Deal. I hung up happy but confused. My mother doesn't have any friends. That's her problem. Ever since my dad left, she spends her nights alone in front of the TV.

Chris said he still needed to refuel before we hit the road. Adam suggested one of those chain coffeehouses everybody pretends to hate. While we waited for our three tall coffees and a couple of brownies, Chris went out to the parking lot to call his girlfriend, Sarah. Adam met her over Christmas break, when he went to visit his mom. I tried to imagine him in California—Rollerblading, hanging out at the beach—but couldn't.

Chris came back flashing a nervous frown. "Did you guys know the city is three and a half hours from here?" he said, showing us the map on his phone.

Adam and I glanced at each other and nodded.

"I didn't," he said. "I thought it was closer. If we leave now, we're not gonna get back until five-thirty, six o'clock, and I've been up since four. I'm thinking driving all night probably isn't the brightest idea. Not to mention Dad'll kill me if the car's not there when he leaves for work." He sipped his coffee. "You're not angry, are you?"

I shrugged. It was probably a bad idea, anyway, to go gallivanting in my parents' footsteps.

"It's not too late to take me home," I said, picking at a brownie crumb. "I'll just say I'm sick."

Adam's face fell. He kissed the back of my hand. "I don't want to take you home," he said.

But sleeping at Adam's was out of the question. Their dad might've been cool with me crashing on the couch. Their stepmother? Not so much.

"We'll sleep in the car," Adam said to me. And then to Chris: "If Dad asks, say I'm at Trent's."

Chris looked skeptical.

"They'll never know," Adam said. "Trust me. Dad and Linda are in bed by ten."

He was right. The house was dark when Chris pulled into the driveway. He shut off the engine and gave Adam the keys. "Checkout's at six. You want a wake-up call?"

"If you could get housekeeping to bring us some extra towels," Adam said.

Chris laughed and got out. Crossing the yard, he tripped the sensor light. He froze mid-creep, like a cartoon burglar, then waved good night and let himself in through the back door.

"Is this your first time car camping?" Adam asked.

It was. It was also the first time I'd ever spent the night with a boy. But it didn't feel weird or awkward. Adam and I belonged together. I knew it in my heart. Everyone else knew it, too. Adam pulled up a movie on his phone, and we huddled together over the tiny screen, shoulder to shoulder, our heads touching. Then our ears. Then our chins. We were kissing—just kissing— when the sensor light flooded the car, scaring the crap out of us. I climbed back in my seat. Adam paused the movie. "Sorry," Chris whispered, passing a couple of blankets and some snacks through the window. When the light went out, I leaned my head against the door and put my feet in Adam's lap.

"Once upon a time," I said. "My parents and your parents were exactly like us. What happened?" I wanted to know because I was happy. And because I was happy, I couldn't imagine what I felt that night with Adam ever ending. Not ever. "What went wrong?"

Adam shrugged. "People change."

"People don't change," I said. "Not really. I think that's the problem: no one changes." If I had to sum up my father's problem in a sentence, it would be this: he was bored. Bored with his job, his wife, and his kids. All of it. Adam's parents split over incompatibility: His mom is a raging type A personality. His dad, a model cubicle rat.

"See," I said. "Your mom probably hoped to light a fire under your dad, and your dad figured your mom would settle down. If either one had changed, they'd probably still be together."

What I loved about Adam was that we could go from kissing

to having a serious conversation to acting like little kids, snuggled up under our blankets, goofing on some lame movie. When the phone died, we talked some more, but then we were drifting, the pauses between getting longer and longer . . .

Branches scratched my leg. I was running through the woods. It's always the same dream: I'm lost and then I see the shack. Only it was different. Something had changed. It was guarded by figures, brightly colored girls towering above it. My heart swelled to see them restored: Rapunzel in her turret, offering up her golden rope of hair; Goldilocks tucked neatly in the just-right bed; Red Riding Hood skipping between the trees. I was running toward them when something sent me scrambling to the surface.

The sensor light again.

Heart pounding, head pounding, I froze, straining to see what set it off. Adam was sleeping soundly. The yard was still. My brain tried reasoning with my gut—*it's probably a cat or a skunk*—and then the light went out. Crouched in the dark, afraid to close my eyes, shards of color pierced the blackness. The storybook girls, looking exactly like they had when I was little. Paint so vivid it blinded. But they had gaping black holes for eyes. I had to go back. To fill the holes. I tore through the shack, searching. Where was the box? Day turned to night, and then Lisa found it. *It's right in front of you, stupid*. I breathed deeply and shook my head, then went from girl to girl with a flashlight, trying to fit the empty sockets with blue and green and brown. The yawning holes swallowed the eyes, and I dropped the flashlight. Dropped the box, too. Eyes scattered everywhere.

I jerked awake. Adam was watching.

"You were having a bad dream," he said and kissed my nose. I filled my lungs and held it. The car smelled like him. Not his soap or deodorant or whatever he used on his hair, but *his* smell. Something dark and sharp and deep. Nothing like Jerk Face. *He* smelled like that obnoxious body spray for guys.

Adam kissed me again. "Are you okay? You look scared. You're usually so tough."

"Me? Tough?" I stretched my arms over my head. My back was killing me.

"Maybe 'strong' is a better word. You look . . . I don't know . . . fragile. It makes me want to protect you." It was something Foley would've said, except I knew what Adam felt was reserved only for me.

"We better vacate the premises," I said, gathering the blankets. "Before your dad gets up."

For the second morning in a row, I got to see the sun rise. I stood out front while Adam ran the keys inside. A garbage truck rumbled up the street, trailing putrid liquid. I checked my breath and popped a piece of gum.

"Breakfast?" Adam said.

"Whatever you want," I said. I had an hour to kill before my mother left for work.

Adam wanted muffins. Blueberry. We walked to the gas station and then walked to the park. Not Hillhurst. The other one. The one around the corner from his house. It's not even really a park, more like a playground with ancient swings and a teeter-totter and these iron animals on springs. I rode the duck. Adam squatted on a hippo. The muffins were stale, so we fed them to the pigeons. When it was safe to go home, Adam walked me to the door and kissed me good-bye. We wouldn't see each other again until tomorrow. He and Chris had to do the family thing: lunch with his aunt; dinner with Grandma and Grandpa. I needed sleep, anyway. Plus, I'd promised to clean. When I finally rolled out of bed at three, I vacuumed and dusted—the works. The place was spotless. I made dinner, too: spaghetti and meatballs.

My mother was impressed. She'd also had her hair cut.

"So who's the friend?" I asked.

"His name's Chip."

"Is he from work?"

"I met him online. Through one of those dating sites."

A hunk of meat went down the wrong way. After I stopped coughing, part of me was like, *Go, Mom!* But another part was just plain sad. Sad that she was lonely. Sad that she was desperate enough to look for someone on the Internet. Sad that she was lonely and desperate enough to pick a guy named Chip.

"Sorry," I mumbled. "I'm just surprised. Why didn't you tell me?"

"You're never home long enough for me to talk to you."

Ouch. Point taken.

I took care of the dishes while my mom got ready, and then I got ready, too. I chose my T-shirt wisely—no inappropriate slogans or band names—and brushed my teeth. I wasn't going to be one of those kids who sabotage her parent's shot at a new beginning. If anybody deserved a little happiness, it was my mom. Maybe Chip had good taste in music and went to a lot of concerts. Or maybe he was really into home improvement—I'm too old for a pink bedroom anymore. Better yet, maybe Chip was the kind of guy who liked to lavish gifts on his girlfriend's children.

Chip was okay—a little stiff. A little beefy in the face and middle, like he'd only recently started working out. He said he had a daughter my age. Maybe I knew her? She went to Nisky, the other high school.

Nisky girls are the worst. All the snobs go there. My interests? Theater. Art. Music. Chip's daughter was into sports. Vol-
leyball, mostly. When the interview was over, my mother was
smiling. I waved good night and made my escape.

It actually felt really good to be home, in my room, in my bed,
kicking back to drool over my favorite food show. I wondered
what Scott would think—about our mom dating. It was weird,
but for some reason I wanted to call my dad. To rub it in his face.
See, Mom's moving on. This is your last chance.

I picked up my phone and stared at his number. I called Lisa
instead. We hadn't talked all day.

"Tracy?" Her voice sounded strained, like she'd been crying.
My first thought was Gabe. He'd found out about Trent and it
was over. I turned down the TV.

"What's wrong?" I said. "What happened?"

Silence and then whispers: "He's been here. I'm scared. What
if he wants to hurt Katie?"

"What are you talking about?" I asked. "Who?"

"The creep from the woods," she whispered. "Banana Man.
I'm gonna go find him."

I shivered, but then I heard my mom and Chip in the kitchen,
pouring drinks.

"Have you been smoking?" I asked.

"I have to stop him," she cried.

"Stay there," I said. "I'll be right over."

What turns a nonbeliever into a believer? For Lisa it was
coming home to a second eye, settled neatly beside the first. Two
starry blues gazing up from her nightstand.

But I couldn't make the leap.

I followed because she was my friend.

Standing at the top of the stairs, Lisa's flashlight trained below, we dashed the silence with pounding feet, the hard snap of rocks hitting tarp. Lisa's fear made her fearless. She shouted herself hoarse—*Leave us alone! Stay away! Touch my sister and I'll kill you!*—but I hung back, clinging to reason. *There has to be an explanation. No one lives there. The place is abandoned.*

And then a shaft of light crossed ours. A long, dark shape advanced. The tight lump of nerves in my chest metastasized, spreading panic through my veins. Brightness snagged my eyes, blinding me. Nails clawed my flesh. Lisa's nails, digging into my wrist, dragging me up the stairs. We chased the beam from her flashlight through the underbrush, running and tripping but not looking back, not until we exploded into the street.

Safe, I thought, like an idiot, like this was some game we were playing. But we weren't safe.

The rules had changed.

Six

after two dates with the Chipster, Mom was ready to call it quits.

"It's . . ." She lifted her turkey sub and put it back down. Glancing around the food court, she leaned in and lowered her voice. "I don't know. It's weird. I'm too old for dating." She took a sip of soda and swallowed. "You've got to remember, I was with your father for more than half my life." Her eyes welled up and she shook her head. "It's like you marrying Adam. No. Longer. It's like you marrying Foley."

Something in me surged. My face got hot. Now I was the one with darting eyes, hoping no one was listening. "Pul-eeze," I said, trying to hide what I was feeling.

My mother smiled around her straw. "You two'll end up together. Once you figure it out."

"Figure what out?"

"C'mon, Tracy. You'd have to be blind not to see how he feels about you."

"You don't know what you're talking about," I said, shaking my head, looking away. "He's like that with everyone. Foley doesn't believe in commitment. Besides, I already have a boyfriend. I don't think Adam would appreciate you suggesting I dump him for another guy."

My mother reached out and chucked my chin. "Lighten up. I'm teasing." She checked her watch. "When's your party?"

"Not until seven," I said.

"Good." My mother stacked our trays. "I really need something for the company picnic. A simple top that covers and shorts that don't ride up. Is that too much to ask these days?"

Watching my mother try on one hideous outfit after another, I wondered if she was right—about Foley. He was going to be at Adam's party. Everybody was going. Everybody except Lisa. She couldn't let go of the eyeball thing. All week she'd insisted on being home when Katie went to bed, which was Lisa's bed now, too. She'd started sleeping in Katie's room. I texted her one last time hoping to change her mind, but she already had plans. Gabe was coming over. Homeless Ryan, too. They were going to the movies. A double date.

By the time my mother dropped me off at Adam's, I had a wicked case of mall head. Chris was out back filling a cooler with ice, his white polo and khaki shorts emphasizing his insanely dark tan. Chugging a can of soda, I spotted Adam's stepmom, Linda, spying from the back window.

"I thought they were going out?" I whispered.

"They tricked us," Chris said without moving his lips. He smiled up at Linda and waved. "Mix-up with their tickets.

Show's *next* Friday. This should be fun. We're playing energy-drink pong."

Adam sauntered from the garage, looking paler than usual, a bundle of torches clamped under his arm. "Just in time," he said, and pressed his mouth to mine. I winced. Twice. Once from the stubble. Again from his breath. It smelled like taco meat.

"You know how to set up the cups for pong?" he asked, dropping the torches at my feet.

"I'm not an idiot," I said, wishing he'd eat some toothpaste. "You put them in a triangle."

Adam looked hurt. "I meant would you do it."

"Sure," I said, turning to avoid another kiss.

"Everything's in the garage," he said. "Shout if you need help with the table."

The garage smelled like motor oil and gasoline. I wrinkled my nose. Dragging the folding table across the cement, I pinched my finger in the stupid leg brace. Sucking my pinky, I unpacked red plastic cups and eggshell-thin balls, a case of gold-and-black cans, and then texted Lisa again. *Please come,* I begged. *Bring Katie and Ryan.* It was bound to be the tamest party ever. Especially with Adam's stepmom hovering. Lisa responded with a frowny emoticon, *Just bought our tickets.*

As if on cue, Linda ducked into the garage with a basket of cheese curls. "Adam said to put some snacks out here," she said, putting down the basket and picking up a can. "I don't know how you kids can drink this stuff," she said, scanning the label. "Oh, by the way, the next time you and Adam sleep in the car . . ."

My face burned. I knew I'd felt someone watching that night. It wasn't my imagination. But it wasn't Banana Man, either. It was Linda—Scary Stalker Mom. Lucky for me, Rachel came dancing down the driveway. I shouted and waved, and Linda gave me a tight-lipped smile before marching back to the house. Rachel's eyes raked the garage. "Where's Lisa?" she asked.

Sometimes I think Lisa and I are too close, and I can't socialize without her. I could never talk to Rachel the way I talk to Lisa. After a few minutes, the conversation fizzled out and we drifted, searching for our boyfriends. Hers was arguing politics with the foreign exchange student. Mine was hooking up speakers. I sat at the picnic table, alone, waiting for someone good to show up. Adam had invited theater people, mostly, but then someone he worked with rolled in with a couple of girls from Nisky. Keira, I think, and her friend Something Snobby. I hated them instantly, with their long, smooth hair and manicured nails, faces looking like they'd spent the day at the makeup counter. They reminded me of Jeanine. Which reminded me of Foley. Warm hands cupped my eyes. Everything went dark. My heart did a little dance.

"It's not so bad," Adam said. "I think everybody's having fun. Trent's got a case in his car if you want something to drink." Adam's skin was usually pretty clear, but that night his forehead was a constellation of angry red bumps.

"What's going on with your face?" I asked, grimacing slightly, and then hated myself for asking.

"It's from the kitchen," he said, dragging his bangs to his chin. "I was on the grill. All that grease."

I brushed the hair from his eyes and kissed him gently. I loved him. I did. Foley meant nothing to me, and I meant nothing to Foley. My mom had it all wrong.

I spent the rest of the party acting like Katie at the pool that day, wading past faces, searching, and then bored. Eventually I parked myself beside Chris and watched him whip one of the Nisky girls at energy-drink pong. When that got boring, too, I wandered out to Trent's car for something to numb the ache in my chest.

"Get in," Trent said. He reached behind the seat and passed me a green bottle. "Listen, I'm sorry I started all this bullshit. I didn't think anybody would actually believe it."

I took a swig and shook my head, confused.

"This stuff with Lisa. About Banana Man. Gabe says she's kind of gone off the deep end."

"You didn't do that thing with the other eye, did you?" I poked him with the bottle, hoping he'd confess, but now Trent looked confused.

"What 'thing' with the other eye?"

He shifted his weight. The upholstery squeaked. In the dark of the car, the closeness made me reach for the door handle, but I stopped, cringing inside, hating my body for overreacting. I hated the way it cropped up like that—the fear. My radar was broken. *He'd* broken it—that stupid jerk from Troy.

But Trent hadn't noticed.

I tucked my hand under my leg and explained how Lisa had found a second blue eye, in her room, on her nightstand, next to the one she'd stolen.

"I'm pretty twisted," Trent said, flicking his lighter. "But that's some sick shit." Two orange tongues reflected off his glasses as he bent to the flame and inhaled. "Who do you think's messing with her?"

"I don't know," I said. "But she's losing it. She really thinks he's stalking her." I thought of the sensor light. *There are no monsters. Only creepy stepmoms.* "The crazy thing is," I said, "she almost had me believing it, too."

I was about to tell Trent about our midnight raid—I'm sure we'd scared the crap out of that poor homeless guy, bombing his shelter with rocks—but a boy with a lip ring knocked on the roof and leaned in. "Bar still open?" he asked.

Trent shuttled the bottles through the window. "Be discreet," he warned, nodding his head toward the Nisky girls, posing beneath the streetlight, finger-combing their hair. But beer ended up out back anyway and so did Linda—to stay, circling the yard like a shark until everyone decided it was time to head over to Eric Stanley's. He was having a party that night, too. His parents were on a cruise, I think. It didn't matter. They had a pool. Foley probably just went straight there. Or he was with Jeanine. Or maybe he was out talking some girl off a ledge. You never knew with Foley. He was like a one-man crisis prevention hotline. Rachel offered me a ride, but I stayed to help Adam throw away cups and cans and cheese curls. It was my penance for being a jerk all night.

While Adam and Chris cleaned up the garage, I went around front and sat on the steps. Why was everything always so complicated? And what did my mom know anyway? When did she become an expert on love? She hadn't even known my dad was having an affair until she found that charge on a credit card. Or that her son was gay until . . . well, I hadn't known Scott was gay, either. Not until he told us. But it didn't matter. She'd ruined my night. It wasn't the first time I'd made myself miserable waiting for Foley, but that was before I had a good boyfriend, before I had Adam. A small voice in me blistered: *You shouldn't be feeling what you're feeling.*

"Don't be sad," Chris said, startling me. "I'll be back at Christmas." Gripping my head, he climbed around me to the next step up and gave my shoulders a squeeze.

I was so distracted all night I'd forgotten he was leaving Sunday. I'd almost gone home without giving him a real good-bye. The porch light winked out and a toad jumped from the shadows. I crouched down and scooped him up. Bumpy and cold, his tiny throat pulsed beneath my fingers.

"I'll call him Chris," I said. And then to Adam, as he came slouching across the lawn: "Doesn't he look like a Chris?"

Adam sat on his heels and chewed a cuticle, considering. "Mammalian Chris is browner than amphibian Chris," he said. I agreed. Chris poked my ribs and then rested his chin on my shoulder and stroked the toad's head through my cage of fingers.

"He's a night creature," Chris said, laughing. "I think 'Adam' is more appropriate—"

A car raced up the street, drowning him out. Brake lights flared. Someone jumped out of the passenger side and waved. "Hey, sorry I missed your party," Foley called, jogging up the walk. He clapped Adam on the back and shook his hand, and then rushed toward me, stooped on the step with my heart in my throat. My muscles went weak. Foley opened his arms for a hug and I lost my grip. The toad wiggled from his cage and hopped away, vanishing in the grass.

seven

To: splendidhavoc@horizon.net
From: blackolcun@horizon.net
Subject: SOS

I just wanted to put the fear of darkness in him.

It's not like we didn't try to get him to stop. We really did.
But he wouldn't. Things kept escalating. We had to do
something.

Please come home.

I understand about you and Justin. Mom does, too. She
didn't mean the things she said—you know how she is.

That was a pretty big bomb you dropped. How was she supposed to know? You had a girlfriend for three years. Lisa took it hard, too. She always had a not-so-secret crush on you. I think she dreamed that someday you'd see she wasn't a kid anymore—your little sister's best friend—and fall in love, just like in the movies. But it's never like the movies, is it? Love?

Sometimes it feels like the ugliest thing he put in me that day is fear. I fight it, I do. But it's there. And it hurts. I'll get over it—I have to, right?—but I don't ever want to hurt again.

I'm rambling. I know. This is turning into one of those e-mails Grandma sends, the ones where you scroll and scroll and never reach the end. It would be easier if you'd just answer your phone. It's so quiet right now. Almost too quiet. I keep expecting the cops to show up any minute, pounding on the door, waking Mom, waking the neighbors, dragging me out to the street in cuffs. But I need help. I need someone to listen. I could go to Foley, but I never want to see him again.

I can't sleep. I'm too afraid.

eight

i f I ever make a movie with a grisly murder scene, I'll film it
in the Hillhurst Park bathroom. It's one of those concrete
block buildings with an L passage and a metal door that gets
padlocked after dark. Inside, there's a curtainless shower and
four stalls with plywood doors you can see over and caged
windows set high in the walls. Post-slaughter, a killer can wash
the gore down the floor drain. I don't know how I'll capture the
smell, which is always something funky.

That day it was rotten eggs.

Washing my hands, I checked my reflection in the polished
metal over the sink. My blue streaks were fading. I needed more
color. I tiptoed around the wet toilet paper stuck to the floor and
held the door for a mother dragging a rabid toddler on a leash.
Cue the screechy violins.

But the places where bad things happen aren't always so

ominous, I thought, stopping to buy a blue raspberry taffy from the Snack Shack. A few days before, a boy with a bee allergy died right here in front of the candy counter.

I took the shortcut through the pines back to the pool. When I'd left, Lisa was propped on her elbows watching Katie practice handstands in the shallow end. But now Katie was crouched on the grass with the towel over her head and Lisa was screaming and gesturing at a woman in a mom bathing suit. The mom flailed angrily right back.

Conflict makes my knees go wobbly. I wanted to climb under the towel with Katie. I caught enough of the shouting to hear that the woman's son had yanked down Katie's bikini bottom. I didn't know if Katie was hiding because everyone had seen or because her sister had morphed into a raging psycho.

"If your son *ever* touches my sister again, I'll break his little arm!" Lisa shrieked. Which was exactly the wrong thing to be yelling when park security showed up to investigate the disturbance. The guard listened to the lifeguard and then the mom. A few minutes later, he was escorting Lisa through the crowd toward Katie and me. I pulled on my T-shirt and then peeked under the towel and handed Katie hers.

"Get this," Lisa said, shoving her book in her bag. "He's asking *us* to leave."

The officer just stood there, clutching his belt, looking bored.

"It's okay," I said. "It's cloudy anyway."

"It's sexual harassment!" Lisa shouted to anyone still listening. "My sister has a right to go swimming without being felt up!" She reached under the towel for Katie's hand and guided her up the knoll to the jogging path. When we got to the play area with the rocket slide, I tugged Lisa's shirt to slow down. I started to apologize, but she cut me off.

"Save it," she growled. She stuck her head under the towel to talk with Katie. "You can come out now," she said gently. Katie's eyes were red from crying. Her breath escaped in uneven bursts.

"Stupid scummy slimeball jerks," Lisa muttered, doing her best not to curse in front of Katie.

Then the sky opened up, pelting the hot asphalt with warm summer rain. A low rumble rippled across the park. Two seconds later, the air horn sounded. Everybody out of the pool.

"Good," Lisa said, finally smiling. "I hope those lowlifes get struck by lightning."

I'd always known Lisa was fiercely protective. Once she'd yelled in our math teacher's face to defend me after he accused me of cheating. I hadn't. I'd just studied really hard—all weekend, at the diner with Lisa. Her reaction today made me wonder what she would have done to the jerk from Troy.

If I'd told her.

Why hadn't I told her?

I'd skulked home that day feeling shivery and brittle, thinking everybody looking at me knew, like what had happened was as visible as a big black eye.

We waited out the storm in the Snack Shack, and then we cheered Katie up with a trip to the big-box drugstore they tore down all those houses to build. She loves that place. Actually, Lisa and I love that place, too. I hate running errands for my mom, but I never complain when she sends me down there. It's in a crummy part of town, but as soon as those sliding glass doors part, you could be anywhere. That day: Alaska. A blast of frigid air turned my skin to goose bumps. I checked my reflection in the giant round mirror in the ceiling and made a beeline for cosmetics.

"I look like a quarterback," I said, wiping the black smudges from under my eyes.

"Cotton Candy Frenzy?" Lisa asked, spritzing my wrist.

I sniffed. "Nice," I said. "If you want to attract clowns and carnies."

I moved down the aisle toward the lipsticks. Uncapping a tester, I asked Lisa if she liked the color. She shrugged. "Not on you." I drew a stripe on the back of my hand. Too dark.

"These are your shades," she said, gathering a handful of tubes and pots.

After she did my makeup, we wandered over to the magazines and browsed fall fashions. It's hard to get excited about boots and sweaters when it's ninety degrees. Everything looked binding and itchy. End-of-summer colors did nothing for me either: brown and ocher and maple leaf.

"I'm getting these," Katie said, running up with a pair of kiwi-green eyelashes.

"Where'd you get money?" Lisa asked.

"Mom."

"Buy me something, too?" Lisa pleaded

Katie counted her bills. "What do you want?"

Lisa came back with a bottle of pearly nail polish.

"Okay," Katie said. "I owe you for sticking up for me. Even if we are banned from the pool."

"We're not banned," Lisa said. "And you don't owe me. He had no right to touch you."

"Pervert," Katie said. "We should tie him up in the woods. Sacrifice him to Banana Man."

"That kid's not a pervert," Lisa said. "Just a horndog. Please don't make me explain the difference." She turned Katie by the shoulders and sent her toward the registers. "Go pay."

"I never should've told her he's real," Lisa whispered. "It's all she talks about."

It's all you *talk about*, I thought. I wanted to take her by the shoulders and say, *Wake up. You're not a little kid. Monsters don't exist.* Instead I said, "You didn't tell her about the eye, did you?"

She picked up a box of hair color and put it back down. "I'm not stupid."

"Doesn't she wonder why you're sleeping in her room?"

"I told her my room's too hot. It's true. She's got the better fan."

I knew it was the wrong time to bring it up, but I told Lisa that my mom wanted her to stay over Friday night, so we could get an early start on Saturday. The company picnic was at an amusement park this year—something new. They used to hold it at the Rod and Gun Club. Hamburgers and hot dogs and contests for the kids. Scott and I always went home with half the prizes.

Lisa sighed heavily.

"If you don't want to go," I said, "tell me now. I'll bring Adam. He hates rides—"

"No, I want to go." She sounded torn. "Can I let you know tomorrow?"

Katie came back waving four dollar bills. Outside, she dragged us toward the yellow arch shining brightly against the storm-bruised sky. "That's a lot of food if we order off the Value Menu," she said. She was right. Four bucks won't buy a grilled chicken salad, but it will buy two cherry pies, a strawberry shake, and a hot fudge sundae. When my mother got home from work, I wasn't hungry. Which was too bad—she was actually planning to cook. Parmesan chicken and the first green beans from the garden. She made herself a frozen dinner instead.

"Can Adam come over and watch a movie?" I asked.

My mom blew on her fork. "Sure," she said. "I need to do some weeding tonight, anyway."

"You don't have to hide," I said. "We won't get anything scary. Nothing sexy, either."

The phone rang. My mother froze. "If that's Chip, I'm not here," she whispered.

I picked up the receiver. "This is Tracy," I said. I looked at my mother; a mouthful of beef tips squirreled in her cheeks like she was afraid whoever was on the other end would hear her chewing. "Chip?" I said. "That's so funny! We were just talking about you. Yeah. Hold on, she's here."

My mother bulged her eyes angrily and swallowed. Putting the phone to her ear, she croaked, "Hi!" As soon as she realized it was a recorded message for some company trying to sell us something, her face relaxed into a smile. "Ha-ha," she said, hanging up. She tossed the black plastic tray in the trash and her fork in the sink. She was smiling. Good. It was the perfect time to ask what I'd been wondering about since the drugstore: "Can we bring Katie to the picnic?"

My mother went to the fridge and pulled a couple of plastic deli bags from the meat drawer. Her silence meant she was considering my request. I got out the chips and stuck a fruit cup in her insulated lunch bag. "She's a good kid," I said, trying to sway her. "She'll do whatever you say."

"Katie's not the problem." My mother chucked a loaf of moldy bread. "I'll have to pay full-price at the gate. And she wouldn't get any lunch. You need a special wristband for that. They came with the tickets I got through work."

"The problem is, Larry might have to do overtime," I said. "If she can't go, Lisa can't go."

I hated lying, but the truth was ridiculous: my best friend was afraid of the boogeyman.

"Let me see what I can do," she said. "Maybe somebody has an extra ticket."

Leaning on the counter, watching her build a sandwich, I asked if she'd ever heard a creepy story about a guy called Banana Man.

"Banana Man? Like the fruit?" She rolled a slice of turkey and popped it in her mouth. "Sounds kind of silly. Where'd you get that from?"

"Never mind."

My mom screwed the lid on the mayonnaise and rinsed the knife. After everything was put away, she sat next to me at the counter and dug into the chips. "When I was a kid we were all afraid of the Hillhurst Demon," she said, crunching. "He stalked the triangle of woods between the park and the hospital. You know where I mean?"

My temples throbbed. The kitchen started spinning. I nodded for her to go on.

"My friends used to say that if you ever saw the creature— even just a quick glimpse—your eyes would melt like wax." My mother elbowed me and then offered me a chip. "Kinda scary, huh? What's your monster do?"

nine

t he last time we went to Action Adventure, my family was happy. At least we seemed happy. I guess if I put it on a timeline, my dad was already cheating, Scott was sorting through some crazy emotions, and my mom was getting all kinds of grief over her promotion to supervisor. And I was plotting the death of my tormentor, a mean girl who nicknamed me Melon Head after a really horrible failed attempt to dye my hair.

A lot has changed since then. The security checkpoint at the gate was new. Plus the rule about no coolers. Then there were these special bracelets they were selling that let you cut to the front of the lines. But we didn't need them. We had my mom. It's her job to know all about traffic and how to deal with it. She snatched a guide from a friendly dinosaur and steered us through the crush of families clogging the winding streets of

Ye Olde Village. Her strategy—go directly to the farthest point on the map—worked. Ghost Town was a ghost town.

"What's first?" my mom asked, surveying the massive metal monsters crouched between the false front buildings and wooden sidewalks. Katie oo-ooed for the swings. Lisa, the free-fall tower. Everybody rolled their eyes at my pick: Tornado Alley, a dark ride through a wind tunnel, with flying Day-Glo cows and hypnotic spirals and air horns. My favorite ride ever, even if it was the cheesiest. My mom's eyes drifted to the giant corkscrew rising up behind the saloon and dance hall. The Gold Rush. My mom is the Roller-Coaster Queen. She'll ride anything: sketchy wooden deathtraps; neck-snapping figure eights—the suspended kind, where the cart dangles from a track above your head.

My mom pulled rank. We ducked under the switchback of ropes and claimed the first two cars.

It's amazing what a jolt of adrenaline can do. My mom was rowdy and giddy, throwing her arms over her head while I gripped the safety bar like a chicken. Maybe this would remind her who she was before my dad left and turned her world upside down. Maybe she'd try dating again. Just because she hadn't hit it off with Chip didn't mean there wasn't someone out there for her. She should add "thrill seeker" to her profile.

"That was sick!" Lisa shouted.

Katie and I bumped fists.

"Who wants to go again?" my mom asked.

After the fourth run, lines had formed behind the chains. We moved on. Log Jam. Tornado Alley. The Tumbleweed. My mom and Katie sat out the Thunderbird because Katie's stomach felt weird. Warm and woozy, we showed our wristbands at the saloon for free soda and hiked down the hill to Jungle Land, which was a rip-off—the one big ride was closed for repairs—but Katie wanted to see the animals.

That was always Scott's least favorite part. Even when we were little, he hated seeing them in their sad, lonely cages. I hated the rope bridge, with its animatronic alligators lurking in the muddy waters below. Once, the bridge bounced so hard I started crying. Clinging to the net, I was sure I'd tumble over and die, impaled on those long sharp teeth. But my dad saved me. Rushing out, he snatched me up and carried me to solid ground.

My mother asked if I remembered the time he won me an enormous pink panda. But I didn't. "You were only two. That thing was bigger than you," she said. "He must have spent fifty bucks trying."

"Hey guys, there's no line there," Katie said, pointing to an oblong wheel ringed with cages—a Ferris wheel on steroids. The Zipper. I'm not afraid of anything, but that ride freaks me out. It's Scott's fault. He used to torture me when we were kids, pointing out rust spots, making me think the bolts were bad. Since Scott wasn't there to torture me, I tortured Katie.

"That doesn't sound safe," I said, furrowing my brow at the creaking noise above our heads.

Lisa buckled us in, and then she got the cart rocking. "You know this thing's gonna flip, right?"

"You guys," Katie whined. "Why are you always mean to me?"

"Mean to you?" I said, bumping Katie's shoulder.

Lisa winked. "Maybe she's talking about the time we read her diary."

"'My hamster died today,'" I quoted from memory. "'It is the saddest day ever.'"

When the guy came around and rattled the cage door, Katie wanted off. She crawled over my lap and flew down the ramp and joined my mother on the bench next to the snow cone stand.

"Is she mad?" I asked. "We were just joking."

"That *was* kind of cruel, making her think that pin is coming loose."

It was just like Lisa to turn things around and make me the bad guy. *She* was the reason her sister was having nightmares. Last night Katie woke the whole house because she thought she heard tapping at the window. But I wasn't going to let Lisa's dumb comment ruin my day. Besides, she smacked her head on the cage. Hard. She got off dizzy and queasy.

My mom went for water and came back with sunscreen. "You're looking a little red," she said. Cupping Lisa's chin, she dabbed her forehead and nose and cheeks. She did Katie's face, too, and then mine. Her fingers felt good—cool and soft.

"I think I'm hungry," Katie said.

My mom checked her watch. "One more ride and we'll head over to the pavilion."

One more ride took thirty-five minutes. The line for the Raging Rapids snaked past the Alpine Slide, with its heavy metal pounding, lights throbbing, the riders a blur of color. Lisa posted a picture of us with a gorilla in sunglasses on her feed. We had eight likes by the time we reached the dock.

I don't know how it happened, but my mom—the one person who didn't want to get soaked—ended up under the waterfall. Lisa and Katie couldn't stop laughing. The shock on her face was priceless. Hair plastered to her head. Eye makeup streaking down.

"You look like a drowned cat!" I shouted over the water slapping against the raft.

"You're a real sweetheart!" she shouted back.

Sluicing through the troughs, the giant rubber doughnut started spinning. My mother cringed at the water sheeting off another fake cliff. "This is ridiculous," she yelled out. Katie tried steering, but she only made it worse. My mom got swamped again.

The rest of us survived—our makeup and hair, anyway. But my mom caught her reflection in a shop window and frowned. I dug through my bag for a tissue. "A lot of good that'll do me," she said, searching the map for a restroom. "I hope my Prince Charming isn't roaming the park."

Judging from the prizes coming out of the men's room, it was safe to say my mother wasn't in danger of meeting the man of her dreams. Ditto for the ones filling their plates under the pavilion. All the guys my mom works with are married or have girlfriends or both. Lisa and Katie got in line while my mom and I made the rounds. A lot of the drivers hadn't seen me since the company Christmas party. There was the mechanic who always brought horseshoes to the picnic, and the driver with the rock-abilly hair and too-strong cologne, and the one with the biker beard who played Santa. I waved to Reese, my driver when I used to take the bus to Troy to visit Jerk Face, and totally snubbed Davis for getting me in trouble with my mother. He's the reason I'll never smoke on a bus route again.

Everybody wanted to know what I was doing all summer. Did I have a job? No. Was my mother teaching me to drive? Yeah, right. No one was stupid enough to ask about my dad, but they all wanted to know where Scott was hiding. I wanted to joke, *Not in the closet!* But I knew my mom hadn't told them. She likes to keep her private life private.

Lunch was a buffet of steam trays loaded with hamburgers,

hot dogs, and corn on the cob. We had to wait for the salads to be refilled, but I didn't mind. I have this thing about mayonnaise. Flies, too. The pavilion was crawling with them. I covered my plate with a plate and plunked down between Katie and Lisa.

"This is way better than the old picnics," I whispered. My mom agreed. She's not big into company functions. The way she sees it, she spends enough time with her coworkers without socializing on her days off.

"Is that all you're eating?" my mom asked Katie. Katie rubbed her belly at the pile of corn cobs and ice cream sandwich wrappers and said she felt funny. I took one look at the shriveled brown puck masquerading as a hamburger and ate the salads instead—at least they were fresh.

"Oh my God!" Lisa shrieked, shoving the park guide in my face. "They've got one of those skydive thingies! It's right out there!"

I followed her finger to the two towers sticking up behind the pavilion next to ours. "No way," I mumbled through a mouthful of coleslaw. "They charge for that ride."

"I've got money!" Lisa pulled a fifty from her pocket. "I'll pay! Please say yes!"

Before I could say no, a burly guy with a yellow mustache and red nose clapped my mom on the back. "Trish, sweetie! You look like you went through the bus wash!" Al Minty. My mother hates Al Minty. He's one of the drivers who make her life miserable, filing bullshit grievances against her.

My mom smiled tightly. He was lucky the fork in her hand was plastic.

"Where's Teddy?" Al asked. "I thought I saw you two together." Teddy is my dad. Al smelled like he'd been boozing it up at the Bavarian Village.

"Wasn't Ted," my mother answered sharply. "Better clean your beer goggles."

Al's nose turned redder. Lisa kicked me under the table. I bit back a wicked grin. It sounds sappy, but I'm sort of proud of my mom, the way she can shut down someone like Al. No one knows she hates her job or that she used to come home crying and make herself ill thinking about work the next day. She's a no-nonsense boss, but she takes a lot of crap being the only woman in a garage full of guys. Not all of them are jerks, just a few. The rest of them treat her like Snow White in some twisted fairy tale.

"Who are these lovely ladies?" Al asked, changing the subject.

Lisa and I exchanged glances.

"You remember Tracy," my mom said. "This is her friend Lisa. And Lisa's sister, Katie."

"You girls having fun?" he asked.

We all nodded, and then Lisa and I pulled out our phones to ignore him. I texted Adam to see what he was up to. He was helping his dad with the yard. *I'd rather be hanging with you*, he said.

"Take it easy," Al said, raising his hand. "Good seeing you, Tracy."

My mom rolled her eyes and then gathered our plates and dumped them in a big orange barrel swarming with bees.

"What was that all about?" I asked, pushing through the turnstile.

"Al just likes to be difficult," she said. "Anything to make me uncomfortable."

He made me uncomfortable, too.

"Rip Cord?" Lisa said. She linked her arm through mine and

dragged me to the fence. "It's not so bad. Look. We'll get the DVD to show Adam and Gabe."

"There's no net," Katie said.

"That's what the pool's for," Lisa said. "If something snaps, we'll end up in the water."

I locked eyes with my mom, hoping she'd rescue me.

"It's up to you," she said. "If you're afraid . . ."

Katie just stood there with her arms folded, shaking her head.

"Fine," I huffed. "Let's do it. Before I change my mind."

Lisa squealed and then flung her phone and sunglasses and jewelry at my mom and then raced to the ticket booth. She had enough for the ride, but not the DVD. My eyes traveled up the lift tower. I wondered what the girl pushing me toward the platform had done with my best friend. There was the death wish thing—that was new—but scarier than that, we had an audience. Lisa hates being the center of attention. It's what keeps her backstage doing makeup and hair. It's what keeps her from auditions year after year. Everybody's eyes were on us as the guy cinched us together in an oversized apron and made us lock arms.

"Has anyone ever died on this ride?" I asked.

The guy tugged on the harness straps, said, "Not today," and signaled the control booth.

My mom and Katie cheered as our feet left the platform. Lisa kissed my cheek. "Wave to the people," she said.

The cable winched us higher and higher. Suddenly, I had to pee. My fear needed an out. The pool below didn't help. Shallow and filled with concrete blocks and floodlights, the image of serenity was an illusion. The water wouldn't break my fall, and the crap at the bottom would break my face.

"We've all got to go someday," Lisa said.

I wanted to punch her, but I was afraid to move.

"That's so not what I want to hear right now," I choked.

The riders stuck at the top of the Ferris wheel looked up and waved. Lisa waved back. Her hip bone rubbed against mine. A jerk in the cable made me pinch my eyes shut. We'd stopped moving. A grainy voice came from somewhere above. One of us had to pull the rip cord.

"Look at all those people down there wishing they had the guts to be up here," Lisa said. "If we can do this, we can do anything."

"All those people are waiting for us to die so they can put it on the Internet," I said.

Lisa reached up and wrapped her fingers around the grip. I couldn't do it. I would've left us hanging there forever. The voice started counting: three, two, one . . .

I've dreamed of falling. Usually it's off a cliff or a bridge, but I'm always startled awake after those first few seconds of weightlessness. I opened my eyes and screamed. Lisa screamed, too. Gravity tugged at my insides. We were gaining speed. My cheeks rippled. Down, down, faster and faster, like a giant bird, wings pulled tight, swooping in on its prey, and then we were soaring up, up. We were floating again. Rising gently. My fear rose, too, and fell away. Lisa and I stuck our arms out like superheroes and screamed just to scream.

"I love you!" Lisa hollered over the wind.

"I love you, too!" I hollered back.

The arc got shorter and shorter, and then the guy on the platform chased us with a hook to pull us in. We landed to clapping. My mom and Katie rushed the gate. "That was the most amazing thing ever!" I shouted. Katie and Lisa bumped fists, my mom dispensed the jewelry and sunglasses, and then we huddled around the map. The sun was brutal. Everybody looked boiled. "How about something gentle?" my mother suggested. "There's that ski lift ride over in Tiny Town."

"Too high," Katie said. She wanted to do the Scrambler—her favorite. We stopped for sodas on the way. One minute Katie was happily guzzling root beer and then she was crying because someone ran over her foot with a stroller. When we got to the Bavarian Village, her stomach hurt again. I was starting to wish we hadn't brought her.

"Maybe no more soda today," my mom advised. "Okay?"

Katie tossed her cup in the trash and plunked down on a bench. Lisa plunked down with her. My mom and I got in line for the ride.

"Something's up with her," my mom said, frowning. "While you and Lisa were on the Rip Cord, she went on and on about some monster that's stalking her and Lisa. She's a little old for that kind of talk, isn't she?"

"Sixth graders can be weird," I said. "Remember when I thought the hall closet was haunted?"

My mother rolled her eyes. The dude running the Scrambler told us to take one of the cars around back. I waved good-bye to Lisa, who was braiding Katie's hair, and climbed in first, which was a mistake. When I was little my mom always sat on the outside, against the padding, so she wouldn't squash me, but I'm not little anymore. I'm bigger than my mom. Taller, anyway. The ride started and I flew across the seat, my bones sinking into the softness of her flesh. I tried to keep from putting all my weight on her, but I was powerless against the forces pulling.

Katie and Lisa sprawled on the bench.

The arcade with its flashing lights and buzzers.

My father buying a bag of cotton candy.

My brains rattled in my skull. Everything blurred as our car punched toward Lisa and Katie again. My mother was screaming and laughing, tugging me closer. I tensed, waiting for that brief lag when everything snapped into focus. A man in gold jackknifed from the high dive. A balloon raced for the clouds. He'd moved, but I found him, aiming a water pistol at a clown's mouth. *Turn around,* I thought. My mother laughed in my ear. *Don't turn around,* I thought.

I waited for the ride to loop back again, praying it wasn't him. It couldn't be. Not unless he'd grown a beard. Not unless he'd left us for an ugly troll with a preschooler.

When we got off, he was gone. So were Lisa and Katie. My mother waited by the Moon Walk while I checked the bathroom. Lisa was at the sink, rinsing Katie's shorts. It looked like she'd sat in something.

"She's part of the club now," she whispered. "You don't have anything in your bag, do you?"

I didn't, but I had two quarters for the dispenser on the wall. I remember the first time I got mine. I was mortified. I didn't want to grow up. Maybe it would've been different if I'd had a big sister. In some ways it was like what happened with Jerk Face: I thought everyone would know. They didn't. It's funny how some of the most traumatic events in your life go unnoticed.

"Now my shorts are all wet," Katie complained behind the stall door.

"No one will care," Lisa said. "You look like you rode the Log Flume."

Outside, my mother was slumped on a bench. She needed coffee. Sometimes I forget that she's almost fifty. Katie told her her news.

"No wonder your belly hurts," she said, giving her a sympathetic squeeze. "Maybe we should take it easy for a while."

Lisa and I suffered through some lame rides for my mom and Katie—the swan boat, the train, the swings—and then we cruised over to Fantasy Land for the Rainbow, but it was shut down for repairs. I'm not a big fan of the Tilt-A-Whirl, but the line was short and I needed to keep moving. I couldn't stop thinking about my dad. The image was like a splinter in my brain. I dug and dug, but I couldn't pull it loose. Finally, I told Lisa. Waiting for the bumper cars, I said, "I think I saw my father."

Lisa looked behind us. "Where?"

"Not here," I said. "Back at the Scrambler."

"Are you sure?"

"Not really. The guy had a beard. He was with some fugly woman with a kid. He better not be seeing someone with a kid." Imagining my dad winning a giant stuffed animal for some home-wrecker's brat made my heart hurt. "He's an idiot if he left us for *that*."

A guy lowered the chain and everyone raced for their favorite color. I beat a girl with stars on her cheeks to the orange car. Lisa jumped in the purple one next to it.

"This is a fun day," she said. "Don't be sad."

"Wouldn't you miss Larry if he just up and left?"

"Not really," she said. "We can trade places if you want."

Lisa is the most aggressive driver ever. There's no way I'm ever getting in a real car with her. Blue sparks sizzled across the ceiling as she chased me around the track. I hate getting bumped. I steered clear of a massive pileup and drove donuts around a pole until the girl with stars on her cheeks rammed me into a corner. And then Lisa rammed her. And then someone—the girl's brother, I think—rammed Lisa. Before we'd backed out of the mess, the track went dead. Lisa and I stumbled out of our cars and across the floor. My head pounding, I walked right by my mom and Katie feeding popcorn to some pigeons.

"Over here," my mom called. The sun in her eyes made her squint. She looked happy, but tired. "I think we've had a pretty full day," she said, her cue that it was time to think about heading home. When I was little, I'd cry and cry, wanting the day to last forever. But I guess I'm not a kid anymore because I was okay with the best day ever ending. Dirty and achy, a hot shower was way more tempting to me than another ride. Katie was the only one who frowned all the way to the gift shop and then took her time browsing, dragging it out.

After nine hours in the sun, our car was a sauna. My mom opened all the doors and let the air conditioner run. Waiting for the upholstery to cool, I scanned the lot for my father's truck. Lisa texted Gabe, and Katie dug through her bag and gave my mom a magnet.

"I got one for my mom, too," she said.

"Suck up," I said, because I'd spent my money on myself.

Katie smirked.

"You guys must be starving," my mom said.

Katie called shotgun. Lisa and I jumped in back.

We stopped at a pancake house on the highway, not the seafood place we'd been going to for years. That was closed. My dad always got twin lobsters. The last time we went there, I was embarrassed by the stupid plastic bib he wore. All our family's favorite places—mini golf, now Captain Jack's—were disappearing. Maybe it was a sign. I was stuck in the past. My mom wasn't the only one who needed to get on with her life.

When we got home, I closed my bedroom door and called my

father's apartment. No one answered. I almost tried his cell phone, but then chickened out, afraid I'd recognize the noises we'd left behind. I asked my mother if we still had the giant pink panda she'd told me about earlier.

"Sorry, sweetie," she said, shaking her head sadly. "He's long gone."

ten

To: splendidhavoc@horizon.net
From: blackolcun@horizon.net
Subject: SOS

I can't sleep. I'm too afraid.

The nightmares keep getting stranger and stranger. I dig
beneath the carpet scraps, endlessly searching. There's
a cop there with me, in the woods—I'm always in the
woods—aiming a water pistol at my head, ordering me
to dig. Heart hammering, I claw at the ground until a
flash of pink fleece fills me with joy. I always think it's my
panda. But instead I find a rusty zipper and long blond
braids. Lisa. Not Lisa now. Lisa in seventh grade, before

she hated pink. Clearing the dirt from her eyes, my chest heaves. I can't breathe. I watch myself collapse into the infinite black of her lifeless pupils. Behind me, scaly fingers claw at the air. The cop just stands there with his pistol, useless against those long gray teeth and waxy lips. That's when Lisa's mouth parts, her blue lips curling into a smile. *If he can do this, he can do anything.*

I need help. I keep replaying what I did over and over. It's the weird, small details that stick. Tonight it was the pattern on one of his dirty blankets. Lambs and stars and moons.

In Troy, it was a chocolate under the couch, wrapped in silver foil and clotted with dust.

eleven

how many times do I have to tell my mom that I'm too old for a pediatrician? I don't care that they'll see me until I'm eighteen. It's humiliating. I felt ridiculous in that waiting room with the picture books and parenting magazines and bright plastic toys. I ignored my mom playing peek-a-boo with a crusty-nosed toddler and looked up stuff about dreams on my phone until the receptionist called my name. A nurse in rubber-ducky scrubs waved from the door.

"Come on back," she said.

My mom held my bag while I stood on the scale and watched the nurse fiddle with the clunky metal slider. I wasn't any taller, but I was a pound heavier.

"Is that okay?" I asked.

"You're within range for your height," she said, leading us down the hall to the room papered with jungle animals. My favorite. When I was six.

"You know I'm old enough to have a baby," I whispered to my mom.

She covered her ears. "Please don't say things like that around me."

I kicked off my sneakers and hopped up on the table. The nurse wrapped a pressure cuff around my bicep. Fingers on my wrist, she watched the needle on the dial and pumped the bulb in her fist. "There's a gown for you to put on," she said over the air hissing from the valve, then dropped my chart in the plastic holder on the wall. "Someone will be by shortly," she said, wrestling the accordion door closed.

"I can see into the hall," I complained to my mother.

"No one's looking at you," my mother said, flipping through a magazine while I undressed. Somewhere in the office a child screamed in pain. My mother made a face like she hurt, too, then dug around in her bag for a mint. "Please tell me you wore semi-new underwear," she said. "Not those holey things I keep finding in the wash. Those need to be thrown out."

I glanced at the faded purple cotton with the frayed elastic and pulled the gown to my knees. A rap on the accordion made me jump. I looked up, praying for Sandy the PA. Dr. Dan poked his head in instead.

"Hi Tracy! Hi Mom! How's everybody doing today?" Grabbing my chart, he plunked down on the wheeled stool and scooted across the room. "Let's see, we saw you back in February. Nasty case of flu. I'm guessing you survived?" He examined my fingernails—Gangrene, my new favorite color—and winked. "Maybe not."

My mother giggled. For a millisecond I wondered if there was a Mrs. Doctor Dan before my brain rejected it. *Awkward.* Listening to my heart, he asked if I exercised.

"Not if I can help it," I said to the ceiling.

"That's not true." I could hear the frown in my mother's voice. "She swims and she walks a lot."

"Walking is good," Dr. Dan said, sticking a black plastic cone in my left ear and then the right. He checked my eyes and nose and throat and then asked me to reach for the ceiling while he felt around under my arms. "We're almost done," he said. "If you'll just lie back." The paper beneath me crinkled. "I'm going to press on your stomach," he said. "Is that okay? Any pain or discomfort?"

"No."

"How's your menstrual cycle?"

My face burned. "Normal," I said.

"You can sit up now," he said. "You want the good news or the bad news?"

"Good news," I said.

Dr. Dan scooted over to the counter and tossed his gloves in the trash. "Dang," he said. "I was hoping you'd say 'bad.' There's no good news. You need a meningococcal booster."

My mother looked mildly smug when I asked her to hold my hand during the shot and then mildly offended when it was over and Dr. Dan asked her to wait for me outside.

"The hall?" She frowned, slinging her purse over her shoulder.

"You can go out to the waiting room," Dr. Dan said kindly. "We'll just be a few minutes."

When my mother was out of earshot, Dr. Dan said he had a few questions that might be easier to answer without my mother present.

"Do you smoke?" he asked.

I shook my head. *Liar.*

"Do you drink alcohol?"

"No." *Liar.* I hedged. "Sometimes. Not often. Just once."

"Are you sexually active?"

Flames of embarrassment licked my cheeks. I pictured Adam guiding my hands to neutral territory and shook my head. I should've told him about the jerk from Troy, but I couldn't. Maybe Sandy the PA, but not Dr. Dan.

Picking at my nail polish, I said, "Can I ask a stupid question?"

Dr. Dan dropped the chart on the counter and returned to the stool. "Shoot."

"Is it normal to keep having the same nightmare over and over? Like a really bad one. The kind you can't stop thinking about." I shivered remembering Lisa's eyes, the way they felt looking at me, emptily. Cold and slippery. It had me texting her at two in the morning: *R U OK?*

Dr. Dan clasped his hands between his knees. "You want to talk about it?"

"It's almost always the same," I said. "I'm running through the woods, from this thing, this monster. There's always this shack, too. When I get there, I think I'm safe, but then I realize the thing chasing me lives there."

Dr. Dan nodded, thinking. He asked if there was anything going on in my life that had me feeling anxious. Boyfriend trouble? Family issues? Was I nervous about going back to school? "Most nightmares are triggered by stress," he said. "Also, believe it or not, eating right before bed can give you bad dreams. Alcohol, too." He smiled, winking. "But you've only ever had one drink." He slapped my knee and stood up. "Try laying off the late-night snacks and see what happens. If it starts interfering with your daily activities— like you're tired all the time or the nightmares themselves are causing you stress—we'll have you come back in. Sound good?"

I nodded.

"Want a lollipop?"

I shook my head.

Dr. Dan unwrapped a green one and stuck it in his cheek. "You sure? They're better for you than cigarettes. Here, take some anyway. For your friends."

On the ride home, I was decorating the toes of my sneakers with glitter stickers when my mother squinted at me. "Did you steal those from the examining room?" She shook her head. "Never mind. Don't tell me. What did Dr. Dan want to talk about?"

"You," I said. "He wanted to know if you're seeing someone."

My mother's cheeks pinked. She pursed her lips. "Why do you always have to be a smart-ass?"

"Because the truth freaks you out," I said. "Lollipop?"

My mother scowled at the windshield. "The truth does *not* freak me out."

Sticking a rainbow on the dashboard, I told her Scott would disagree. A shadow passed over her face. I wish I could talk to her, like *really* talk to her. I would've told her about my dad's evil twin at Action Adventure. I would've told her about my nightmares. I might've finally told her about what happened in Troy.

But some things are just easier to deal with on my own.

My mother drove the rest of the way in silence. When we got home, I called Adam. He was at the bank, cashing his paycheck. He wanted to take me out to eat. Someplace nice, he said. My pick. I suggested the new Italian place on Eastern Avenue.

"You might need reservations," my mom said after I'd hung up.

There you go again, being nosy about all the wrong things. But I stayed quiet. She was already moody from my comment about Scott. She frowned at the stack of mail, picking up a postcard.

"This makes me feel old." She groaned. I peeked over her shoulder and read the announcement. Her high school reunion was coming up in August. Thirty years. I wondered if my dad had gotten one, too.

"You should go," I said.

Not going seemed like one of those things she'd regret. My mother sighed, but then hung the invitation on the fridge. There was hope. I'd work on her later, I thought, opening the freezer. Adam was coming at six, but I was already hungry.

My phone rang. Foley.

"Whatcha doin'?"

"Making a toaster pastry," I said.

"Are they tasty?"

"Delicious," I said. "Want one?"

"Do you deliver?" I could almost see him, his grin a little crooked, messy hair in his eyes.

I made a lot of bad decisions that day, but the first was asking Foley what flavor. *Raspberry or apple?* The second was lying to Adam. *My mom already has dinner started. Can we do tomorrow night?* The third was meeting Foley at his house instead of the park because the sky looked stormy. The fourth was putting a hot toaster pastry in a plastic baggie. The one I brought Foley was soggy by the time I got there, but he ate it anyway while cuing up a playlist. Watching him I started to feel guilty.

Lightning crashed close by, making me jump. "Relax," Foley said, turning off lamps. "We're safe." As he pulled me to the couch, my eyes drifted toward the door. But then we were sitting, just sitting. Me with my feet on the coffee table. Foley with his head on my leg, air drumming a song I only know because it's the theme to my mom's favorite crime show.

We're just friends. I'm allowed to have friends.

"We hardly ever see each other anymore," I said. "When did you pierce your ear?" I nudged the silver hoop with my finger and told him I liked it.

"Jeanine did it," he said.

A clap of thunder rattled the living room windows. I shivered.

"Is she your girlfriend?" I asked.

Foley laughed. "I'm sensing some jealousy."

"She is, isn't she?"

"Jeanine's not my *girlfriend.*" He made a face. He hates anything that reeks of possession. He also hates dishonesty. Foley never lies. He's the most truthful person I know.

Staring up at me through his curls, he smiled and said, "I'm happy you came over."

I twirled a lock of his hair. *It doesn't mean anything. You play with Lisa's hair, too.* Rain lashed against the window. A volley of ear-splitting cracks rattled my insides. Foley's knuckles grazed my chin and we locked eyes. Another kind of explosion sent my heart rate higher. That's when I realized my mother's vision was sharper than mine. She'd seen it—that gaze. No one else had ever looked at me that way. Adam was always dragging his eyes away, like he was afraid to let himself feel. The jerk from Troy—his eyes were hollow pits.

Foley reached up and pulled my face to his, and my insides turned to jelly. I didn't try to fight it. Instead, I reached blindly up and closed the drapes, not wanting to see the bolt of lightning that would strike me dead of guilt.

It was nothing like the first time, like that day in Troy. The word "no" never entered my head. Everything was in perfect balance. No pleading. No bargaining. Pressed together under the couch blanket, it was last Saturday all over again. The fear of falling and then I was soaring. Higher and higher. It was far from graceful—our clumsy fumbling. But it felt right. Foley's hands (not on my mouth, not on my throat) skimming over me. My hands (not claws, not fists) circling him. All arms and legs twisting, not elbows and knees digging. He must've known I was somewhere else because his voice gently questioned, *Are you okay? Is this okay?* I nodded, powerless to stop my brain from spinning out even as a sweetly surging heat burned my face. I was melting. The world was melting. But then the images behind my eyes finally stilled and I was filled with a strange calm. Not the distant calm of having just escaped your own body, but a present one, the kind that reminds you that your life is yours and it's good. Really good. Foley smiled shyly and kissed my neck, and then we stayed like that—tangled together, breathing in one another—until the clouds parted and the rain stopped. A ray of light shone through a gap in the drapes.

Slipping into my shorts and shirt, I wasn't ashamed or anxious or fearful. I wasn't anything but alive. I kissed Foley goodbye and then smiled and blushed all the way to the corner. I tried holding on to the floating all the way home, but then gravity pulled me back to earth.

Adam.

How could sleeping with Foley be the rightest thing and the wrongest thing at the same time? I went from feeling strong and sure to sick and weak. A crushing shame that made my stomach ache. Was that how my father felt the first time he cheated on my mother? *No. Because he wouldn't ever have done it again.*

When I walked through the front door, my mother was in

her bathrobe on the couch with a bowl of ice cream. Her eyes were red from crying. On the coffee table was the invitation to her reunion.

"What's wrong?" I said.

"Nothing." She shut off the TV and patted the cushion next to her. I plunked down and stole her spoon. Peanut Butter Fudge. My favorite. I was starving, but that was my own fault. I was supposed to be at that Italian restaurant with Adam. I gave her back her spoon.

"I've been thinking," my mom said. "You say I hide from the truth, but you're wrong. I just choose not to dwell on the ugly ones. Like that your father has someone to take to that stupid reunion and I don't." Her voice cracked.

I tugged at a thread on her robe. "You've got time," I said. "Maybe you can find a date. That would blow his mind, wouldn't it?"

She shook her head, hopeless. "You want the truth?" she asked. "Here it is: my son won't talk to me because I didn't throw a parade when he told me he was gay. I was in shock. What was I supposed to do? And you? You're growing up way too fast. You think I don't know what you do, but I was sixteen once, too."

I blushed like there was a sign flashing above my head. Where was her intuition when I'd needed it before?

If you'd fought harder there would've been something for her to notice.

"That's how it's supposed to go," she continued. "Your kids grow up and move out, and you and your spouse get to be people again, husband and wife—your life is your life again. But now everything's changed."

She pulled a tissue from her bathrobe and wiped her nose.

"When you leave, what's left?" She squeezed me to her, and I winced. My arm was still sore from the shot.

"I don't know where I'm going anymore," she said, sounding as lost as I felt.

twelve

*t*he one night I wanted to stay home, Lisa called, begging
me to drag myself out of bed and over to Trent's. I told her
I was in my pajamas. She told me to bring them because I was
sleeping at her house anyway. I frowned at the T-shirt and shorts
balled at the foot of the bed and sighed.

"Your lover boy's here." Lisa giggled. "Say hi."

I panicked—Foley?—but then Adam's voice asked sweetly,
"Hey, you feeling any better?"

Earlier, I'd canceled our dinner date—again. I hadn't felt
good all day. My stomach was tense and fluttery and I had this
strange urge to hide. The thought of seeing Adam made me
dizzy. There was no way to undo what I'd done. I had to move
forward, but someone had tied cement blocks to my ankles. I felt
them dragging behind me on the way to Trent's, scraping the
sidewalk, catching on hydrants and curbs. It took forever to get
there. But not long enough.

I was barely through the door when Adam tackled me to the bed. I struggled to free myself, but then everyone closed in on me. Rachel flopped down and inspected my roots. Lisa frisked me for gum. Gabe pried the cap off a bottle and knocked it against my ankle. I broke through the tangle of limbs and chugged. Whistling, Trent offered me another.

"I'm good," I said, checking my phone. It was pushing nine-thirty, and Lisa's curfew was ten. "We have to go soon, don't we?"

"Larry pulled his back at work." Lisa smiled. "He's zonked out on painkillers. We can stay as late as we want."

What about Katie? But maybe Lisa had come to her senses. "In that case . . ." I grinned, making grabby hands for the pint on the dresser.

"Wait," Adam said, tugging on my shirt. Scissoring his legs, he launched himself upright and took my hand. "Come with me. I want to talk to you for a minute." Our palms clasped together, he led me to Trent's brother's room—didn't he ever stay home?—and locked the door behind us.

"Remember when you asked me to always be honest with you?" he said, circling my waist with his arms. I did—when we first started seeing each other. Dealing with the aftermath of all that had happened with my dad, and then Scott, I was on an honesty kick. Alarm shot up my spine. Did Adam know I'd cheated? His arms were like a Chinese finger trap: the more I pulled away, the tighter he held. In the dark, his lips shivered across my collarbone. His hand crawled up the back of my shirt and I stiffened. "Whoa," I said. "What's this all about?"

"I've been waiting to make sure this is real," he said. "This is me being honest. I love you."

No. No, you don't. Take it back.

For the first time ever, I was the one wiggling away. This was what I'd wanted—for him to want me—but I was suddenly paralyzed by my secrets. I could feel them both—Foley and Troy—slowly leaching the oxygen from my blood until my lungs seized and my heart stopped pumping. I couldn't breathe. It was too hot in the room, too hot in his arms.

"I'll be back," I said. "Give me a minute."

I followed the steady buzzing coming from Trent's room. It sounded like my father's shaver. Close. Electric clippers. Rachel was cutting Trent's hair. The pint on the dresser was gone. I found it in Lisa's lap, who was in Gabe's lap.

"Where's your sweetie?" she said.

I snapped my fingers for the bottle and tipped my head back and let the fiery liquid rush down my throat. My stomach kicked. My limbs tingled. I drank until my face went numb. I was rubbing Trent's stubble when Adam came looking for me. I exhaled in his face and he winced. "Minty," he said. "Are you okay? How much did you drink?"

I touched the top of the red-and-white label and slowly dragged my finger down, down.

"Have you eaten?" Adam looked concerned.

My head flopped heavily. My hands started shaking. Then a quivering in my belly started as my insides began to lurch upward. The bathroom was on the second floor. I'd never make it. I pushed past Adam and Rachel and slipped on Trent's hair. Lurching down the hall, I tried holding down the rising sickness. It couldn't be stopped. My throat opened as I clutched the radiator for support. I managed to make it down the stairs and out the back door before I puked again.

My stomach was a mess, but my head was even messier. If I didn't love Foley, then why didn't I want to undo what we'd done? Some of what I felt was guilt, but mostly it was fear. I was afraid of getting caught. I was a coward, just like my father, slinking, sneaky. I got down on my back and slithered under Trent's car, into the shadow of its underbelly.

The porch door creaked. Someone rustled the bushes. "Come out, come out, wherever you are," Lisa called. I was pretty sure I was invisible, but then there was a bagel in my face. "Eat it," Lisa demanded, peering around the tire. "It'll soak up the alcohol."

I didn't think it would stay down, but I took a small bite. All I tasted was oil and gas. The sharp tang of corrosion. I concentrated on chewing and waited for my stomach to protest.

"What happened?" Lisa asked.

I love the sound of crickets. I listened for a pattern in the chirping and managed another bite.

"Do you want to talk about it?"

More crickets and then the neighbor's dog barking through the fence.

"Do you want to go for a walk?" Lisa asked. "Do you want to write it down?"

I didn't want to talk or walk or write. I wanted to be left alone. I didn't deserve Lisa's concern. Me, Miss High-and-Mighty, throwing the stuff about Trent in her face, and then riffling through her calendar that night at the diner to see if she'd lied. What I had done was so much worse.

"Are you mad at me?" she asked.

I shook my head.

"Is it so bad that you can't tell me?" she said. "Tell me."

But I couldn't. *Breathe in, breathe out.* I didn't want to be sick again.

"Come out from under there," she said softly. She felt around and then stuck her finger in my side. I hit my head on something.

"Ow!"

"Remember the rule?" she reminded me. "No cars when we've been drinking. In them or under them."

Lisa assisted me up and brushed the gravel off my back, helping me down onto the grass because my legs were shaky.

"I belong with Adam," I said. "I do. I really do."

"Why does that make you sad?" she asked. "Why are you shaking your head?"

My neck was a spring. I bobbled around until Lisa steadied my head on her shoulder and softly sang me a song about wind and wings and friendship and strength.

"Why are you still crying?" she asked.

"Because you're beautiful."

"Okay, Drunky McDrunk. It's time to go. You wait here. I'll grab you another bagel and say good night. Where's your bag?"

I don't know how Lisa got me home. I don't remember walking. We must have passed the woods, unless she took the long way, which I couldn't imagine. When we got back to her house, Larry was snoring in the recliner. It's weird seeing a friend's parent sleeping. It's like running into a teacher at the mall or catching your father in his underwear. Lisa put her finger to her lips, and I swayed in place, trying not to giggle as she grabbed a couch pillow and raised it above Larry's head. *Dare me?* she mouthed. Larry's leg twitched, knocking the remote to the floor. I froze. Behind me, the studio audience laughed at something stupid. Lisa slowly lowered her arms. Lower, lower, until Larry was breathing his own breath. The menacing set of her jaw made me think she'd do it. Eyes wide, I silently commanded her to stop. If she woke him, I was dead. I was too drunk for Larry to ignore. He'd call my mother and she'd ground me. Some lame catchphrase sent the audience into convulsions. Lisa tossed the pillow on the couch. Everyone applauded.

"I think there's pizza in here," Lisa said into the wedge of light from the refrigerator.

"I think I need to be flat," I said. "Where are we sleeping?"

"Katie's room," she said. "Do you mind?"

I shook my head. I think I shook my head.

"You want something to eat?"

I'm pretty sure I shook my head again.

"Go on," she said. "I'll be there in a minute."

I dragged my bag down the hall toward the buttery light spilling from the open door. Katie was sprawled on a comforter on the floor. I flopped down on the bed and inhaled Katie's smell—fabric softener and ranch dressing—which started my stomach churning. I tried my back, but the stars on the ceiling started spinning, faster and faster. I struggled upright. That's when I saw them resting on the plastic crate Katie used for a nightstand. My head spun. Choking back the sickness rising up in my throat, I hid them in my bag where no one would see. I thought they were meant for me. They were the right color—brown, just like Foley's. His warning was as cold and clear as those eyes. *I'm watching you, too. I know your secret.*

thirteen

To: splendidhavoc@horizon.net
From: blackolcun@horizon.net
Subject: SOS

In Troy, it was a chocolate under the couch, wrapped in silver foil and clotted with dust.

Our mother is so nosy. *What are you doing on the computer? Who are you e-mailing? Can't it wait till morning?* No, it can't wait. I have to go back. To the woods. None of this feels real. I keep hoping it's just another nightmare, but I know it's not. It was an accident. It's not like we went in there with a gun or a knife. Our only weapon was a flashlight. We used our hands and feet,

too. I guess that's evidence, the bruises on my knuckles.
I don't know how to explain what happened, what came
over us. Do you think we could claim self-defense?
Because that's how it felt, like we were defending
ourselves. Like we were fighting for our lives. But he didn't
fight back. Like me that day in Troy. But the guy in the
woods didn't have a chance, cocooned in that musty
sleeping bag, buried beneath those blankets.

What's my excuse?

fourteen

t racy got busted!" Lisa sang as she pocketed her phone and relieved me of the armload of dresses I'd been schlepping around the thrift store for her. I covered my face with my hands, trying to ward off the panic. All afternoon I'd been trying to figure out how to confess. What happened with Foley was gnawing at my insides. I had to tell someone. "I was going to tell you," I said.

"Really?" Lisa cocked her eyebrow. "You were so wasted, I'm surprised you remember."

My brain sputtered. If not Foley, then what? The eyes? No. I'd hidden them that morning after lying to my mother about losing my keys. While the locksmith was there, I put them in the one place she never cleans: my old steamer trunk. It's my landfill of mistakes: my ninth-grade third-quarter report card, the portrait I drew of my dad but never gave him, a box and stick

from a pregnancy-test kit, a slip of paper with a 1-800 number
Foley had given me after I told him about the jerk from Troy.

"I think it's funny," Lisa said, puckering her lips at a vest
straight from a seventies sitcom. "Gross but funny. Trent? Not so
much. Gabe said he's pissed at you."

"Trent?" I said. "Why's he pissed?"

"His mother made him clean it up," she said, staring at me
quizzically. "The puke behind the radiator?"

My shoulders relaxed as I followed Lisa around a rack of tops,
my nose wrinkling at the bitter smell of fumigated polyester. I
love thrift stores but hate the stench. Lisa pulled a sweater dress
from a hanger and held it up in front of me. "This is so ugly it's
cool." And then, eyeing the belt in my hand: "Are you getting
that?"

I traded her for a psychedelic scarf and then hopped up on an
ottoman and lip-synced the cheesy song coming from the ancient boom box by the register. A guy hugging a TV nodded
his approval, but Lisa shaded her eyes in embarrassment. "Stop
shaking your love," she hissed, threatening me with a fondue
fork. I jumped down, but she poked me anyway, and that's when
I blurted it out, right there between a rack of scuffed pumps and
a grimy collection of hot-air popcorn poppers.

Lisa did a double take. "Wait," she said. "Did you just say
Foley?"

I snatched the fondue fork from her fist and pointed it at her
heart. "You can't ever tell anyone," I said. "Promise?" Lisa nodded eagerly. She wanted details. "Remember the night I was supposed to go out to dinner with Adam?" I said. "Well, Foley
called. I hadn't seen him in a while. I see Adam all the time. We
ended up at his house, and . . . yeah."

"Have you seen him since then?" she asked.

"God, no." I covered my face. "I don't want to see him. I just want this to go away."

"Is that why you were being such a freak last night?" she asked, rummaging through a bin of purses.

I nodded.

"Stop it," she said. She dropped her armload of clothes in a shopping cart and put her hands on my shoulders. "This doesn't make you a bad person. It doesn't make you anything. It's just sex. It doesn't have to mean anything if you don't want it to."

But it still means I'm a cheater.

Toeing a loose tile in the floor, I asked Lisa if she was mad at me. "I was a jerk about you kissing Trent," I explained, trying on an iridescent smoking jacket. Lisa kicked off her flip-flops and stuffed her feet into some strappy silver sandals with acrylic heels. She shrugged and then shuffled up behind me in the mirror.

"I *should* be mad, but I'm not," she said over the top of my head. She looked down at her feet. "What do you think of these?"

"Do they come with a pole?"

Her elbow jab was fast and sharp. Rubbing my arm, I climbed into the cart with her clothes. As Lisa pushed me around the store, I told her how Adam and I were supposed to go to dinner later, how we had reservations and everything.

"What's the problem?" she asked. "Nothing's changed. Go."

If sleeping with Foley didn't have to mean anything—if it didn't mean anything—then why couldn't I stop thinking about it? Later, getting ready to go out, my cheeks blazed with the memory of the two of us on the couch. And I smiled, thinking of him, until I remembered the eyes in the steamer trunk. I pushed the image away.

I was surprisingly relaxed when Adam came to pick me up. But then we got to the restaurant. I've only been in a courtroom once, when Scott got sentenced to community service for resisting arrest, but I felt like I was waiting for a verdict as the maître d' scanned the book on the stand. Picking at my nail polish, I glanced around uneasily. In the dining room—all crystal and low light and starched linens—silverware clinked. Someone actually guffawed. The maître d' looked up and shook his head. No reservation, but we were welcome to wait. And wait. And wait.

I suspected finding us a table wasn't exactly a priority, not with the way we were dressed. Me with my blue streaks and a thrift store shift that made me look like one of those black-and-white cookies, only not so round. Adam in his oxford, buttoned but untucked. Both of us rockin' our Cons. I kicked myself for leaving the glitter stickers on my toes. "C'mon," I said, grabbing Adam's hand. "I've got somewhere better. You'll love it."

I'd never been there without my parents, but Hal's was our go-to place when everything or nothing was going right. We went there after Scott broke his arm and when my mom got promoted to supervisor and the time I found our cat, Snickers, flattened in the road. Hal's was my favorite, but I'd never shared it with anyone, not even Lisa. I don't know what made me think of it, except I wanted that night to be special. From the outside it isn't anything, just a short flight of stairs to a basement door and a hand-lettered sign—OPEN 24 HOURS UNLESS WE'RE CLOSED— but the inside is something else.

It's a little overwhelming at first, the way the walls nearly vibrate with the doodles and signatures of everyone who's ever been there, but Adam lit up instantly, marveling at the confusion of graffiti. "I knew there was a reason I picked you," he said, squeezing my hand. "How did I not know about this place?" Squinting, he scanned the tangle of names and dates and declarations of love until a waitress clutching a couple of menus led us to a booth in back. Plunking down, he tipped his head and laughed at the ceiling, at the overlapping hearts competing with skulls and peace signs and a jumble of names too faded to read. "This is crazy," he said. "I love it."

"There I am," I said, pointing to my shaky fourth-grade cursive. "Right under 'Uncle Clay Hates Cats.' My dad had to put me on his shoulders to reach."

"It's so us," he said, reaching across the table for my hands. Lisa was right: nothing had changed. While Adam looked around, I looked at Adam, but then his eyes dropped down suddenly and met mine. "I'm going to miss you," he said.

My stomach nose-dived. My face burned with shame. *He knows.*

"When I go to California," he continued. "My dad made my reservation. I'm leaving in two weeks."

Relief collided with sadness. I'd forgotten about Adam's trip. Before I could ask him how long he'd be gone, the waitress came back to take our order. Adam quickly scanned the menu.

"You want the jelly omelet," I said. The cook leaning in the pickup window agreed.

Adam shrugged. "Sounds questionable. But I trust you."

After the waitress retreated to the kitchen, I told Adam I wished he didn't have to go at all.

Folding a corner of his paper place mat, he said, "Me, too."

"When are you coming back?" I asked.

"That's the good news," he said. "I'll only be gone a week. Chris convinced my mom that I'll be miserable without you, and

I'll just make everyone else miserable, too. We owe him. When he comes for Christmas, we should bring him here."

My heart did a little dance, but a deeper part of me—the part that had been blindly grasping at something that wasn't there yet—relaxed. We had a future—the two of us. Adam said so. December was a long way off. And because December was a long way off, I had nothing but time. Plenty for me to sort out my feelings, that chaotic snarl that was as unreadable as some of the messages on the diner's walls. We weren't The Perfect Couple—not yet—but we could be. In my head, I chalked up the last month to a false start. This was my do-over. There was time to make things right.

As I was searching my bag for a pen, our omelets arrived. My mother always says you can dress me up but you can't take me out. I frowned at the dribble of jelly I almost immediately got down my front. Luckily it was the black half of the dress and not the white. But the bathroom had air dryers instead of paper towels. Wetting toilet paper was a mistake. I was still brushing little gray spitballs from my chest when I returned to the table.

"Don't forget to write something," I said.

"I did," Adam said. "Find it."

My eyes swept the busy wall, searching for his block print.

"Give me a hint," I said. "Or we'll be here all night."

I followed Adam's finger to my name and traced a black thread channeling through a maze of doodles and autographs. Up, up, up. I had to stand on the bench to see. There, between "Noel" and "Suck it," an eyeball beside a heart beside a puffy animal with stick legs and a tiny tail.

I scrunched my face. "I love sheep?"

"It's a ewe," he said.

Groaning, I plunked down on the bench. "You're such a corn-ball," I said, grinning. "I love ewe, too."

Some people are addicted to drama, to pain and fear and sadness. Not me. I'm all about lip-syncing to cheesy songs and writing silly messages and acting like an idiot. That's who I am—the real Tracy Kolcun. Adam kissed me and my heart felt light. I don't know why I did what I did with Foley, but I would not be dragged down by some freak that lived in the woods. Who did he think he was? Watching me, judging me with those eyes. I made a mistake. People do. It doesn't make you a bad person. It just means you're human.

After dinner, Adam walked me home, but I didn't go in. I waited until he turned the corner, then ran to the garage and raided my dad's workbench, digging through coffee cans of nails and screws and bolts. In the bottom of his tool bucket I found what I was looking for: his old jackknife, rusted shut and smell-ing like pennies.

It was almost dark when I got to the edge of the woods. Rage marched me through the brush. I got into a slapping match with the branches, but the stinging scratches only made me angrier. *I will bury you,* I thought, but then thunder rumbled overhead. The clouds curdled green and yellow. The dying light ground the edges off everything, smudging the pines and rocks and mossy logs. I stood at the top of the stairs and watched the black tarp bleed into night. The ropes I could see, white webs between the trees. Clutching the jackknife, I imagined sawing the lines, watching the house deflate like a black balloon, listening to him struggle under the weight of all that plastic.

A cold wind raised the hair on my neck, stippling my skin. The tarp rippled like an oily wave. I stood there, my courage shrinking, wishing for Lisa, while the sky above me twisted purple and green. A wicked storm brewing. Worse than the one that night at Foley's. A putrid light ringed in darkness. A vortex forming. A booming crack sent my hands to my ears, and the knife went skittering down the stairs. The only thing to do was hike up my dress and run.

Hands trembling, I fumbled my new key in the new bolt. My mother was in her bedroom watching TV. I ran from room to room, pulling the fans, closing the windows, screwing down the locks.

"What are you doing?" my mother demanded, shuffling into the kitchen with an empty glass and a Popsicle stick. "It's a thousand degrees in here."

"There's a storm coming," I said. "Huge. Check the Weather Channel."

My mother went out on the porch and came back shaking her head.

"Are you high?" she asked, and I think she meant it, because she examined my eyes before she marched me outside and showed me the stars.

fifteen

Sometimes I wish Lisa came equipped with a sensor so I'd know the kind of mood she was in before I agreed to hang out with her. It sounded like fun—roller-skating. We used to go all the time when we were kids. Just because it was a birthday party for Katie's friend didn't mean we couldn't skate, too. I hate the word *turd*, but that's what Lisa was being, parked at the snack bar with a popcorn and soda, paying more attention to her phone than to me.

"C'mon," I said, tugging on her wrist. "This is your favorite song."

"No it's not."

"Well . . . it's somebody's favorite," I said.

I swiped some of her popcorn and watched Katie twirl around under the disco ball and fought the fidgety feeling surging in my chest—the kind I used to get when my mother kept me out of the pool while I digested my lunch. I waited two full songs before asking, "Why aren't you talking?"

Lisa raised her face. Her eyes were blank and cheerless. "I don't have anything to say."

She had to be punishing me for Foley. For being a hypocrite. I sighed. "Fine. I'm going for a spin."

Nothing drives home the absurdity of roller-skating like being out on the floor without a friend. Now I know why nobody goes alone—it's boring. Going round and round with no one to pull or push or bump. No one to tell you how awesome your shirt looks under the black light. No one to whisper in your ear about that cute guy or that mean girl.

Katie glided by, wheels weaving a double helix as she crouched into the turn. "Show-off!" I shouted, struggling to stay upright. Her friends blew past me, too, shouting the words to the song that had become their summer anthem. I suddenly felt old and out of place, trying to keep up with the sixth graders. But it was either that or the moms over in the party room, fussing with the birthday girl's cake and presents. I waved at Lisa every time I passed the snack bar window, but she just sat there, her head on her fist, looking bitchy. Maybe she was mad because I'd ditched her for Adam two days in a row. But how many times had she bailed on me to be with Gabe?

I passed a girl crying under the disco ball and moved aside for the boys gliding to her rescue. Boys were everywhere throwing signs. I tensed. The rink had suddenly grown hot and uncomfortable, infused with the electricity of a fight brewing.

As I skated toward Katie and her pack of friends, someone grabbed my butt. I stiffened. Wheeling around I came nose to forehead with a little Romeo in a basketball jersey and gold chains. My brain crackled and popped like an amp with too much distortion. I wanted to embarrass him the way Lisa had embarrassed the kid at the pool that day, but I knew I'd only end up embarrassing myself.

"Sorry," the kid mumbled, stumbling along, his arms stretched out before him. It was an accident. He could barely stay upright. My stupid radar was malfunctioning again. I palmed the rail to the exit, my legs vibrating when the floor changed from wood to carpet.

"You know Adam's leaving in a week," I said, winging up to the counter where Lisa was chewing her straw. "We should do something. Go to the city. Just you and me. We can look for Scott."

"Maybe," she said. "I don't know."

I checked my phone for messages, then scrolled through the *M*s in an online dream dictionary—macaroni, manatees, milk, moccasins. I wanted to read her what I'd found about monsters.

"Sometimes I hate my life," she said.

"What part?"

"All of it." She glanced at me before turning away again. "I can't wait to graduate and get the hell out of here. Maybe I won't wait to graduate. Maybe I'll just go. I'll be like Scott. One day I'll just disappear. Move to the city so no one can find me."

Katie and her friends flew past the window with their eyes crossed and their tongues hanging out. Lisa shook the ice in her cup and said, "You ever just wake up one morning and wonder how your life got so effed up?"

Right then I wanted to tell her. About what really happened that night in Troy. How ashamed I felt. How stupid I felt for being ashamed of something that wasn't my fault. I'd been treating that day like a snag in my tights. Like I could dab it with nail polish and forget about it. But the hole kept growing. Part of me wondered if that was the cause of my nightmares. Maybe telling Foley wasn't enough.

"Don't worry," she said. "I'm not going anywhere. I can't leave Katie. You either, dummy." She shoved me lightly before glancing around the snack bar furtively. "I have to ask you something," she whispered. "Have you been back in the woods?"

My face got hot. I couldn't tell her without telling her about the eyes he'd left for me. After the other night, I decided ignoring him might make him go away. That's how I got Jerk Face to stop calling. I pretended he didn't exist and eventually it was like he didn't. Poof. Gone. Like magic.

I answered her question with a question: "Why?"

"No, it's just . . . I found a jackknife with your dad's initials. What are the chances?"

"You found it in the woods?" I said. "What were you doing there?"

Lisa shrugged.

"You've got to stop this," I said. "You're going to get hurt. Why are you stalking him?"

Lisa's face turned stony. "*He's* stalking *me.*"

"Then go to the police."

"With what? I don't have any proof. A glass eye doesn't prove anything. It's just a feeling. Like I'm constantly being watched. I want him to know I'm watching, too."

I just sat there, chewing my thumbnail, rolling my feet back and forth nervously. I was as guilty as Lisa for believing in him. I told my mother I'd lost my keys so she'd change the locks. How demented is that?

"What?" Lisa huffed. "I can see you want to say something."

"It's a myth, Lisa. A dumb story. My mom said when she was a kid they called him the Hillhurst Demon."

But a story can't leave things for you to find . . .

"What about the eye?" Lisa challenged.

"It could be anybody," I said. "Remember when we all watched that scary movie that pretended to be a documentary, and then we all woke up the next morning with piles of rocks on our lawns?"

"I still think it was Rachel," Lisa said.

"Me, too."

The punch in the back startled me. Lisa's cup crashed to the floor, ice flying.

"Jesus, Katie!" Lisa said. "Stop much?"

Rubbing her wrist, Katie said we could have some cake if we wanted. The birthday song came on and Katie shot out of the snack bar and across the rink. Helping Lisa scoop up the ice, I longed for the days when Banana Man was just a creepy story we told at sleepovers and cake could fix anything. Maybe it still could. I grabbed Lisa's hand and dragged her toward the birthday room, toward Katie and her goofball friends fighting over frosting flowers.

sixteen

i'd just stopped sweating when Adam met me in the hospital cafeteria. He looked paler than usual and didn't stop to kiss me, just tossed his head for me to follow. I did—up the service stairs, down the hall with the gift shop and the pharmacy, through the lobby and the sliding glass doors, and out into the clinging humidity. A taxi coasted into the drop-off lane. An ambulance screamed across the lot. My body, loath to quit the cool and the quiet, turned instantly sluggish. Adam lowered his hair against the blistering sun and parted the heat waves rippling off the asphalt. Keeping up was an effort.

"You really need to work on a base tan," I joked.

The muscles in his jaw pulsed like he was working a wad of gum. He unrolled his sleeves. "I wash dishes in a basement all day. I don't have time to lounge around, catching rays." There was an edge in his voice I had never heard. Out on the street, he lit a cigarette, blew smoke at the sky, and trudged up the hill.

Watching his back, his oxford billowing behind him, I wanted to run up and throw my arms around him and beg him to tell me what was wrong.

"Where are we going?" I called.

He didn't answer. Not his house. That was in the opposite direction. Up ahead, tree shadows darkened the sidewalk as a flock of birds swiftly scattered. We needed to cross soon. When Adam stepped off the curb, I let out the breath I'd been holding against the woods. Cars zoomed past. A helicopter shuddered overhead. Adam waited by a hydrant for me to catch up.

"What did you want?" he said. "What was so important that you had to send me sixteen texts?"

What I wanted was to see him, to know if he wanted to meet me for coffee at that little place on lower State Street. It was open mic night. Music or poetry, I wasn't sure. It didn't matter.

"Yeah—no." He squinted into the smoke swirling toward his eyes. "I'm not really up for hanging out tonight."

We were silent all the way to the middle school, two strangers who just happened to be walking in step. A crew was sandblasting graffiti off the fifth-grade wing, so we kept going, past the main entrance to the playground. A couple of boys were kicking a ball around, and Adam stopped to watch. Leaning against the chain-link fence, he lit another cigarette off the one he'd just finished.

"I'm leaving for California on Friday," he said casually.

My shoulders fell. "I thought you weren't going for another week?"

He shrugged. "I'm leaving early. Staying longer, too. The rest of the summer."

"But the rest of the summer is forever," I whined. "What happened?"

"I should be asking you that," he said coldly. His lip curled in disgust, and suddenly I knew. *He* knew. I started shrinking then, my brain scrambling for excuses. Adam raised his hand. "I'll save you the embarrassment," he said. "I won't ask. I'll just tell you. I know you cheated on me with Foley."

My stomach lurched. The weightless terror of missing a stair, when it's too late to stop yourself from falling. I looked to the woods. *No*. Then who? *Lisa?* Her words: *Wait till you slip up*.

"Adam, please," I begged, my voice breaking. "I'm so, so sorry."

Growling, he turned and rattled the chain links. The boys froze mid-pass. "Chris was right," Adam said, nodding slowly. *Chris? He told Chris*. A second wave of shame washed over me, like I'd somehow betrayed him, too. I'd earned his approval and then made him look stupid for liking me.

"Chris said some girls can't handle being treated right," Adam said. "They don't know what to do with a guy like me. It's like they enjoy being used. They want someone who makes them feel like shit about themselves."

"That's not fair!" I cried. "You don't understand!"

"No!" Adam shouted, jabbing his finger at my face. The harshness in his voice made me recoil. "You don't get to be mad. This is your fault. You did this. We were supposed to go to dinner that night and you lied. You lied so you could . . ." He pulled at his bangs. "I can't even say it."

The softness in his eyes was dying. He inhaled a shaky breath and blinked once more and it was gone, replaced by something cold and hard. Silent tears stung my face. The boys on the playground smeared. Everything went foggy. I don't know why, but all I could see was Lisa and me on the steps at graduation, firing finger pistols into the air, like finishing middle school was some big accomplishment. I slumped down on the hot sidewalk and wished for the days when the worst things possible were forgetting your lunch and being nicknamed *Melon Head*.

"For future reference," Adam said, grinding his cigarette into the sidewalk. "The next time you cheat, do it with someone who's not compelled by honesty to confess every wrong he's ever committed."

Watching him walk away—my heart already aching for what I'd lost, for what might've been—my shame turned to rage. If you could be imprisoned for murderous thoughts, that's where I'd be for what I wanted to do to Foley. It started as a rumble in my throat, a low snarling that grew and grew, until my jaw slackened and I was howling. A woman pruning bushes across the street stopped and stared. The kickball rang against the fence. I pried myself off the sidewalk and cried all the way to Lisa's.

"What happened to you?" Larry asked, his face knotting with concern as he let me in. "Are you hurt? Did someone hurt you?"

I looked around the living room and wiped my cheeks with the palms of my hands. "Boyfriend," I said, my voice cracking. My lips started trembling again. "Is Lisa here?"

Larry looked distressed, like my dad used to when I'd skinned a knee. I think if he'd tried to hug me, I would've hugged him, too, but he was holding his lower back like it pained him.

"You need anything?" he asked gently. "You look thirsty. We've got some juice boxes."

Shaking my head, I flashed him the OK sign, then hurried down the hall before I lost it again.

"Lisa?" I shouted over the music behind the bedroom door. I leaned against the cool wood and knocked with my forehead. "It's me. Can I come in?"

The bathroom door behind me popped open and Lisa stepped out.

"What the hell happened to you?" she mumbled around the toothbrush jutting from her mouth.

I pushed past her and yanked a bunch of tissues from the box on the counter, slumped down on the edge of the tub, and dried my stinging face.

"Adam," I said. "Foley told him."

Lisa bulged her eyes and then spit in the sink. She dropped her toothbrush in the holder, unwound a strand of floss, and tossed me the little white box like I needed to floss, too.

"Did you guys break up?" she asked the mirror.

"What do you think?"

Examining her teeth, she flashed me a look: *You don't have to get snotty.* She raised a tube of toothpaste and said, "This stuff foams like crazy. Try it. You'll like it."

What was wrong with her? My life was going to pieces and she was carrying on about dental hygiene. She was acting like one of the witnesses in that crime show my mom loves. Nobody ever has time to talk to the police. *Hello, people, there's a dead body in the alley! Stop stuffing your face with hot dogs! Put your cell phone away!*

The tears started again and Lisa hugged my head. She knelt down on the bath mat like she was about to give me her undivided attention, but then Katie barged in with a pencil under her nose.

"It's popcorn! Wanna smell?"

Lisa stood up and took a sniff. "It *is* popcorn. Does the taco smell like taco or feet? Remember those stickers we used to get?" That question was for me, but I didn't answer. I turned my face away and focused on a cracked tile behind the toilet. "My favorite was the pink soap," Lisa said. "Tracy's was candy cane. Right? That and root beer."

Lisa and Katie were going on and on about their favorite smells when Larry knocked.

"Are you guys having a party in there?" he asked.

Lisa gave the door the finger. Katie snickered behind her palm and then asked Lisa to straighten her hair for her. Two seconds later their mother was calling down the hall: "Don't forget, it's garbage night!" And then, "Are you almost done? I have to get ready for work."

"Gabe's taking us to Thursday in the Park," Lisa said, fishing the flatiron out of the basket beneath the sink. "Ryan, too. Wanna come?"

A mix of shock and disappointment, but mostly hurt, turned my face to stone. She didn't even care enough to cancel her night to be with me, her *best friend* who'd just had her heart broken. The air around me suddenly became heavy and cloying. My face shriveled and I was crying. Again. Squashed in that tiny bathroom with the two of them, I'd never felt so alone. I had to get out. I needed a break from the Grants—Katie *and* Lisa. A long one.

When I got home, my mother was in her bedroom watching TV. Thank God. I didn't think I could stop the shuddering in my chest long enough to hold a conversation. I turned off my phone and pulled the shades, wrapping myself in Adam's oxford—the one I'd never washed—and crawled into bed with the remote. My mother looked in on me once, on her way to the kitchen, but I pretended to sleep. She was the last person I could go to. *Oh, Tracy. How could you?* The hopelessness and loss building and building, I switched to some inane comedy. There was a slight delay, but my mother was watching the same thing. Both of us stuck in bed, trapped in the light of a TV, our long faces frozen in blue.

seventeen

Our garden was brown and weedy. Everything was dying. I wanted a tomato for my sandwich but the bottoms were black with rot. I'm not into growing stuff—that's my mother's thing—but I squeezed between the rows, searching for a pulse. My face sagged at the squash leaves, brown and mildewy, plastered to the soil like wet newspaper; the pole beans she'd started from seed shriveling from atrophy; the willowy carrot tops a matted nest of yellow. Scott's the Rescuer of All Things Helpless, but I'm not totally heartless. It's hard to stand passive in the face of neglect. I plucked a dandelion and tossed it over the fence. It was probably too late to save anything, but once I started I just kept going, down on my knees in my pajamas, yanking, tossing, the wilting pile growing and growing.

It's not like I had anything else to do. Adam was gone. Drinking iced coffee on a boardwalk with Chris, hating me, moving on. I imagine it's hard to stay sad in California, with the sand and the surf and all those palm trees gently swaying. And Lisa . . . I was still pissed at Lisa. I hadn't called or texted, and neither had she. What was her problem? The silent treatment is my thing, not hers. She hadn't even liked the throwback picture I'd posted of the two us huddled beneath a poncho on the eighth grade camping trip.

I put my phone aside and grabbed the hose coiled against the garage. I didn't need a green thumb to know that a good soaking wouldn't hurt—nothing had been watered in ages. Setting the nozzle to mist, I sat there with the water trickling down my arm, wrapped in the smell of sun-warmed dirty hair and earth and vegetation. I'm not sure how long I was outside, but the tops of my feet were starting to pink so I went in. After baking in the sun, the house felt cool. I was going to wash up, but I sort of liked the soles of my feet black, my fingernails ringed with soil. My palms, stained yellow from pulling weeds, stung like I'd been climbing ropes in gym. I filled a glass with ice water and sat down at the computer. I wanted to find something about reviving tomatoes, but I clicked on my mother's dating site bookmark instead. She had three unread messages, all from decent-sounding guys who wanted to meet her. One of them was a volunteer fireman who liked dancing and horses. The other two listed interests like long walks and quiet Sundays. If she started now, she'd have a date for her reunion, but she had no intention of going. The invitation was in the trash by the desk.

Enough was enough.

I was still grimy when I knocked on the door, a million different emotions rioting in my chest. The hallway smelled of stew and cigarettes. Decades of traffic had darkened the carpet from one stairwell to the other. I'd changed out of my zebra-striped pajama bottoms, but my pajama top was just a T-shirt so I hadn't bothered. I stood there wiggling my dirty toes, a nervous fluttering in my belly, as I listened to a chain rattle against wood. A bolt clunked. The door creaked open.

"Tracy!" my father said, sporting a beard that made me want to punch him and run.

"When did you grow that?" I asked. "You look ridiculous."

My father's brow crinkled with confusion. I could tell by the creases on his face he'd been sleeping. *Maybe he thinks he's dreaming.* Just like me that day at Action Adventure. Only it turns out it wasn't a dream. Behind him, in a cardboard frame, I could see a picture of my father and that ugly woman and her stupid child on the Log Flume.

"You can't go to your reunion." I glared.

My father rested his hands on my shoulders. I shrugged them off.

"Your high school reunion," I said. "Did you get an invitation? You can't go because I want Mom to go." I hated how whiny I sounded.

"Get in here," he said. "I'm not having this conversation in the hall." He turned and disappeared behind the door, expecting me to obey, which I did. It wasn't my first time there, but it still felt strange. Your parents' things are your things, but everything in that apartment was foreign. The faux leather couch and glass coffee table and new appliances. I felt like I was visiting my grandmother's: look but don't touch. My eyes skated from room to room. The place was neater than I'd expected. No stray socks or dirty glasses. An empty pizza box was tucked behind the trash can and all his World War II DVDs were neatly stacked. On the back of a chair hung a uniform shirt with an embroidered badge. He was still working as a night guard.

My father came out of the kitchen with a blue and white box of chocolate chip cookies. At least that hadn't changed. We had the same box on the microwave at home. It made me want to go through his fridge and cupboards, to see if he still ate the same spaghetti sauce and cereal. Like a good guest, I took one cookie instead of a handful and closed the lid.

"You walked all this way to tell me I can't go to my own reunion?" my dad asked.

I nodded, unable to peel my eyes from the picture in the cardboard frame. I don't know why, but her being ugly made it harder to take. "Do you love her?" I asked, pointing. My father followed my finger. "Are you going to marry her?"

"Her name's Cindy," my father said after a brief pause. "We're not getting married."

"Then why did you leave?"

My father plunked down on the couch and gave me another cookie.

"You know, those people were my friends, too. What you're asking, it's not fair."

"Doesn't matter." I shrugged. "You made your bed." I knew what I was talking about because I was in the same situation. When Adam returned, I couldn't ever go to Trent's again. Even if Lisa went, it was forever off-limits as long as Adam and Trent were friends.

"Listen," my father said. "I don't want to bad-mouth your mother . . ."

I flashed him a scalding look. "Then don't."

"Look, she's not perfect, either," he said gently. "She loves me, but she wasn't *in* love anymore. It's not the same thing. You'll understand when you're older. Maybe. I hope."

"The romance is gone, so you just abandon her? Me, too?"

My father sighed, rubbing the back of his neck like he had a kink. "The last time I saw you," he said, "you called me some pretty nasty names."

"I'm your kid," I said. "You have to love me even if I hate you."

"No," he said. "I mean, yes, I have to love you. I do love you. There will never be a question about that. But, I *don't* have to put up with your crap."

"You would if you lived with us," I said. "You wouldn't have a choice."

My father picked a crumb off the floor. "Have you heard from Scotty?" he asked, changing the subject.

"No," I said, helping myself to another cookie. "You?"

My father took one, too. "I got a card, but I haven't talked to him."

It was awkward, sitting on a strange couch with my dad, watching him chew. I wanted everything to go back to the way it was before our lives got so broken. When the universe revolved around my next play or Scott's latest campaign to save the world. Back when my mom and dad used to sit on *our* couch, eating *our* brand of cookies during the eleven o'clock news, the two of them taking bets on whether or not Scott and I would make it home for curfew.

"I've got to go," I said.

"Let me give you a ride," he said, reaching for his keys.

"I'll walk," I said. "I need the exercise."

My father offered me the box of cookies, but I refused them, too.

"Don't be a stranger," he said, kissing my nose. "You're welcome here anytime."

I didn't think I ever wanted to see him again, not after I walked in on my mother crying silently in our kitchen. There's nothing sadder than watching someone iron her own tears. That's what she was doing, hunched over the ironing board, eyes overflowing, staining the wrinkled shirt draped over the pad. The metal plate sizzled. She looked up and sniffed. "I didn't hear you come in," she said.

"Did you see the garden?" I asked, picking through the mail, hoping we'd gotten something from Scott, too.

"I did. Thank you." My mother leaned into a cuff and zig-zagged around the button and then glanced up. "It's your father's birthday today," she said flatly. "You should call him."

The needle on my rotten-daughter meter pitched toward the red zone. That's why Scott had sent him a card. "Is that why you're crying?" I asked. "Because it's his birthday? He's probably out celebrating with that sleaze. They're probably—"

My mother shot me a look. "Don't start," she said.

I tossed my hands in the air. "God, Mom, get over it! I saw your account on that dating site. You're never going to meet any-body—"

My mother slammed the iron on the board. "Get over it? Get over it? You don't *get over* twenty-eight years of marriage, little girl. This isn't one of your high school romances. I'll *get over it* when I'm damn good and ready." Her face dark and stormy, she clobbered the collar, pounding it flat.

I ran out of the kitchen, afraid that if I stayed I'd start crying and make it worse. I closed my door, but my mother's voice pen-etrated the walls: "And stay off my account, or I'll ground you from the computer!"

I hammered my pillow and then sank like a rock to the floor. I was a jerk. I'd been soothing my conscience imagining Adam in a better place than me. Jealous, almost, that he had Chris and California while I was stuck here, alone, in this dying city. One

of the things that killed me about my father was that he'd oblit-
erated our family without punishment. The universe wouldn't
punish me, either, for what I'd done to Adam. Karma is a fiction
victims invented to find comfort in suffering. It doesn't exist. If
it did, Jerk Face would've been in an alley getting the snot kicked
out him instead of answering my text: *Meet me @ Pyramid Mall.*

It was too hot to ride my bike, so I took the bus. I was hoping for Reese or Davis, but Al Minty was driving, my mother's
nemesis. "Hot date?" he asked, as I trudged up the steps with my
pass out. I knew he was joking—my hair was a wreck and my
T-shirt and cutoffs were limp and grungy. But I stared at him
coldly. *Don't mess with me.* I slid into a seat and watched the fes-
tering city swarm my reflection and wondered what the hell I
was doing. Sleeping with Foley hadn't fixed anything. I'd been
an idiot thinking what happened with him and what happened
in Troy were opposite sides of the same coin. And facing The
Jerk wouldn't change anything, either, but when the doors
shushed open, I still got off. I didn't think he'd show. But there
he was, in the food court, by the carousel, his thumbs working
his phone. My vision tunneled and I started sweating. I remembered him taller, bigger. More muscles. Not one of those
puppy-dumb boys from that band Katie loves. Everything about
him screamed weak: the green plaid shirt, the skinny jeans, and
white sneakers. That hair sticking up as if his dad had tousled it
on his way out the door.

The phone in my pocket chirped, startling me. *Where r u?* But
my entire body had gone numb. I stood in the shadow of a kiosk
and watched his eyes search the tables, my veins flooding with
the hatred and shame of that day, trapped beneath him, writh-
ing, struggling, and then giving in. I wanted to slink out from
hiding, slowly, steadily, and then leap, claws extended. To drag

him out behind the mall, behind the Dumpsters in the deepen-ing dark, and rip and tear and grind, hissing, *How do you like it? How do you feel?* But that's the difference between boys and girls—*that* boy and *this* girl, at least. He'd enjoy it.

The next bus wasn't for an hour. I shut off my phone and waited in the shelter. The orange streetlights turned my skin a sickly purple. I needed a shower badly. I picked at my nails and faced the truth weighing on my heart: there was a reason why Foley was the only one who knew what happened. No one else would've believed. It seemed unbelievable to me, too, that I hadn't been able to defend myself. But I hadn't. The killing part, the part that kills me inside: I won't ever be able to fight him off now.

He's with me forever.

eighteen

Lisa's house was the only one on the street that didn't look like the people inside had given up on living. From the end of the block, their yard was a green raft in a sea of scorched grass. It was all Larry, out there every night, spraying, killing, coaxing. Our yard used to look just as nice—not a scrap of paper or stray weed—until my dad moved out. The yard was the last to go. First it was a shutter we lost in a storm, and then a broken porch board, and then the paint started peeling off the garage. For a while we had Scott to send up on a ladder or handle the heavy lifting. But now that Scott's gone, too, my mother's bar for what's acceptable keeps getting lower and lower.

I was wondering what it would take to get on one of those home makeover shows when Lisa's storm door swung open and Foley stepped out. My brain backfired: *What's he doing here?* The urge to tackle him was strong but so was the need to run. I spun in place and shot across the lawn, not caring about Larry's grass.

"Hey, Trace!" Foley called, pounding down the stairs. His sneakers slapped the sidewalk behind me, but I gave him the finger and kept going. "C'mon, Trace," he pleaded. "Wait up." I refused to look, but I knew he was gaining on me. I cursed my stupid flip-flops and lengthened my stride. I hustled through the crosswalk just in time, but Foley wasn't so lucky. The screech of brakes stopped my heart. I wanted him dead but not like that, with his beautiful head crushed beneath the wheel of a truck. I slowly turned, expecting blood, but Foley was on his feet, smiling and waving at the woman behind the windshield. The driver shook her fist and took off.

I took off, too, but Foley caught up, grabbing me from behind and wrenching my shoulder. My anger restored, I wheeled on him, my hand connecting harshly with his cheek. Foley dropped to his knees, cupping his face. I rubbed my wrist.

"Damn!" he wailed. "I know. I know. Lisa told me Adam broke up with you."

"Dumbass!" I shouted. "What did you think he'd do?"

A girl with massive hoop earrings and black lip liner watched nearby. Glaring at her didn't work. She smirked, folding her arms, and leaned against a telephone pole. Foley got up and kneaded his neck. "I did it for you," he said. "After what happened, you needed someone safe. Adam was a crutch, but now you have to walk on your own."

"What are you, my effing shrink?"

Foley's eyes looked so warm, so kind. Something in me weakened and I looked away. I watched a stray dog bob along the curb, and then I stared straight at the sun.

"You didn't love him," he said.

"I did love him." I blinked. "I still love him."

"No, you don't."

"Yes, I do."

Foley shook his head.

I seized a fistful of curls, and he cried out, squirming, trying to pry my fingers loose, but I locked my grip. It felt good hurting him. Really good. The sound of someone cracking up made me turn. The girl was still there, laughing behind her phone, recording the whole thing: Foley twisting in pain, whimpering for me to let go.

"Mr. Sympathetic Ear," I said, dragging his face to mine. "Mr. Problem Solver. You go around acting like your motives are innocent. You're only there to help, right? I'm not stupid. You get off on damaged girls." My knuckles started to ache so I released him. Foley stumbled back, rubbing his scalp. "You're pathetic," I hissed.

Lacing his fingers on top of his head, he stared into me, those heavy eyelids creased with pain. It was the same look he'd given me the day I told him everything.

"Enlighten me," I said sharply. "How many messed-up girls have you slept with? Besides me."

Foley smiled weakly, like I'd told a bad joke, and made a zero of his thumb and finger.

I inhaled sharply, darting across the street before he could follow. Storming toward Lisa's, I turned back. Foley—*Foley, who never lies*—was gone. The girl was using her phone to talk now, holding her belly and laughing. I rushed up the walk. One of Katie's friends answered the door. Katie was in the living room with a game controller in her hand, trying to keep up with the faceless dancers on the TV screen.

"Where's your sister?" I asked.

Katie rocked from foot to foot, popping her chest. "Bedroom."

Lisa and I hadn't talked in a few days, but I'd been stalking her feeds for posts. Other than some random pictures of shadowy figures, she'd been silent. I'd been stalking Adam, too—palm trees, a guy juggling fire sticks on the beach, everything he ate—until he blocked me.

Wailing, I busted into her room and flopped on the bed beside her. "What was he doing here?!"

Lisa sat up, surprised. "Who?"

"Foley!"

Lisa shrugged. "He was in the neighborhood."

"It's my neighborhood, too. He didn't come to my house. Why are you in your pajamas?"

"I'm kind of sick." She pulled the sheet up over her legs. "My period's been all messed up. I had to have this thing done, a D and C." Her upper lip curled. "It didn't hurt, but it was weird."

I scooped up Lisa's eyeballs from the nightstand and shook them like dice.

"Seriously," I said. "Why was Foley here? Did you guys talk about me?"

Lisa turned away. "Not everything's about you."

"C'mon. Yes, it is. What did he say?"

"He loves you, stupid."

I let that sink in and then sank my head in her pillow.

"He has a retarded way of showing it," I mumbled.

A knock, and then Larry poked his head in the door. He was thinking barbeque chicken for dinner. Was that okay? Lisa nodded. Had Lisa taken her antibiotic? She nodded again.

"I don't have the energy to deal with your little drama right now," she said, rolling out of bed. "You're making this way more complicated than it has to be. Adam's gone. Foley loves you. You love Foley. Simple."

"It's not simple," I said. "Everybody loves him. Everybody needs him. You know Foley. If somebody sends out an SOS, he drops everything. It'd be like dating a superhero. I'd always be fighting for his attention."

"Poor you," she said, faking a frown. "It's tough being Tracy, isn't it?"

I slammed the eyeballs on the nightstand. "What is wrong with you?" I asked. "Why are you being such a bitch?"

Lisa threw a pillow at me.

"Fine." I shrugged. "Call me when you feel better."

The whole way home I wondered what I'd said to piss her off. Lately, Lisa was getting harder and harder to read. We'd been through rough patches before, but this felt different, deeper.

"I thought you were going out with Lisa?" my mom said.

"She's sick," I said.

"Then I guess I've got to feed you," she said, pulling leftovers from the fridge.

I sat at the counter and poked at a bag of hamburger buns until my mother took them away.

"What's a D and C?" I asked.

The wrinkled brow of suspicion was her response.

"That's what Lisa had to have," I explained.

My mother looked stunned and then tried hiding it by messing with the keypad on the microwave. Fear blossomed in the silence. Flashback to health class—alphabet soup diseases and cysts and cancer. "What?" I asked. "Is it bad?"

My mother's face pinked. I had the strange sensation that she was about to spring something awkward on me. The microwave dinged. She pulled out one plate and stuck in another. "Is Lisa sexually active?" she asked.

"Mom!"

I couldn't say yes. I know how my mother's mind works: *If Lisa's having sex, then Tracy must be, too.* I wasn't about to open that door.

My mother started cutting the food on my plate like I was a toddler again. "Are you sure? It's just . . . that's a procedure," she stammered. "That's a clinical term for . . . sometimes . . . for abortion."

My brain wheeled erratically, like a kite in the wind. It explained everything: Lisa's moodiness, her absence, her total lack of interest in my problems. "She's not having sex," I said defensively. "So you're wrong."

My mother shrugged, the worry lines on her forehead softening. For some reason I wanted her to force the truth from me, grill me until I weakened and confessed everything. But the issue was dropped. She set the table, but I wasn't hungry. I went for a walk instead. Not far, just the park with the hippo and the duck where Adam and I fed muffins to pigeons after we spent the night in his dad's car. Wrapping myself around the cold, hard ostrich, I rocked back and forth, the creaky spring drowning out the sounds of me missing Adam. There should be an expiration date on grieving—like milk, so you have some clue how long it's going to last—because I didn't think I'd ever stop feeling sad and sorry and miserable.

I kicked off my flip-flops and dug my toes in the dirt. I was about to call Foley when a toddler waddled over, offering me a fish cracker. The mother was sitting on a bench with a baggie in her lap. She smiled at her son like he was the most precious thing on the planet, and then she smiled at me like I was supposed to think he was precious, too.

I babysat once and I hated it. I called Lisa every five minutes for help. Why didn't she tell me she was pregnant? I would've made the same choice had the second pink line bloomed on the test stick hidden in my trunk.

I rested my head on the steel beak, hoping the kid would disappear. When I opened my eyes, I was alone. It was that time of evening when everything turns shadowy. Something had set the swings rocking—invisible legs pumping, kicking the bruised sky. My ear caught the warped music of an ice cream truck in the distance. I slid off the ostrich and frisked my pockets for change and then froze as something small and hard and shiny rolled from the shadows and stopped at my feet. A glass eye. My hands tingled.

He's here.

Another eye followed, clacking against the first.

"Who's there?" I hollered, trying to sound tough.

Giggling erupted behind the slide. A shadow stole across the playground.

"Lisa?" I called.

A second shadow exploded into view. Mangled hair. Light reflecting off lenses.

"Trent?"

More laughter and then Lisa was rushing headlong, arms raised, fingers clawing the thick air. Crashing into me, she tickled my sides and pecked at me with her nose. I tried wrestling out of her hold, but my limbs were still quaky. I grabbed her wrists and squeezed.

"We need to talk," I said.

"Not now," Lisa said. "I'm on a mission." She plucked an eye from the dirt and wiped it on her shirt. "Come out, stupid!" she called behind her. "She knows it's us!"

Trent sprang from the jungle gym, his long legs making longer shadows.

"We're going back," he said. "One last time."

"I'm returning these." Lisa scooped up the second eye and tossed both to Trent. "I don't want them anymore. They're useless."

"Can't we do it during the day?" I pleaded.

"I've got work tomorrow," Trent said, vaulting the fence. Lisa used the gate. I checked my phone. The battery was dead.

"C'mon," Lisa called, and I followed, the two of us skipping along to the ice cream truck music until it was replaced by sirens. We were nearing the hospital. The huge lighted EMERGENCY sign seemed brighter than usual, eerie almost. Suddenly, the pop-pop-pop of firecrackers sent me ducking for cover. Lisa and Trent laughed, but it wasn't funny. My nerves were shot. I shuddered through the brush and vines and clinging branches, thinking I'd never make it down those rickety stairs, not with my legs like rubber. Lisa took my hand. "One step at a time," she said gently.

At the bottom, just beyond the boulder, a bulging black trash bag twisted from a limb. The guy's food, probably. Scott used to do that, too, when he camped in the backyard. Hang his snacks to keep the skunks out of it. Trent grabbed a stick and swung. The thing burst like a piñata. A black buzzing cloud ascended as hundreds of white twigs and white rocks scattered at our feet. Rice followed, raining down like confetti, squirming over the twigs and rocks. No, not twigs. No, not rocks. Tiny bones and tiny skulls crawling with maggots.

Lisa screamed.

My head hit something hard.

The ostrich.

I looked up at the stars and looked down at my feet, trying to loosen the kink in my neck. My cheek was numb. I shakily crawled off the ostrich and scanned the empty park, labeling everything—slide, jungle gym, swings, bench, trees—until my eyes stopped on something familiar but nameless. Long and dark and thick, cocoon-like except for the way the light shining through suggested arms and legs. It was a shape I'd seen before, in pictures. The shadowy figure Lisa kept posting. A low metallic throbbing sounded from the edge of the park. Danger of a different kind. The blue neon of under car lights swept the street. The cocoon receded, shrinking into murky darkness. Before summer started, I would've shrunk, too. Alone after dark, in a park surrounded by decrepit houses and shady bars and homegrown churches. It's funny the way fear can shift, how the thing I used to dread most—gangbangers cruising the streets, flashing cryptic signs from smoky windows—made me feel strangely safe.

nineteen

teetering on my toes in Lisa's driveway, strumming the window screen with my fingers, I called in a singsongy whisper, "Rapunzel, darling, let down your hair." Slowly, the blinds levered open. Lisa squinted against the sun. She was wearing eye makeup—a good sign.

"What are you doing?" she asked.

"Wooing you," I said. "I was kind of a jerk yesterday. I brought you a present."

I held out the lone cherry tomato I'd picked from our garden.

Lisa snorted. "Dork."

"I grew it," I said. "Sort of. I didn't let it die."

Lifting the screen, she snatched it from my palm and popped it in her mouth.

"Was I supposed to share?" she mumbled through her fingers.

"No. That's okay." I smiled. "Is it good?"

She nodded. "Are you going to hang outside my window or come in like a normal person?"

"I'll use the window," I said. "Give me something to stand on. You got a crate or something?"

Lisa reached for my hands. "Put your feet on the siding and climb."

"Don't let go," I pleaded, the thought of my head cracking open on the driveway making me shiver. With Lisa pulling, I scrambled up until my shoulders were through the window. My belly followed. I wanted to rest, but the metal tracks were digging into my skin.

The last thing I needed was an audience, but Katie drifted in with a bag of chips as Lisa was dragging me by the belt loops up onto the sill. I don't know how gymnasts do it. My body seesawed, pitching toward the floor, but my hands flew forward before my face met the carpet.

"You are the weakest person ever." Lisa grunted, drawing my legs through the window.

"I know, right?"

Lisa pulled down the screen. I pulled down my shirt. Katie flopped on the bed.

"My window's easier," Katie said matter-of-factly. "You can stand on the hose thingy."

Lisa shot her sister a threatening look. "I better never catch you sneaking in or out."

Hand on her chest, eyes wide, Katie pantomimed innocence.

"I'm serious," Lisa said. "Don't make me kick your butt."

The doorbell rang and Lisa ran to answer it before it woke their mother. I sat next to Katie and examined my shins, scraped all to hell.

"It's my emergency exit," Katie said, crunching a chip. "I've never had to use it. Not yet. I've done drills, so I know I can do it."

"What do you mean?" I asked, going through the lotions on Lisa's nightstand.

Katie licked her greasy fingers and wiped them on Lisa's comforter.

"You know," she said. "Like if I ever wake up and he's actually *in* my room. I've got an escape."

I fumbled the brightly colored bottles and tubes and then set them straight.

"You think I'm crazy, don't you?" Katie asked.

I absently opened Lisa's nightstand. There was my dad's jackknife—the one I'd lost in the woods. Did I think Katie was crazy? No. Because the paranoid part of me was wondering if that's how he'd gotten in that night. The night he left me those eyes, the ones hidden in the bottom of my trunk.

"You should keep your windows locked," I said, closing the drawer.

Katie shook her head. "That won't help."

Before I could ask why, Lisa stormed in with finger pistols firing. Smiling slyly, she shot her sister in the heart. "Ry-an's here!"

Katie bounced off the bed, scattering chips everywhere. She frowned at the mess, but Lisa just rolled her eyes and told her to go. A squealing Katie twirled out of the room.

"Young love," Lisa said dreamily. "It's official now—sealed with a kiss just last night."

"Aww," I cooed, grateful to talk about something normal. "I remember my first kiss."

Lisa shuddered. "Wasn't it that spaz, Joel Shoemaker?" she

asked, picking chips from the carpet and putting them back in the bag. Knowing Lisa, they'd find their way into Larry's lunch.

"Joel wasn't bad," I said, defensively. "For a nerd. Is Ryan cute?"

Lisa hooked her finger for me to follow. Creeping down the hall, she pressed her finger to her lips. Joel Shoemaker was my first boyfriend, but not my first kiss. That distinction belonged to Foley. He had tasted like hot cocoa. From the shadows, we watched Katie and Ryan standing close. Not touching, just talking. Katie was describing some viral video when she stopped and said: "I know you guys are there. I can hear you breathing."

Lisa elbowed me like it was my fault.

"We just came to see . . . yeah, um," Lisa stammered, searching for an excuse. She threw out her hands. "You, Ryan. Okay? We came to see you."

I showed myself and waved. Ryan smiled shyly. He didn't look homeless. His clothes were clean and his hair was combed. He even smelled of soap.

"It's Dollar Day at the Dog House," Katie announced. "Can we go?"

"Go," Lisa said. "But don't go crazy. Mom's making that cheesy chicken thing for dinner."

While Katie ran to find shoes, Lisa told Ryan that there was enough if he wanted to stay for dinner. His face lit up in a way that made me sad and angry all at once. Sad that he lived in a van with his dad and sisters. Angry that all over the city perfectly good houses were sitting empty. I wondered when the last time he ate in a kitchen was.

After Ryan and Katie left, I kicked back in Larry's recliner. Lisa sprawled on the couch and fanned herself with her hand. "You seem like you're feeling better," I said.

"Yeah. A lot." Lisa chewed her thumbnail. "It's crazy, I slept like thirteen hours last night. I don't think I've slept all summer. Not like that."

I wasn't surprised. Dr. Dan said stress can disrupt sleep, and Lisa had been under a lot of stress. How many nights had she struggled with her choice before reaching a decision?

"If you ever need to talk," I said, "and I'm being a total jerk, you have permission to slap me."

The corners of her mouth turned up. "What if you're acting like a partial jerk?" A car door slammed out front. Lisa's smile shrank. Larry clomped in with his lunch cooler under one arm, a rolled-up newspaper under the other, and tossed his keys on the TV. "Which one of you walked through my flower bed?" he asked.

Biting my lip, I raised my hand.

Larry swatted my foot with his newspaper and smiled. Clomping toward the kitchen, he announced that he was going to take a quick shower and then take Katie to get her new bike.

"Katie's not here," Lisa called. "She's at the Dog House with Ryan."

Silence and then the sound of Larry dropping his cooler on the counter. The clomping turned to stomping. Bottles rattled in the fridge door. Lisa mouthed, *one one-thousand, two one-thousand.* Larry mumbled something unintelligible and then barked her name. I wanted to stay where I was, but she dragged me with her. Larry was waiting with his hands on his hips. "Did you even think to ask my permission?" he asked.

Lisa grabbed a bottle of water from the fridge and chugged. "Since when does Katie need permission to go to the Dog House?" she asked.

"I don't like her hanging out with that boy," Larry said.

"Too bad," Lisa said. "I invited him to dinner."

Huffing, Larry stomped toward the sink to rinse his thermos. I moved out of his way and he smiled kindly, imagining, I thought, how much easier his life would be with me as his step-daughter.

"Ryan's a nice kid," Lisa said. "Just because his dad lost his job doesn't make him a dirtball."

Larry made a face like *whatever*. "What kind of guy lets his kids sleep in a minivan?" he said. "Moving from parking lot to parking lot like a bunch of gypsies?"

"First, what does that have to do with Ryan?" Lisa leaned on the counter and crossed her arms. "Second, having a nice house doesn't mean you're a good parent." She rapped the counter with the empty plastic bottle. "You own this place."

Boom.

Larry glanced at me and then aimed his gaze at Lisa, his face turning redder and redder, like he was slowly burning from the inside out. I wanted to backtrack down the hall, but I was stuck in place. Larry and Lisa were stuck, too, the three of us trapped in a freeze-frame until Mrs. Grant shuffled into the kitchen, massaging her temples.

"I swear, you guys are like oil and water," she said. "Why does everything have to turn into a confrontation?"

Larry sucked his teeth. Lisa shrugged. Mrs. Grant wiped the sleep from her eyes and pressed the button on the coffeemaker. "Seriously," she said. "What is it with you two?"

I wondered the same thing as Lisa shoved me toward her room.

"I am so sick of his shit," she said to the mirror. "He's just jealous because Katie went off with Ryan instead of waiting around for him."

I was trying my best to listen only to Lisa, but the Grants' walls are thin, thinner than ours. There was no tuning out the sound of Larry pounding his fist on the table, grilling Lisa's mom: *Do you even know where your youngest daughter is right now? Do you?*

Lisa put her hands on her hips and listened, too.

C'mon, Larry, it's my first Friday off in a month. I don't wanna fight.

The clatter of silverware followed by the clink of plates. Mrs. Grant unloading the dishwasher. The back door slammed. Once. Twice. Shading her eyes, Lisa spritzed her head with hair spray. I thought it was over, but then Larry started in again:

I thought we agreed, Sharon, no dating until high school.

You can make all the rules you want, Larry. She'll just go behind your back.

So let her run wild? Do whatever she pleases?

That's not what I'm saying.

She's too young for a boyfriend! Case closed!

A car drifted up the street, rattling the house with its thunderous bass. Larry's voice followed, equally thunderous: *Unless you want her to end up like Lisa!*

My heart stopped.

Lisa exploded. The hairbrush hit the mirror, cracking her reflection.

I wanted to grab Lisa's hand and leave the way I'd come in—through the window—but she towed me through the kitchen, past her mom and Larry, and out the back door.

"Where do you think you're going?" Larry hollered from the steps.

"Away from you!" Lisa shouted.

I'd seen Lisa hurt—bumps and bruises, her heart broken—but this was something different. A weariness reserved for adults. The pain in her eyes crushed any notion I had of comforting her. Fists clenched, her stride grew longer and longer. Helpless, hopeless, the tears flowed. And then the curses: "I hope he dies," she choked. "I hate him. I hate him so much."

Listening to her strangling on her own grief, I would've given anything for words. The right words. The wrong words. Any words at all. My silence ballooned, filling the space between us. I wanted to be the one leading us wherever, but it was all I could do to keep up.

"You have no idea, do you?" she asked over her shoulder.

"I think I do," I said. "My mother told me."

Lisa stopped in her tracks, confusion warping her brow. A car blew by and honked.

"My mother knew what it was, the thing you had done," I confessed. "You could've told me."

Lisa's eyes turned flat and cold, pupils fixed, just like in the nightmare. Instead of dirt, though, I found myself wiping away black mascara. Lisa flinched as if I'd stung her.

"Who else knows?" she asked.

"No one." I raised my right hand. "I swear."

Lisa mumbled something and marched on. I thought I knew where she was going, but she took a left instead of a right, toward downtown. Nobody walks there from where we live—that's why we have buses. It isn't just far, it's dangerous. Any other day I would've defected, but Lisa needed to walk off her rage. Heads low, eyes lowered, we moved quickly, quietly, past blocks of forgotten houses and dismal stores and graffiti-covered billboards, ignoring the scarecrows in basketball shorts and baseball hats thumping their concave chests. Bus after bus lumbered down the hill, but we trudged on—like one of those dreams where the hallway keeps getting longer and longer—until the houses turned into apartment buildings and the billboards were dwarfed by office high-rises.

This is downtown: hot sidewalks dotted black with gum, racks of discount clothes, broken windows and garbage and pizza. I smelled them before I saw them—the homeless sprawled on blankets and newspapers, withering in the heat. A simmering Dumpster took my breath away. It isn't any better where Scott is—cities are cities—but at least he has the bright and shiny to distract him from the stench.

"I'm not complaining," I said, stopping to tie my sneaker. "But I think my blisters are bleeding."

"You should've said something," Lisa scolded. "We could've hopped a bus."

I wrapped my sweaty hands around her sweatier neck and pretended to choke her. Tongue lolling out of her mouth, Lisa crossed her eyes and went limp, then pried my fingers loose and led me around the corner to a pizza shop. It wasn't any cooler inside. The heat from the ovens made my temples throb. Lisa waved to the guys tossing dough behind the counter.

"Gabe here?" she asked a woman hunched over an order pad, a phone pressed to her ear. A floury finger directed us to the empty dining room in back. My legs felt like jelly as I powered through the final stretch of our death march and collapsed on the first vinyl chair.

"Hey!" Gabe said, abandoning a gray tub of dishes to wrap his arms around Lisa's waist and give her a spin. While they were kissing, I sniffed the plastic flowers and then examined myself in the gold-spattered mirror above the table. My shoulders glowed. My nose looked cauterized.

"Why are you so red?" Gabe asked. "Did you walk here?"

Lisa's eyes wandered as she whistled aimlessly.

"Hold on," Gabe said. "Let me get you some drinks."

Plunking down across from me, Lisa wrinkled her nose and then sniffed her armpit. She picked up a paper menu, scanned it, tossed it, and then reached out and pressed her thumb into my shoulder. "Ouch," I whined, watching the red seep back into the white oval.

"Sorry." She winced. "Thanks for sticking with me, Trace. You're the only person—" Lisa fell silent as Gabe returned with a water pitcher and cups. He poured from the side instead of the spout, giving us lots of ice. Pushing one cup toward me and the other toward Lisa, he ordered us to drink. "I hope you guys didn't come all this way for the pizza," he whispered. "It's not that good."

"Actually," Lisa said, "I was hoping to get a little something." Making tweezers of her thumb and finger, she raised it to her lips.

"Aren't we going to Trent's?" Gabe asked.

"It's been a bad day." Lisa gritted her teeth, then grinned, batting her lashes. "I need something *now*."

I fished a chunk of ice from my water and swabbed my collarbone. Gabe refilled our cups. "I don't have anything on me," he said. Lisa's whole body sagged as though finally feeling the effects of walking miles in the heat. "Hang on." Gabe's chair scraped the tile floor. "Let me see what I can do."

When he came back, he had something clutched in his fist. He palmed it to Lisa, who peeled her thighs from the vinyl seat and pressed her body against his.

"I'll thank you for this later," she whispered.

Gabe's face pinked. "You want some sodas?" he croaked, then cleared his throat. "To go?"

Jumbo paper cups in hand, we trudged back out into the heat. I took the lead this time, winding down side streets and alleys, searching for the sunken plaza where Foley and I first kissed one snowy winter evening. It was deserted this time, too. We hid behind a brick planter anyway, in the shadow of an office building. My father worked in one of them, patrolling dark halls with a flashlight and radio.

"I'm the only person?" I asked, rattling the ice in my cup.

Lisa squinted. "You're the only person, what?"

"Back there, you said—"

Lisa flicked the lighter in her fist. "You're the only person who knows. About . . . you know." The thin white paper crackled as Lisa inhaled. Examining the glowing red ember, she said, "Except my mom and Larry. And your mom, too, I guess."

"You didn't tell Gabe?" I asked.

Lisa shook her head. A light went on in mine: *Trent?* I took a smoke and then sipped my drink. "Is it possible it wasn't . . ."

The hatred in her eyes made me swallow my words. She leaned back and laughed harshly. "You think I'm a slut, don't you?"

"Like I've got room to talk." The smoke expanded my lungs. My vision expanded, too. I'd never noticed the fine red threads branching from the creases where Lisa's nose flares. "I think you're brave," I said. "There's no way I could've told my mom. I don't know what I would've done."

Gone running to Foley, probably.

Lisa snatched the lighter from my knee and took another hit. "Did you hear about that woman who left her baby baking in the car while she was at Bingo?" she asked. "You should need a license to have a kid. You need one to own a gun or drive a car. Hell, you need one to own a dog."

I laughed, releasing a puff of white smoke. My head grew light as if filled with helium.

"Nobody told me you can't give gum to a three-year-old," I said, referring to the one and only time I babysat.

"See what I mean?" Lisa slapped her thigh. "That kid could've died, and you'd be in juvie for neglect or whatever."

Church bells echoed in the distance, tolling the hour, but my mind drifted and I lost count.

"I don't think I want kids," I said. "Not because I'd be a sucky parent. There's just too much I want to do." I poked the bendy straw between my lips. The empty cup gurgled. Lisa offered me hers. "Scott's the opposite," I said. "Which is sad because he'll probably never have any unless he adopts."

I leaned my head on Lisa's shoulder, my body sinking into a sweet acceptance of heat and pain. Maybe the combination of smoking and clearing the air with Lisa would help me sleep. Dr. Dan had told me to come back if the nightmares started interfering with my days. And I'm pretty sure nodding off in the park the other night counted. "What about you?" I asked. "You think you'll want kids someday?"

Lisa raised the smoldering stub to her lips, but the sound of feet pounding jerked us upright. Lisa swatted the smoke curling above our heads. I peeked around the planter as a cluster of pigeons exploded. Just a panting jogger cutting across the square. Heart drumming, I leaned back and laughed nervously at the inky-blue sky. Suddenly, a lonely sunken plaza in the middle of desolate downtown seemed like a dangerous place for two wasted girls.

"We should get out of here," I said. "Before it gets dark." I checked my phone. If we hurried, we had a shot at catching the 8:06 uptown. Tossing our cups, we stumble-rushed toward the sound of traffic, then sprinted for the shelter. I knew we'd make it—the bus was a block away—but Lisa started waving like she was hailing a taxi.

"Act normal," I begged, gulping air. "Seriously. My mom finds out *everything*." The bus rocked to a stop. Paranoia set in. "Quick!" I pinched Lisa's chin. "How do my eyes look?"

The doors hissed open. Lisa started giggling. "Purty," she drawled, kissing my cheek.

I didn't know the driver. I flashed my pass while Lisa pumped her money into the fare box. Bumping down the aisle, Lisa made chicken sounds until we fell into a row behind a guy eating french fries. My stomach rumbled for the cardboard scoop of fat and salt. Lisa walked her fingers along the top of the seat like she meant to swoop down and snatch one. My head was pretty messed up, but I had enough sense to know she'd get her hand broken. I bulged my eyes for her to stop, but Lisa just shrugged and cleared her throat. "Excuse me?" she said, leaning around the seat. I drove my knuckle into her leg and she snorted. "My friend wants to know if she can have a fry."

The guy turned and smiled and raised the cup. I hesitated, wondering if he was a serial killer who preyed on girls with the munchies. Biting my lip to keep from giggling, I drew first and then Lisa. I got an extra-long one, the kind you have to bend to fit in your mouth. Lisa frowned at hers, brown and short and shriveled. As the giggles passed from me to Lisa and back again, I had one of those lightbulb moments: laughter is a lot like fear—highly contagious. Katie'd caught it, too. Poor thing. Imagining her crazy escape drills made me laugh even harder until I saw the driver watching in the mirror.

As the bus trundled uptown, the blue lights came on, purging all trace of red. Something about that eerie wash always magnified Lisa's stark beauty. I leaned my head against hers and snapped a picture with my phone, but the flash ruined it. I looked like a clown with my bright nose, my eyebrows arched ridiculously high, and Lisa's pupils were enormous. She deleted it, then leaned over and tapped the buzzer. Gripping the handrails we stumbled toward the stairwell and waited for our stop. The bus bucked and the doors jerked open. Descending into darkness, we giggled and skipped like idiots the last couple blocks to Trent's, where his spacey mother let us in. The sub-bass frequencies droning from the third floor magnetized us up the first flight, but then the rising heat took hold, weighing us down. The stairs stretched on forever. We'd never reach Trent's room. Ever. The hallway grew longer and longer as we swam toward the light. My brain was trapped in a cement mixer, turning and turning, until the music stopped. Time and space collapsed. A platinum-pigtailed Rachel flicked her hand lazily, too hot or too drunk to wave. Kicking a pile of clothes out of the way, Trent hugged Lisa and then glowered at me. "You look like hell," he said.

I wiped the sweat trickling from my hairline. "This *room* is hell," I said. It was the first time I'd been to Trent's since Adam and I had broken up. A few things had changed. The fist-sized hole in the wall beside the closet—that was new. And the drum set was under the window now. In its place was a small black fridge plastered with band stickers. And then there was Rachel's hair. Actually, it was more like Lisa's hair on Rachel.

"What are you drinking?" Trent asked. "Beer or beer?"

While Lisa pretended to mull it over, Trent tossed me a generic cola. I didn't know if it was punishment for puking behind his radiator or cheating on Adam until he cozied up to Lisa and showed her a picture on his phone.

"This is what our boy is up to in California," he said. "Is she a hottie or what?"

Lisa stared blankly at the screen and shrugged.

Winking cruelly at me, Trent zoomed in with his fingers. "Seriously," he said. "Look at her." He was hoping I'd ask to see, but something fiery and inflexible—pride, maybe, jealously, probably—hardened my jaw. I squeezed the soda can with both hands to keep it from flying at his stupid smirking skull. Lisa swiped the screen and asked if the next picture was the same girl. I couldn't help it. I peeked.

"You could park a car in that dimple," I said. Lisa and Rachel laughed, but Trent started barking at me in a way that made me hate him and fear him at once. "You don't get to be bitchy!" he shouted. "Look at that hole! Look at it!" I obeyed because I was in Trent's house, in Trent's room, with Trent's hand driving my head toward the wall. In biology we learned about the fight-or-flight instinct. I must be genetically defective because I don't possess either. I stared into the black void, waiting for Trent to tell me what I was seeing. "That's you," he hissed. "Adam did that after he found out you cheated."

A thunderous rush filled my ears. My eyes filled, too, with blinding rage. But I didn't move. I couldn't. "Let go," I whispered. "Please let go."

"Don't be a dick," Lisa said, chucking a bottle cap at him. "Leave her alone."

Trent's fingers tensed and then fell away. I waited until he'd stomped out of the room and down the stairs before turning. The bathroom door slammed below. Lisa gave the empty hall the finger, but Rachel cocked her blond head and frowned. "Don't be mad," she pleaded. "He was just . . . I don't know. It was a shock. You and Adam. You guys were the perfect couple."

"Nothing is perfect," I responded icily.

I wasn't pissed at Rachel—well, actually I was, a little, for defending him—but I was furious with Trent for being a hypocrite. Maybe he didn't count kissing as cheating, but I was damn sure Rachel did.

"C'mon, let's go," Lisa said. She chugged the last of her beer and checked her phone. "I don't care if Adam's his friend. That was a shitty thing, what he just did to you."

"I'm fine," I said, still feeling the ghost of Trent's palm gripping my head. "You sure?" Lisa asked. I shrugged. Rachel passed me her cigarette and promised to make Trent behave, which wasn't necessary. When he returned, he was someone else. There was still an edge to his voice, but it was the edge of someone trying too hard to be nice. "I think I've got one of those lemony things you like," he said, rattling through the fridge. "Yep. Last one." He twisted the cap with his T-shirt and held the bottle before me—a peace offering. I took it, reluctantly, and drank it. *One less for him.* Bottle in hand, I jumped on the bed and tugged Rachel's pigtail—the same shade as Lisa's, except Lisa's didn't come from a box. "I like the new color," I said. "It totally works." And then, smiling innocently: "Did Trent pick it?"

Beer shot from Lisa's nose. Grinning wickedly, Trent mouthed *Touché.* I waited for a glassy-eyed Rachel to ask what was so funny, but she clinked her bottle against mine like she was in on the joke. As I wrinkled my face at Lisa—*Does she know he has a thing for you?*—Lisa inhaled sharply, her torso convulsing like she'd been shocked with a Taser. Another creaky gasp. Her chest quivered. The four of us burst out laughing. Lisa hiccupped again. And again. And again. The faces she made made us laugh harder, our bodies racked by those deep, uncontrollable jags that only seem to strike at life's lowest moments. Suddenly, everything felt right again.

"Stop it, you guys!" Lisa gasped, jerking with another spasm. "I can't breathe!"

Trent quit laughing long enough to take her by the shoulders and help her to the bed. Chest heaving, he panted in Lisa's face. "Hold your breath."

Lisa recoiled, swatting the air between them. "God, Trent, hold yours!"

"I know! It's wicked, right?" Rachel shrieked and then lost it all over again, flopping on the bed in a fit. Arms flapping, Trent descended, roaring like a fire-breathing dragon. I crawled beneath their feet, rescuing tipped beer bottles. Lisa slid off the mattress and slumped on the floor, her body jerking every few seconds like invisible fingers were poking her ribs. "Please make it stop," she moaned, and then, "I think I peed my pants." As she ran for the bathroom, Trent called, "Drink water! There's a cup on the sink!"

"Water won't work," Rachel said. "We need to scare them out of her." Thinking, we sipped our warm beers and then froze at the sound of someone heavier than Lisa stumping up the stairs. Gabe in his work boots, reeking of pizza. He went straight to the fridge for a drink and then looked around the room, confused. "Where's my girl?" he asked, flicking the bottle cap through the hole in the wall.

"Bathroom," I said. "Wicked hiccups."

Trent's eyes sparkled fiendishly behind his lenses. "I've got it," he whispered. "This is brilliant. *Brilliant.*" Gabe raised the bottle to his lips, but Trent snatched it away. "You. Under the bed," Trent ordered. Gabe complied. Rachel grabbed her phone so she could record it. The three of us hushed and hissed as Lisa rasped violently up the stairs and down the hall, then keeled over on the bed, clutching her middle.

"This—" Her body quaked, gripped by another spasm. "Is torture!"

I was dangerously close to cracking up again. Rachel, too, behind her phone, pretending to use the camera as a mirror. Not Trent. There's a reason why he's always cast for the best roles. Ignoring Lisa's hiccups, he chugged Gabe's beer, then plunked on the floor and picked at the loose rubber on his sneaker before launching into his setup: "Hey, Leese, did you ever get your flip-flop back?"

It was supposed to be funny, our attempt to cure Lisa. What was Trent doing? I silently shook my head at him. *Don't go there.* Lisa clasped the pendant at her neck, as if remembering the original she'd lost that night along with her flip-flop, and chirped, "No. Why?"

"It's just . . . well," Trent hesitated. "Maybe it's not even yours."

Lisa eyed him suspiciously and then turned to me. Lips twitching, I fought the giddy burbling in my chest and shrugged, feigning cluelessness.

"Okay, I'm just gonna say it," Trent said. "Wednesday night, when I got home from work, there was this box. And there was a flip-flop inside."

Between hiccups, Lisa asked, "Where?"

"That's the freaky part," Trent said. "It was on my bed. It's under it now."

I didn't know if it was the hiccups or Trent's story, but Lisa looked stricken. That's not true—I did know. I also knew it was time to pull the plug on Trent's joke. But I didn't. Instead I waited silently as my best friend dropped to her knees and pitched toward the black beneath the bed. It was priceless at first, the way Gabe's hands shot out and Lisa, in a blurry frenzy, did one of those full-body screams, with arms and legs flying in all directions. But then something in me shifted—my view, I guess. Suddenly I was Lisa, shrinking from strange faces. Distorted. Ugly. It was one of those moments when you're painfully aware of yourself: my laugh craggy and grating. My features alien, grotesque. The part of me that found Lisa's shock hilarious seized up. "Are you okay?" I asked.

Gabe mopped his face with his T-shirt and then wrapped his arms around Lisa's waist, but Lisa just stood there stiffly, lips quivering.

"This is gonna get a million hits!" Rachel screeched, fumbling with her phone.

"Admit it," Trent laughed. "You thought it was Banana Man."

I think everyone expected Lisa to start laughing, too, once the confusion wore off. I know none of us expected her to explode the way she did, slashing Trent's face with her nails.

"Mother—!" Trent snarled, pressing his palm to his cheek. "It was a joke, Lisa!"

"A joke? You think this is a joke?" Lisa turned, raising the back of her shirt. The skin across her spine was striped purple and yellow. Gabe's face buckled. He reached to touch the fading bruise, but Lisa yanked her shirt down. "Sweetie," he cooed. "What the hell happened?"

Trent didn't care. Lisa had drawn blood. Pinpricks of red seeped from the claw marks. Rachel went for bandages and antiseptic. It wasn't an overreaction. It was pretty nasty—the wound—but Trent was even nastier. Clenching his fists, he ordered Gabe to get his psycho bitch out of his house.

I'd always considered Lisa lucky to have a guy like Gabe, but right then, not so much. Scaring the crap out of her was one thing—we'd all been in on that—but failing to defend her was just plain wrong. I took one look at his big dumb head—grudging and sad that Lisa had wrecked his night—and said, "Stay. I'll take her home."

Passing Rachel on the stairs, she begged us not to leave, but we kept going until we were out the front door. The cool air tickled my neck and I shivered. I'd spent all summer trying to convince myself that Banana Man didn't exist, but I had to ask: "Did he do that to you? The bruises on your back?"

Lisa rushed into the murky darkness beyond the porch. She waited until we reached the next pool of light to speak. "Yes and no," she said. "I went back to get my stuff and fell down the stupid stairs. I want this to be over, but he's got my stuff. That dumb necklace. My flip-flop. It makes me sick, knowing he's got them, not knowing what he's doing with them. You know what I mean?"

There was a desperate loneliness to her voice. I understood. Knowing that someone has something of yours, a piece of you you'll never get back, it jigsaws your insides. But you have to let it go. Eventually.

"He's not real," I said gently. "The guy who lives in the woods is a man, not a monster. He doesn't know who we are, what we're thinking. He's not watching us. He doesn't know where we live." I reached for the button on the pole, but Lisa pulled me back.

"You've felt it, too," she whimpered. "You've said so."

"I know," I said. "But listen. I think it's something else. I think it's everything you've been going through. The . . . you know."

Lisa marched across the street, ignoring the DON'T WALK light. Like an idiot, I tripped after her, racing an oncoming car.

"You think *I* started this?" Lisa demanded.

I took a deep breath, trying to calm my nerves. "No," I said. "Of course not. Trent started it. Remember when we were little, though, how we used to get ourselves all worked up over the stupidest things? I know it sounds weird, but stress, fear, hallucinations—all that's stuff's catching." I stuck my finger in her ear, trying to get a laugh, but Lisa brushed my hand away.

"What about the eye?" she asked.

Eyes.

Picturing the two in my trunk, I blinked away the image and lied because it was the only explanation that made sense: "It was Trent," I said. "And Gabe," I added. "Trent put him up to it. Just like now. You think it was Gabe's idea to hide under the bed?"

Lisa stopped short and put her hands on her hips. "Gabe?" she asked. "Did he tell you that? Did he actually say he did it?"

I knew what Lisa needed. Taking her hand, I nodded firmly, definitively, before we raced toward the next dash of light in the long ribbon of darkness.

twenty

Sometimes I feel like my life is held together with spit and wishes. It was supposed to be a perfect day: back-to-school shopping, frozen yogurt, then open mic night with Lisa. But everything fell apart, starting with our junky car. It just quit running, without warning, while we were waiting for the light to change. My mother turned the key a few times. A rapid clicking noise sounded. "That's just great," she groaned, hitting the steering wheel. The car behind us honked. My mother stuck her arm out the window and waved angrily for the guy to go around.

"Now what?" I said, gazing helplessly out the window. A few drivers slowed as they passed, checking out the losers stranded in the middle of the busy street. My mother unbuckled her seat belt. "We can't stay here blocking traffic," she said. She popped the door and got out. "I'll push, you steer."

I climbed over the armrest and gripped the wheel at ten and

two, just like she'd taught me the one time she took me driving. I knew it was useless, but I tried the key anyway, hoping the car had magically healed itself. Nothing. Dead.

"Foot on the brake," my mother directed through the window. A truck blew by, ruffling her hair. She flattened her body against the door and leaned in. "Now put the gearshift in neutral. The *N*," she said, jabbing her finger at the center console. "*D* is for drive."

"I know," I snapped, clutching the knob. "I'm not stupid."

My mother stalked to the trunk and then stalked back. Reaching in front of me, she cranked the stiff wheel, aiming the tires toward the lighted ENTER sign for a burger place. The rubber beneath me shuddered, skipping over the pavement. "Hold it tight," she said, nodding for me to take over. Back to the trunk she went. In the side mirror, she waved, shouting, "Take your foot off the brake!"

The car started rolling slowly. I could walk faster than we were moving, but I still felt out of control. In the rearview mirror, all I could see was the crooked part in my mom's hair. Glancing to my right, I caught a minivan trying to nose ahead of me. Some soccer mom in a hurry for the drive-thru. Instinctively, I hit the brake. When I looked back, my mom was slapping the trunk in frustration. I cringed. We'd lost our momentum. She'd never be able to push the car up the slight rise ahead. Watching her there, hot and miserable, trying to summon the strength to get us going again, I was ready to call my dad when another head appeared next to hers. Clean-cut face, deep laugh lines, pilot sunglasses. My mother instantly perked, relieved by the small break the universe had granted. With the two of them pushing, the car glided forward, bumping up and over the asphalt lip. The stranger shouted something I couldn't hear. I think he wanted me to steer, because my mom jogged to the window and took the wheel, aiming the car toward an empty spot beside the Dumpster.

"Thank you so much. That was really nice of you," my mother gushed as the stranger came around the car. "I really appreciate it."

"Not a problem," he said, extending his hand. "I'm Jim."

"Trish," my mother said. "This is Tracy."

I waved from the driver's seat. My mother opened the door for me to get out, then reached in and grabbed her phone. "Guess we're gonna need a tow," she said.

Jim thunked the hood with his knuckle. "You want me to check it out?" he said. "I don't mind."

"It's the alternator," my mother said confidently. Jim seemed impressed. "This car's been nothing but trouble," my mom griped. "Look, I've got the towing service under 'favorites.'"

Jim laughed. My mother pulled a wad of crumpled bills from her pocket. "Tracy, go get some drinks," she said. I assumed she meant three—one for each of us—but standing before the fountain dispenser, I realized Jim hadn't said what kind. Not that it mattered. Shouldering the glass door, I expected to find my mother sitting on the car bumper alone, but I was wrong.

"Root beer. Lemon-lime. Orange," I said, directing my nose at each of the cups in the carrier. Prying the root beer from the cardboard, Jim thanked me and then poked a straw through the plastic lid. The three of us stood there in the blistering parking lot, sipping and sweating, until Jim pointed his cup at my mother and cocked his head. "Trish, right?" My mother nodded. "You look really familiar," he said. My mother flexed her eyebrows in surprise. "That's funny," she said. "I was thinking the same thing about you."

They spent the next five minutes playing the Where-Do-I-Know-You-From game. It turned out my dad was the connection. They'd played softball together forever ago. There was an awkward moment after my mother said they were separated, but then the tow truck roared into the lot, breaking the silence. A guy in a grimy work shirt dropped from the cab. The way he watched me gave me the creeps. I didn't think it was my radar giving me another false positive. I went inside to escape his slimy gaze and use the bathroom. When I returned, the front end of our car was suspended by chains. I hated seeing it like that, strung up like some enormous dead beast. Maybe it was a heap of junk, but it was *our* heap of junk.

"Can we ride with you to the garage?" my mother asked the driver, who was marking something off on his greasy clipboard. I glanced inside the cab—cramped and grungy—then glanced at the driver with his pit stains and hairy forearms. Suddenly my shorts felt too short, my T-shirt too sheer.

Jim tapped my mother's shoulder. I noticed his ring finger, bare and tanned. "I'll give you a lift," he said.

I locked eyes with my mother, pleading silently, *Say yes, stupid!*

"If it's not a problem," she said hesitantly. "I don't want to hold you up."

Unlike our car—full of dents, with fries on the floor and stickers on the dashboard—Jim's car was clean and new, with a sunroof and tinted windows. It made me wonder what he did for a living. He didn't say. He didn't get a chance. My mother blathered the whole way about all the things that were wrong with our life, everything old and broken and neglected, including herself.

When we got to the garage, I leaned between the seats, between my mother and Jim.

"Do you like roller coasters?" I asked.

"I guess." Jim looked puzzled. "Why?"

I shrugged and got out. As Jim's car pulled away, my mother swatted me with her purse.

"He likes you," I said, waving at his taillights.

My mother blushed. "Don't be stupid. He was just being nice."

"There's nice and then there's *nice*," I said. "He didn't have to give us a ride."

She didn't argue. The tow truck growled into the lot, dragging our sad car behind it. While my mother paid the driver, I went inside where it was cool. Dark, too. Just like the bathrooms at Hillhurst Park. Nothing had changed since the last time our car had died. Same stack of worn magazines. Same gumball machine filled with ancient gum. Same pot of burnt coffee. I plunked down in one of the molded plastic chairs and checked my messages. Lisa had sent a video. It was hard to hear over the whir of air-powered tools, but I knew she sounded good. She'd been rehearsing since Monday. If she could make it through open mic without choking, auditions for the fall musical were next week. Even if she didn't get the lead, I knew she'd make ensemble. Any part on stage was a start.

"Is that Lisa?" my mother asked, angling to watch. "I didn't know she could sing."

I played it again and then played a game. My mother bought a soda from the machine and asked to take a crack at slicing fruits. I took the game back after she beat my all-time high. All those years of wagging her finger at me and Scott had given her an unfair advantage.

"I know it doesn't have all the stores you like," my mother

said. "But if these guys hurry up and let me know what's going on, we can catch the three-forty to the Pyramid Mall."

A chill went down my spine. The Pyramid Mall. I hadn't been back since I'd made Jerk Face meet me there. Somehow it seemed tainted now, like the way you can't bring yourself to eat a certain food after you've been sick, even if that food wasn't the thing that made you sick.

"Don't get too excited." My mother folded her arms, annoyed. "I'm just saying, today doesn't have to be a total waste."

But she was wrong. The 3:40 came and went. And then the 4:10. Every time my mother slapped the bell on the counter, another mechanic appeared and promised they were working on it. Four-thirty. Four forty-five. The garage closed at six. I imagined the manager shutting off the lights and locking us in for the night. Mom bought a candy bar from the honor snack box and wandered outside. A few seconds later the glass door whipped open. Trish had her game face on. Shoulders squared, eyebrow arched, she bypassed the bell and marched straight into the garage. Familiar territory for her, but judging from the reaction of some of the mechanics, you'd think she'd barged into a men's locker room. "Excuse me," she said sharply, ambushing the nearest guy. "Do you think I'm an idiot?" The mechanic looked around nervously, afraid to answer. "Nobody's even looked at my car," my mom said. "It hasn't moved an inch. It's sitting right where the tow truck left it."

The guy tossed a wrench and wiped his hands on a rag. "Let me get my boss," he said. A few minutes later a man in a polo shirt was leading my mother back to the waiting room. "Sorry about the confusion," he said. "We're pretty backed up today."

"I understand you're busy. That's not the problem," my mother said, her voice low and steady, one supervisor to another.

"But someone could've told me that an hour ago instead of leaving me sitting here. If you can't get to it today, just say so. Ignoring me or saying you're working on it when you're not—that's just bad service."

The manager apologized again, but his eyes said something harsh and ugly. A word men reserve for women like my mom, strong women who won't be pushed aside.

"Here's my number," she said, unaware or undaunted or just plain immune after all her years with the bus company. "Call me when you know something."

I followed my mom out into the harsh sunlight. "I guess we're walking," I said. Other than the bike path down by the river, I couldn't remember the last time I'd walked anywhere with my mom. She drove these streets daily, but walking is different. You notice more of the things you'd rather not. As we passed the park with the animals on springs, my mother whispered, "Are those guys dealing drugs?"

"Welcome to our neighborhood," I said in a singsong.

My mother clutched her purse tight to her side. "You don't walk this way at night?" she asked.

I lied, afraid she'd change my curfew back to nine. When we got to our corner there was no reason to go home. I begged my mom for some money and went to Lisa's instead. I figured she'd need some support. Open mic was a big deal—for me and for her. For years I'd been telling her to stop hiding her voice. If this thing backfired, she'd never speak to me again.

"How's my makeup?" Lisa asked the bathroom mirror. "Too much? Too little? Maybe a little more eyeliner." She raised the liquid pen and extended the wings trailing from her lids.

"You look good," I said. "Really good. I like your top."

"Katie picked it. She said it makes me look like . . ." Lisa leaned out the door and shouted down the hall. "Who'd you say I look like, Katie?"

"The woman on that cooking show! The one with the boobs and the teeth!"

Lisa plumped herself in the mirror. "Yeah. Her."

I freshened up quickly, borrowing Lisa's deodorant and running a brush through my hair.

"C'mon. Let's go," she said. "I want to get there early so we get a good seat."

I caught her arm and examined her eyes. "Did you take one of Larry's pain pills?"

Lisa stared right back. "No. Why?"

"You just seem really calm . . ." I trailed off.

"I'm just ready to do this," she said. "I'm done being afraid. What's the worst that can happen?"

The worst that could happen? Open mic night was canceled. The guy who usually runs it was away on vacation. Apparently, we weren't the only ones who hadn't gotten the memo—a couple of head bangers wandered in after us, looking for the sign-up sheet.

"I guess it wasn't meant to be." Lisa shrugged, scanning the coffee menu. She ordered some crazy frozen thing—more dessert than drink—with whipped cream and chocolate shavings. I only had enough for a small coffee. "I'll be glad when you find a job," she said, getting one for me, too. Waiting for our order, we snagged one of the high tables in back and watched a few more musician-types trickle in.

"You're still going to the audition, right? Actually, don't answer that. You're going." Lisa didn't argue. She went for straws instead. Watching more and more people come in, I tried to ignore the gnawing in my chest. I'd wanted so badly to hear her sing, for this to be her night. There was always next week, but next week seemed so far away.

Lisa poked a straw through my whipped cream, and I sipped. My cheeks imploding, I mumbled, "Does this thing have caffeine in it?"

"That would be the *-uccino* part—"

Her eyes had caught on something.

I turned and then stiffened.

"Why's he here?" I hissed.

Lisa waved Foley to our table. "He wanted to watch," she whispered. "I couldn't say no. I didn't say anything because I knew you'd be pissed."

Pissed didn't even begin to describe how I felt when Foley came up from behind and put his hands on my shoulders. "Don't touch me," I snapped. Lisa made a pouty face and flicked Foley's earring. "Open mic's canceled," she said. "There's nobody to run it. I would've called, but I forgot my phone."

"You could've used mine," I said.

Foley scanned the cafe. It wasn't exactly packed, but there was a decent crowd, big enough for him to convince the guy behind the counter to let him emcee for the night. I sat there silently fuming while he set up the microphone and amp and then went around with a sign-up sheet. I should've known he'd find some way to save the day. "Nothing's changed," I growled when he returned. "I still hate you."

Foley ignored me. Lisa wrote her name on the list, taking the fourth slot, which was perfect: enough time for everyone to get settled, but not enough for her to change her mind.

"I owe you," she said, hugging Foley. "Thanks."

Foley shrugged. He glanced at the couches and tables filled with intense-looking hipsters and punks, preening and tuning. "It's funny how no one was willing to step up," he said.

"Doesn't your arm ever get tired?" I asked Foley. I slurped the chocolate sludge at the bottom of my cup and gave him a shove. "Stop patting yourself on the back and get this thing started."

I'm sure there were some ridiculously talented people that played before Lisa, but my world had shrunk. It's happened before, during auditions, my mind drifting to some faraway place where it's only me and the lines in my head while I wait for the director to call my name. That night was all about Lisa, but it still had a tunnel effect as I watched her, blanched of color, restless knees bouncing. Her eyes widened unnaturally when Foley introduced her.

"You've got this," I said. "Don't think. Just sing."

Everyone clapped as she made her way to the stool in the corner. Wiping her palms on her thighs, she smiled painfully and looked to me. *Say something,* I whispered. Lisa nodded but when she opened her mouth to speak, the espresso machine drowned her out. My heart stalled. Foley ran up and adjusted the microphone. The guy polishing the steamer wand shouted, "Sorry!" and then my phone rang. It was Lisa's ring tone, which meant it was probably Katie calling to tell her she'd left it at home. I shut it off. Foley slapped his arms together like a movie set clapper. *Take two.*

I wasn't surprised that Lisa's voice was a little shaky at first, but I was surprised when after a few bars she cut short the bubbly pop song she'd been rehearsing and asked to start over. *What are you doing?* I thought. But Lisa was already somewhere else, swaying gently, tapping her foot to an imagined melody. Smiling shyly, she locked eyes with me as the first line to a different song escaped from her lips. My brain sparked with recognition. It was one of her favorites. Mine, too. Part love song, part lullaby, she'd sung it hundreds of times after we discovered it back in eighth grade, acting like it was new even though it had been around since our parents were in high school.

Foley slipped into the chair beside me and scooted closer to see over all the heads, but I didn't care. I was busy burning the moment into my brain, a permanent recording of my best friend at her best. Something about that song always fills me with this heavyhearted longing. It isn't just the lyrics—a dream of childhood, of warmth and safety and blue skies—but the way Lisa sings it. Softly, sweetly, her voice building and building, gathering strength for the final verse when the song shifts from sweet memories to unanswerable questions about the future. I'd wanted to hear that song so badly the day I'd returned from Troy feeling stupid and small and scared. I'd wanted Lisa to sing it to me. She probably would have, too. If I'd asked. If I'd gone to her. If only I'd gone to her.

Nobody ever gets booed at open mic, but you can tell when someone knocks it out of the park. Classic rock is always a hit but it wasn't just the song. Lisa had nailed it, making it her own. Her voice stronger than ever.

Or since.

I leaned over and whispered in Foley's ear. "Don't take this the wrong way, but thank you."

Stumbling through the maze of tables, drunk on applause, Lisa high-fived Foley as he went up to introduce the next person on the sign-up sheet. The rest of open mic was one big yawn. I felt sort of sorry for the people who went after, especially the singers. Nobody paid much attention. Everybody was up getting coffee or out smoking cigarettes. Even the ones who stayed in their seats kept glancing back at our table.

"I was so scared," Lisa said later, after the last musician gave a shout-out to Foley and packed up her guitar, after the guy running the coffee shop shouted last call, after everyone spilled out into the humid night air. "The way nobody clapped at first, I thought maybe it sucked."

"Are you kidding?" Foley said. "They were in shock. I was in shock."

Lisa batted a moth circling her head. "Seriously?"

"When have you ever seen the guy behind the counter stop pumping coffee to watch?" I asked.

Lisa smiled at her feet and then up at the stars. "Yeah, I was pretty awesome."

The neon sign in the window extinguished, and Lisa thanked Foley again.

"You're welcome, my dear," he said with a smile, but then he glanced at me and his eyes dropped sadly. I think the truth of us was just sinking in. Foley's power to fix anything extended only so far. The one thing he needed to fix was beyond fixing. "C'mon, Wonder Boy," I said, the bitter knot in my chest loosening a little. "Walk us home."

"Sorry," he said. "I've gotta run." In typical Foley fashion, he didn't offer a reason, just bowed to Lisa and then bowed to me and took off. I watched until his shape fused with the shadows before checking my phone. Katie had called twice more, but she hadn't left any messages.

"We should go, too," I said.

"I'm never gonna be able to sleep tonight," Lisa said. "I'm practically vibrating."

Singing and squealing, we floated up State Street hill, past the drugstore and the yellow arches and the church where my parents were married. When we got to my corner, Lisa put her hands on my shoulders. "Remember that day at the roller rink when you said we should take a bus to the city?" she asked. "I've been thinking we should do it. Just you and me."

It was a perfect ending to what started out as a less than

perfect day. The old Lisa was back, but there was a new Lisa, too. I went to sleep with the ghost of her voice ringing softly in my ears. That's why I thought I was dreaming when I opened my eyes and heard Lisa's pitch in my room. But she wasn't singing. She was crying. Not in my room, but outside my window. Heart knocking, I slipped through the kitchen and met Lisa out back. There was a book in her hand—Katie's diary. Before she even opened it, I knew it wasn't good, whatever she wanted to show me. I led her into the garage and turned on the light and then leaned against the tool bench and read the last entry, written a few hours before, while Lisa and I were hanging out in front of the cafe with Foley. We should've protected her. Little Katie. My knees felt weak, the weight of her words pulling me down. When I looked up, Lisa was glaring, waiting for me to speak, but I couldn't. What do you say? What can you say? I said what was in my head, the looping line of the last verse, the one that sang me to sleep: *Where do we go now?*

twenty-one

To: splendidhavoc@horizon.net
From: blackolcun@horizon.net
Subject: SOS

What's my excuse?

I know what you'd say: violence is never an answer. But what did you expect us to do? Go to the cops? With what? A sixth-grader's diary and several glass eyes? Maybe he's not the monster from my nightmares, but he's still dangerous. Sometimes you have to act. Someone had to take charge. Does that make me the perpetrator? I guess Lisa will get charged as an accomplice. I don't know how this stuff works. I don't want to go to prison. Like that kid

from your class, the one who shot that girl while robbing a
sub shop. His life is over. *I'm not him.* I'm a good person.
We were *protecting* Katie. There was no one else who
could. Sometimes I hate being a girl. I hate it. I hate it. I
hate it. Remember how Mom used to send me to those
Girl Power classes? What a load of crap—girl power.
It's a myth, just like Banana Man. I have no control over
anything, my own body, even. It was strange the way I
felt outside myself tonight. Like I was watching myself on
stage. Like I was playing a part.

But I had no choice.

twenty-two

i felt gutted reading Katie's diary that night—like someone had taken a vacuum to my insides. Flattening the spine on the tool bench, I'd wanted so badly to find the stuff of an eleven-year-old girl's dream summer—afternoons at the pool and roller-skating parties and ice cream and first kisses. Instead I found a nightmare.

I was in the shower when the bathroom door creaked open. I saw a shadow on the ceiling and thought it was Lisa—home from her thing at the coffee shop—but when I called her name, the shadow didn't answer. I froze, water running down my face, shampoo stinging my eyes, afraid to look around the curtain because I knew it was him—the monster. I knew he was

watching. I don't know what he was waiting for,
but it felt like forever. The hot water ran out and
I started shivering and then there was this creepy
groaning noise and the bathroom door closed.
I know he'll be back. Maybe not tonight, but
someday. I need Lisa so bad right now. She's the
only one who'll believe me. I tried calling, but she
forgot her phone. I called stupid Tracy but she
didn't pick up. I hope Lisa gets home soon. She's
supposed to protect me. I'm too old to be scared of
the dark, but I am.

"Why didn't you answer your phone?" Lisa shouted angrily. She punched the air in frustration, sending the lightbulb above her head swinging crazily. The shadows followed, lurching and shrinking.

"I didn't know," I whispered. "I didn't think it was anything. Where is she now?"

Lisa dropped her voice and covered her eyes. "Home," she said. "Sleeping."

"Did you check her window?" I asked. "Is it locked?"

"Read," Lisa demanded. Clutching her head, she paced the garage while my fingers struggled with the dog-eared pages— the important entries, the ones Lisa wanted me to see. I stared dumbly at the words, my brain dulled by shock and fear. Like a child's drawing of a gruesome scene, something about Katie's chunky, kiddish handwriting only made me feel sicker.

Last night there were two glass eyes on the crate
next to my bed, just like the ones Lisa thinks I
don't know about. She was supposed to be home

*by ten—that's her curfew. But I don't know what
time she got home. I fell asleep. This morning the
eyes were gone.*

I read the entry again and again, trying to make the words
stick. He left them for Katie. Not me. This wasn't about me. I
wanted to wake Katie and wrap her in my arms and apologize for
everything. For doubting, for lying, for making excuses, for always believing there's a rational explanation. I'd tried so hard to
ignore what the pit of my stomach knew: he's real. I focused on
the blackness beyond the garage window and then lowered my
head. I had to tell Lisa. "Katie's not making this up," I said. "I
found the eyes. I have them." Lisa's inky shadow spilled across
the diary. Hand shaking, she ripped a page while turning to the
next entry.

*Lisa's all freaked out. I heard her talking to
Tracy. She thinks Banana Man's been in our
house. She thinks he left a glass eye for her, just
like the one she stole from his house. She's been
sleeping in my room. She says I have the better
fan, but that's not why. She wants to protect me.
I think it's working.*

But why was he stalking Katie, too? She was innocent; she
had nothing to do with what we did. I turned to the final creased
corner and read:

*Lisa would kill me if she knew I went into the
woods with Ryan. I think I saw him. Banana
Man. He was watching from behind a tree.*

When I looked back, there were tears running down Lisa's face. My blood turned cold as I remembered my mother's words: *If you see the creature, even just a glimpse*— I closed the diary.

"You said it was Trent," Lisa hissed. "You said it was Gabe. You lied. Why didn't you tell me?"

"I—it had to be them. Nothing else fit." My eyes skittered around the garage, taking in the relics of a former life. "This can't be real," I said. "This isn't us. Things like this don't happen to girls like you and me. How was I supposed to believe we were being stalked by . . . by what? I don't even know what to call him."

"You know what to call him," she said. "You know what he is."

I did. I stared at the moths flinging themselves at the bare bulb and then grabbed a flashlight from the shelf. That night, as Lisa and I ran blindly through the woods, Katie was my sister, too. There was no right or wrong or consequences. Those words had lost their meaning. The last time we'd entered the woods together, armed with rocks, screaming like banshees, our fearlessness took us only so far—within throwing distance—but now we were possessed by something unbending, stony, a cold, calm nerve that carried us to the threshold of his house and somewhere darker, deeper. A place no one should ever go. Lisa lifted the flap of screen. I shone the light inside. The smell was awful.

"Do you think he's here?" I whispered into the crook of my arm.

"He's here," Lisa hissed. "I feel it. Don't you feel it?"

I did. Something electric, a pulsing current, like when you know there's a TV on in another room, even if the sound's muted. A thunderous rumble shook the ground, shook the trees. The black tarp walls rippled. I bounced the light around the living room, searching, my heart hitching with the hope and dread of finding him sitting calmly in the flowered armchair, sharpening his fingernails, or hunched over the piano, licking his gray teeth.

I've been waiting for you, Tracy.

The walls stilled. An eerie expectant silence thrummed in my ears. I let the flashlight linger on the initials Adam had carved into the blackened piano case until Lisa tapped me on the shoulder and pointed toward the back. She followed the carpet scraps, and I followed her, past the ancient washing machine and the step stool, every muscle in my body taut and quaking, braced for the inevitable. That he didn't rise from the shadows only made me more anxious. I dropped the light, but Lisa kept going, into the kitchen. Everything was exactly the same as last time. Not the way we'd left it. The way we'd found it. Clean and orderly. I shone the light on the plates Lisa had smashed, webbed with cracks now, but whole again, stacked neatly on the table with the crackers and oatmeal and coffee. A gust of wind made the tarp walls shudder, and then another sound—not wind, not walls—made Lisa and I lock eyes. The sound of metal on metal. The sound of rusty springs creaking. Lisa motioned toward the bedroom, and I trained the light on the ground. Slowly, cautiously, we crept across the kitchen and peered around the gap. My heart skipped. There, on the iron bed frame, was the long gray cocoon. There he was. Breathing peacefully, sleeping peacefully, in his cocoon of musty bedding. Lisa and I locked eyes again. Suddenly, we were back in middle school: *I'm not going! You go! No, you go!* The demon stirred, shifting its weight. *Now!* I mouthed, but Lisa hesitated. I didn't. Rushing the bed, I struck the first blow, hard and fast.

It's something I'll never forget: the feeling of bone on bone.

It's messed up to say it felt good, but it did. My brain knew it was wrong, but my fists didn't care. Once the fuse was lit, all I could do was stand outside myself and watch my body explode. Lisa's, too. Our shadows on the tarp, black on black, a dark frenzy of arms and elbows and knuckles, punching, bashing, crushing, knocking the air out of the thing beneath the blankets. Our voices shrieking in rage and frustration, drowning out the demon's long, painful cries until another low tremor rolled through the woods, vibrating the walls and the bed. As it echoed up my legs, I glanced at Lisa. I half-expected the ground to open up and swallow us whole. I wish it had because I can't ever erase what I saw: Lisa, beautiful Lisa, a maddened clawing animal, possessed by something that chilled me. Sickened, I turned away, but as I did, the blankets slipped down to its chin, forcing me to face another awful truth.

The thing about monsters is, nothing prepares you for how plain they look. Ordinary. Not some gray, scaly thing with a twisting mouth. No. Pale blond hair and pale wiry beard, a long thin nose and thinner lips. The only thing out of the ordinary was the empty socket beneath his right eyebrow. The left eye was there, wild and frightened. Not the soulless eye of a demon, but the eye of a man, searching my face for sympathy or leniency or compassion, all things I'd lost that day in Troy when a boy knocked me to the floor and held me down and forced my legs apart with his knees. I want to believe that everything I did that night was for Katie. But it wasn't. A deeper rage was thrashing out. Staring into that yawning socket—deep, dark, jagged as the hole Adam punched in Trent's wall—made it easier to do what I had to do.

I brought the flashlight down upon his head, shutting his one good eye forever.

twenty-three

h unched over the computer, I listened for my mother, the cursor on the minimize box in case she came barging in again. I'd been trying to contact Scott for the last hour—the longest hour of my life. He'd know what to do. Maybe. Maybe not. I typed anyway, ignoring the acid eating away my stomach, the panicky surges rising in my chest. Keeping my fingers moving helped.

I feel like I left something behind. I need to find it
and put myself back together.

But there was no going back. Not to the woods, where a body lay cooling quickly, the blood in its limbs turning to jelly. Not to the corner, where only hours ago Lisa talked about making that trip to the city. Not to open mic and Lisa's shining moment and a thousand reasons for being happy and hopeful. Things we took for granted. It felt like the sun would never rise again. Like I'd never close my eyes again. Every time I did, his face was there, alive and frightened, begging, pleading. It was the worst kind of nightmare. The kind you couldn't wake up from.

Maybe I could come stay with you. No one would find me.

A police siren screamed in the distance and I froze, my heart beating wildly. That sound had always signaled some abstract tragedy, some faceless offender's shame and ruin. Now it triggered visions of my own life crashing down. Nearer and nearer, the siren wailed. My legs started shaking. My insides throbbed with a strange prickling. I wanted to hide, curl up into myself, but I couldn't move. I couldn't even call for my mother. All I could do was sit there, my finger hovering above the escape key, paralyzed by the loneliest fear in the world—the fear of getting caught. As the siren passed our street, my lungs released a shuddering breath. Our neighbor's dog barked. My phone chirped a text alert. Lisa.

Come over. Now. Use back door.

I deleted the e-mail to my brother. I should've hidden the flashlight, too, but I didn't bother. What did it matter? My life would be over in a few short hours. At most, a few days. As soon as someone went into the woods searching for a lost dog. As soon as someone saw the halo of vultures above the trees. I imagined my parents' reaction: denial at first, until the evidence proved otherwise, and then a slow, bitter acceptance that their daughter was a monster. What Lisa and I believed wouldn't matter. We'd killed a man, not some oily-eyed demon with claws and teeth. We'd crept into a homeless man's home and beaten him to death in his sleep.

I wanted the walk to Lisa's to last forever, so I took the long way, touring the bleak, forgotten streets I normally avoided. But I shut my heart to the ugliness and focused on the beauty: a cluster of tiny white flowers struggling at the base of a hydrant; on the sidewalk, a chalk drawing of a horse with wings flying through broken glass. Everything seemed so sharp, so clear, the moon and the stars, the chill in the air. Summer would be over soon. My eyes flooded with the sadness of endings as I circled back and headed toward Lisa's. I hesitated at the corner, afraid to find blue-and-red lights slicing the front of the house, a couple of officers leading Lisa out in cuffs. But I only found Larry's lawn with its almost unnatural glow. The street was silent, deserted. I crept down the driveway, keeping to the shadows, past Lisa's window and then Katie's, the same path he'd taken earlier. Which window had he used? What if it wasn't him but someone else? It could've been anyone.

What if we'd killed the wrong—?

The screen door creaked as I slipped into the darkness of the Grants' kitchen. There was just enough light for me to recognize Lisa's shape at the table, but not enough to identify the black slab in her hand. As she flung whatever it was at me, I flinched, expecting something denser, but it was light and flexible. Her missing flip-flop. A new wave of sickness washed over me as I imagined Lisa going back into the woods, rooting through the dark, alone with the stiffening body.

"He's not dead," she said.

The flip-flop tumbled from my grip. I'd spent the last hour at the bottom of something dark and brackish, fighting for air. Those three words were all it took to shed the weight pulling me down. I breathed again, deeply, as I broke through the dread.

"Oh my God, thank God," I breathed, my shoulders sagging with relief. "Are you sure?"

"I heard him groaning," she said flatly. "He's hurt, but he's alive."

I rushed Lisa and wrapped my arms around her, but she just sat there stiffly. Something in her eyes silenced the shrieking joy in my heart.

"We have to go back," she whispered. "You have to go with me."

I jerked upright. "No! Why?"

"Shh!" She glared. "My necklace. I have to get my necklace."

I started shaking my head, slowly at first and then faster, as Lisa glided to the counter and opened a drawer. The moonlight through the window glinted off something metal. The bluish tinge of steel. My brain danced and sparked.

"No, Lisa, no." I grabbed her wrist. "Don't be stupid."

"We can't go unarmed," she said with a steely coolness I found frightening. "He'll be ready. He'll put up a fight."

A soft click flooded the kitchen with light.

"Who'll put up a fight?" It was Larry, in his boxers, sluggish and squinting. "Tracy? What are you doing here? What are you two doing?"

I stood there, rooted, blinking at Larry. Lisa's leg jounced nervously. I had no business being in their kitchen in the middle of the night, but I rummaged for an excuse anyway: "I was just . . . I . . ."

Larry shot me a look—not his normal frown, but something harsher—and then fixed his red-faced gaze on Lisa. "What are you doing with a knife?"

Lisa turned toward the drawer. I expected her to drop it and then face Larry, empty hands raised—*What knife? I don't see any knife*—but Larry bolted across the kitchen, bare feet slapping, and gripped her elbow, his voice booming, "Answer me, Goddammit!"

Legs quaking, I counted the steps to the door, readying myself to slip quietly out. In a way, I was glad Larry had found us. Now there would be no danger of Lisa returning to the woods tonight. In the morning, everything would look clearer and Lisa would be thankful, too.

At least that's what I imagined.

But Lisa whirled on Larry, the knife still clutched in her first.

Larry jumped back.

I raised my hands.

Lisa advanced, the knife raised. "Don't you ever touch me again," she snarled.

"Put that down," Larry said calmly but firmly.

I inched toward the door, frightened and unsure. Larry was frightened, too. His hand shook as he reached for the phone. Lisa let out a barking laugh. "What are you going to do?" she asked. "Call my mother? The police?" Larry's red face deepened a shade. "I'm not scared," Lisa said, her voice starting to break. "I'm not anything. There's nothing left, Larry. *You took it all.*"

My brain cartwheeled, afraid to land on the dark truth. I tried to speak, but Lisa's rage was a vacuum, sucking all the air from the room. I wanted that moment to last forever because there was no good way for it to end. Not with Lisa bent on making Larry pay for something I was only beginning to understand. It was the woods all over again, with Lisa possessed by something terrifying.

"Stop it, Lisa. Please," a small voice whispered from the hall, breaking the spell.

Lisa flinched. A pained look crashed her face. She lowered the knife and then lowered her head.

"Go back to bed, Katie," Larry said sternly, trying to mask his fear with authority.

Katie stepped forward, into the light. Her eyes looked scalded. She took another step and then another, carefully placing one foot in front of the other like a tightrope walker.

"Katie, get in bed," Larry pleaded. "I'll be there—"

"No!" Lisa hollered. Katie and I jumped. "Go near her, and I'll kill you!"

Clutching her ears, Katie ran through the kitchen and out the back door. I followed, calling for her to wait. Gripped by a dizzying sickness, I ran until Katie suddenly stopped short. She'd stepped on something sharp. Clutching her foot, she toppled sideways onto a shaggy front lawn. When I caught up, I fell beside her, my legs buckling with the weight of what I should've known. Kneeling beside Katie, I cradled her head to my chest.

"The stuff in your diary," I whispered into her hair. "It was about Larry?"

Katie wrestled from my arms. She brought her foot into the light and examined the sole. Whatever she'd stepped on hadn't pierced the skin—the wound was invisible—but she winced when I touched it. "There is no Banana Man," I said. "That part's made up."

Driving her head into my ribs, Katie mumbled, "I did that stuff with the eyes, too. I found them. With Ryan. When we went in the woods. I wanted Lisa to think Banana Man had been in our house, so she wouldn't leave me alone at night. I wrote it in my diary in case . . ."

"You could've told her it was Larry," I said. "Why didn't you tell her?"

Katie's eyes met mine, only this time it wasn't pain that I saw but my own helpless rage reflected back at me. "I didn't think anyone would believe me," she said. I closed my eyes and rocked Katie gently, listening to the night sounds and her muffled sobs, waiting again for the sound of sirens, the police responding to a 911: *I think my stepfather's dead.*

But Larry's truck peeled out at the corner, breaking me from my thoughts, and drove right by us—Katie and me—still hugging on a stranger's lawn. We stayed like that, frozen, until the red taillights disappeared.

"What if Larry . . ." Katie sputtered, struggling upright. "You don't think . . ." She took off running. But before I could catch her, Lisa came around the corner, her body hunched over like she was carrying a load of bricks. She didn't say what happened in the kitchen. It was evident from the mark on her cheek.

"C'mon, Katie," she said weakly. "Let's go."

"You can't go back," I said.

A porch light came on behind us. The face at the window warned us to start moving. Lisa glared angrily and grabbed Katie's hand. "Where are we supposed to stay?"

"My house," I said.

"What about tomorrow night?" Lisa asked, her voice high and tight. "And the night after that? Where are we supposed to sleep then?"

She was right. It wasn't a solution. There was only one solution. She had to tell her mom.

Lisa huffed like I'd told an old, unfunny joke and started marching. "You think it's that easy?" she said. "I've been trying to tell her for years. I can't. I don't know how." At the corner, she stopped, gesturing wildly. "Listen, I'm not trying to be mean, but you don't understand. I know you're just trying to help, but there's nothing you can do. Just go home. Please? Go home."

As they disappeared into the shadows, I looked up at the stars. Where was the sun? Our darkest fears have a way of shrinking under daylight. Was this our punishment for what we'd done in the woods? To be suspended forever in night?

twenty-four

Iife has a way of forcing you to keep moving.

The morning after I realized I had it in me to hurt another person, after I learned Larry belonged in a cage, I wanted to stay in bed. Forever. But my head and hands cried out for aspirin and my stomach rumbled. In the kitchen, my mother was dancing to the radio. I shuffled to the freezer for a toaster pastry but the box was empty.

"We're out of bread, too," my mother said when I reached for the basket on top of the fridge. "I've got some shopping to do when I get the car back."

It was almost lunch so I made myself a sad sandwich of peanut butter and jelly on a hot dog roll. My knuckles—stiff and swollen—made it hard to hold the knife. My mother shimmied to the counter and cleaned up my mess.

"How was open mic?" she asked cheerily.

Open mic. I snorted.

"Not good?"

"No, Lisa was awesome. It's just . . ."

It just seems unimportant. Now at least.

"Did you guys have a fight?"

I bit into my roll and shook my head. I wanted to tell her about Larry, but I didn't know how.

My mother shrugged and went on. "You'll never guess who called this morning."

Scott? No. Why would Scott call? I'd only left him a thousand messages. What if I really needed him? I *did* really need him.

When I didn't respond, my mother smiled slyly. "Jim."

"Jim who?"

An impatient eye roll accompanied by that annoyingly high voice she gets when she thinks I'm being deliberately stupid. "Jim from yesterday. The guy who helped push the car? He wanted to know how I'd made out at the garage." My mother waited a beat before batting her eyelashes and delivering her news—the real reason Jim had called: "He wanted to know if I have any plans for tonight!"

Any other day I would've danced around the kitchen with her, but instead I just forced a smile. "You're a real joy today." She frowned, chucking the sponge in the sink. "What's wrong?"

A gnawing sickness turned my stomach. As I tossed my half-eaten sandwich in the trash, the phone rang.

"She's not here," my mom said cryptically after answering, and then, "Yes. Hold on."

I was surprised when she handed me the receiver. Nobody calls me on the house phone.

"You don't know where Lisa is, do you?" It was Mrs. Grant.

"Larry said they had a fight last night and she took off with Katie. I thought maybe they were with you."

My mother planted herself in front of me, making those concerned eyebrows. I turned away.

"No," I said, twisting the phone cord. "Have you tried Gabe?"

"He hasn't heard from her," Mrs. Grant said. "She's got her phone, but she's not answering. If she calls you, please tell her to call me."

I'd barely hung up when my mother started with the interrogation.

"What's going on? Is Lisa in trouble?"

I sighed.

"Something's going on. Why were you all jumpy last night? Who were you e-mailing at one in the morning?"

Grabbing my cell, I ran from the house. The back door slammed behind me.

"Tracy Louise!" my mother shouted through the screen. "If I find out . . ."

Find out what, Mom? You never find out anything.

Plunking down in our pathetic garden, I texted Lisa. I wanted the world to stop, but I also wanted it to go on like normal. I wanted Lisa to respond with something ordinary, like, *We're at the pool* or *Meet us at the Dog House.* But I knew after last night there was no going back. Why didn't she come to me? Why didn't she tell me where she was going?

Because you suck at dealing with the hard stuff.

It's true. I can't help it. And I was doing it again. Waiting when I should've been out looking. Sometimes our city seems small and suffocating, but right then it seemed huge as I thought of all the places where Lisa might be hiding. I stared at my phone, a million "what-ifs" screeching through my brain. What

if I'd gone to Lisa after what happened in Troy? Would she have
opened up about Larry? Or are some things too horrible to tell
even your best friend? That's how I felt when I told Foley—
   Foley.
   Waiting for him to answer, I plucked an aphid from a leaf and
crushed it between my fingers.
   "Hey, what's up?"
   I could tell by his voice that he'd been sleeping.
   "Have you heard from Lisa?"
   "No."
   I watched a bee crawl inside a wilted squash blossom. Poor
garden, I'm not good with silent things that need attention. It
was my fault that everything was dying again.
   "Trace?" Foley said. "You still there?"
   "I need to see you," I said. "Can you meet me at the park?"
   Foley sighed. "Listen, I can't do this . . . whatever this is . . .
this thing with you."
   "It's not about me," I said. "It's about Lisa. It's bad. I don't
know who else to talk to."
   Foley didn't hesitate. "Give me ten minutes," he said. "I'll
meet you by the fountains."
   Brushing dirt from my shorts, I ran inside to change. My
mother was at the table making a grocery list. "I'm going out," I
said as I passed through the kitchen.
   "Whatever," she responded, still hurt. "I'm going to get the
car."
   Listening to her mumble something about me fending for
myself for dinner, I closed the bedroom door and texted Lisa
again. Nothing. I threw on clean shorts and a shirt and ran to
the garage for my bike. A fine layer of dust coated the seat. The
chain was stiff with rust and the tires needed air, but it would do.

Zigzagging down the driveway and into the street, I pumped hard, not toward the park but toward Lisa's. My legs burned.

I think part of me expected the house to look different somehow, contaminated, all that sickness throwing an eerie cast over everything. But the car was in the driveway and the truck gone. Shades drawn. Front door closed. Same as always. Mrs. Grant was sleeping. Larry was working. Maybe I had it wrong. I didn't want to believe something so ugly had been happening to Lisa. It's a survival mechanism, the way we look toward the light, refusing to adjust to the dark.

We can't handle the dark.

I pedaled harder, faster, my vision blurring as I flew down Cutler and strained up Parkwood, the same route Lisa and I had taken the night before, only now I was gripped by guilt as the looming woods swallowed my shadow. I could barely breathe. There were people everywhere, smiling, oblivious to the darkness siphoning the air from my lungs. I almost turned back, but a voice called out. Foley was straddling his bike beside the paddle boats. Jerking his head for me to follow, he led me behind the basketball courts, to a picnic area set back in the pines. Wearily, I leaned my bike against one of the cast-iron grills nobody uses. Foley climbed onto a picnic table, soft and damp with rot, and pulled me up beside him, holding onto my hand gently, but firmly.

What is it about Michael Foley that always makes me open up? Even when I want to hold back, I can't. I stared at my knees and told him everything, starting with Katie's diary and ending with the red mark on Lisa's cheek. When I looked up, shock and anger had hardened his kind eyes. I knew what he was thinking, what he'd like to do to Larry. There's a killing part inside each of us. Until last night, I didn't think I was capable of hurting someone like that. But I am. Foley is, too. Cursing, he drove his fist into the table. Sweet, gentle Foley. I took his hand and told him to take a deep breath.

"He's got to be stopped," he said. "What are you gonna do?"

My mouth went dry and my heart started pounding. The feeling of being on stage and forgetting my lines. I shrugged. Foley flashed me a look. "You've got to do something," he said quietly. "You can't just shut down."

Gritting my teeth, I dropped his hand. "What am I supposed to do?"

"You have to tell Lisa's mother."

"No way. Absolutely not." I jumped off the picnic table and grabbed my bike. "Were you even listening? I almost killed a guy last night. The wrong guy. What if I'm wrong again? This will hurt Lisa's mom so much. And Lisa never actually said it, that Larry . . . you know."

Foley's eyes softened as though he understood. I wanted him to come over and take my face in his hands and tell me I was right, but instead he gripped the handlebars and leaned in, whispering gently, *"You've* never actually said it, Trace, that you were raped. But that's what it was, what that guy did to you."

"Go to hell," I growled, shoving the bike at him. I wanted to claw his face, but he grabbed my wrists. It was the nightmare all over again, only now I was the one who'd been buried alive. All I wanted was to rest in peace, but Foley was digging deeper—*If you can't say it, maybe Lisa can't, either*—clawing the ground—*Say it, Trace*—clearing the dirt from my eyes—*Say it.* From the bottom of a dark hole, I looked up through the trees, at the cloudless sky above, and I said it.

Raped.

I was raped.

He raped me.

I said it again and again, waiting for the change. Finding your voice to speak the truth is supposed to be empowering, but I didn't feel powerful. I felt weak and fragile and small. My brain turned to dandelion fluff and floated away on the wind. *Make a wish.* My body wanted to follow, but when I tried to right my bike, it weighed a ton. I could barely hold it steady enough to climb on. I stepped hard on the pedal, but the tires skidded on the pine needles and I lost my balance. Foley caught me.

"Sit back," he said, swinging his leg over the crossbar. "I'll take you home."

"What about your bike?"

Foley shrugged.

Giving in to exhaustion and grief, I wrapped my arms around his waist and pressed my tear-dampened cheek to his back. How did I become this shriveled clinging thing? Foley and I used to be equals. Back before the world started taking me apart, piece by piece. Once upon a time there was the plaza in winter where two rosy-faced children sat, sipping hot chocolate, steaming the air with their laughter and the sweet awkwardness of first kisses. Where did that go? Where did I go? I wanted to stretch toward the sun and feel the wind on my face, but I stayed curled inside myself until Foley led me inside my house and tucked me in bed.

I don't remember falling asleep, but when I woke, my room was awash with the bluish light of nightfall. I checked my phone for messages. My text clouds were stacked like thunderheads—all delivered, but none read. I tried calling, but Lisa didn't answer. *Maybe her phone's dead. Maybe she's dead. Maybe. Maybe. Maybe.* I called her house, hoping Mrs. Grant had found a note explaining why and where they'd gone, but Larry answered. *Maybe Larry killed them.* I fumbled the phone and pressed the end button. Shaking, I watched the screen go dark. *Safe.* But then the phone lit up. My ring tone chimed. I took a deep breath and answered.

"Tracy? It's me. We got cut off. Have you heard from Lisa and Katie?"

I expected Larry to sound different, more threatening somehow, but he sounded exactly like he always had. Like the same Larry who gave us piggyback rides around the living room when we were little or took us for ice cream after school. The Larry I always liked. The one I never understood why Lisa hated.

"Is Mrs. Grant there?" I asked timidly. "Can I talk to her?"

"She's at work," he said. "She's hoping the girls will show up there. Listen. About last night. I don't what Lisa's been telling you—"

"Lisa hasn't told me anything," I shot back.

Larry sighed uneasily. "I know things got a little crazy," he said. "But this is a family matter. Okay? We just want Lisa and Katie to come home."

I looked to the window, at the rapidly fading light. "Maybe you should call the police."

"I just said it's a family matter," Larry said sharply. My heart kicked. There was an awkward silence. Then Larry spoke again, his voice measured: "If you hear from them, you'll call me first, right? Tell them I'll come get them, wherever they are, no questions asked."

I heard myself say, "Okay," and then I heard a noise in the kitchen. "I've got to go," I said, abruptly hanging up.

I sat on the edge of the bed and listened to our cupboard doors opening and closing, over and over. My mother searching madly for something. Annoyed, I opened the bedroom door. The sound grew louder, faster, a familiar rhythmic beat. *Definitely not*

cupboards. Definitely not Mom. I shuffled down the hall to find
Foley, white cords trailing from his ears, drumming along to
whatever song was blaring in his head. I waved my arms. Foley
stopped thrashing and yanked the buds free. "Was I really loud?"

I shrugged.

"You hungry?"

I nodded.

Foley went to the freezer and brought out a new box of toaster
pastries. "Mom went shopping," he said, tugging at the cardboard zipper.

I looked around. "Where is she?"

"Out," Foley said. "She went to dinner with some guy. Jim
somebody. I told her you were sick. She wanted to cancel, but I
told her I'd hang with you. I must look trustworthy." He winked.

I smiled halfheartedly before shuffling to the bathroom to
wash my face. My eyes felt raw and crusty, my skin tight from
crying myself to sleep. When I came out, Foley was tossing a hot
pastry from hand to hand, muttering under his breath. He
lobbed it on a plate and blew on his fingers, then cut the corner
off an icing packet and piped out a big gooey star. Two forks, one
strudel. We leaned together and dug in.

"These things are much better when they're hot," Foley said
wryly.

I blushed, remembering the two of us in his living room, on
the couch, falling, soaring. There's a thin line between love and
hate, and my heart was jumping double Dutch again.

"Is this okay?" Foley asked. "I can make you a can of soup."

I shook my head. "This is fine," I said. "Thanks for staying."

Foley licked his fork and put it down. "I wasn't here the whole
time," he said. "While you were sleeping, I went back for my
bike." Foley scooped up my hands and squeezed. Staring at the

bruises on my knuckles he said, "Plus I took a detour. To check on your guy."

Something in his tone made me think it wasn't good, whatever he was about to tell me. Lisa was wrong—he was dead. An icy chill filled me. I jerked my hands free and squeezed myself tight.

"Just say it, Foley. Whatever it is, say it."

Foley stepped back like he was afraid I might hit him. "There's garbage everywhere," he said. "Old furniture and tires and stuff. But there's no house made of tarps. Nothing like you described."

I closed my eyes but the image of my flashlight striking his head made me open them again. "It wasn't my imagination," I said defensively. "Or Lisa's. Or Adam's or Trent's. They saw it, too—his house. Trent's the one who found it."

Foley raised his hands. "I'm not saying it wasn't there. I'm just saying it's gone. He's gone. That's a good thing, Trace."

If it was a good thing, then why did I feel so lousy? Probably because going to jail sounded easier than doing what I knew I had to do. I dumped the forks and plate in the sink and checked my phone again. Still nothing from Lisa.

"Will you go with me?" I asked.

Foley looked out the window. "It's almost dark. I'll show you tomorrow. First thing."

"Not the woods," I said, swallowing the lump in my throat. "The diner. Lisa's mom's at work."

twenty-five

how many nights had Lisa and I spent in the diner where her mom waitressed? Weeks, if you added up all the hours. Maybe even a whole month. I'd always thought of it as just a hangout, but staring at my reflection in the silver siding, I realized it was way more than that for Lisa—the diner was her refuge, a place to get away from Larry.

"You can do this," Foley said, opening the glass-and-chrome door. I took one step. And then another. Foley's guiding hand on my back was the only thing keeping me from turning around. I inhaled the familiar smells—coffee, gravy, fried everything—and tried to calm my breathing, but my legs started shaking when I spotted Mrs. Grant updating the specials easel. I think part of me had hoped that the diner would be packed, with Lisa's mom being pulled in a hundred different directions. Whatever I had to say would need to wait until morning, when she got off work.

See, Foley, I tried. But the place was nearly empty. Capping her marker, she called my name and trotted over.

"Did Lisa call?" she asked.

I shook my head at the floor, at the black and white tiles that needed mopping. Mrs. Grant lifted my chin. "Did something happen?" she asked. "What's going on?" I tried to answer, but the worry in her eyes silenced me. Foley spoke up. "Listen, Mrs. G.," he said. "We need to talk."

Mrs. Grant frowned at Foley and then at me. "What's this about?"

When we didn't respond, she said, "Fine. Hold on," and then to Val: "I'm gonna take my break."

When the diner was dead, Lisa and I always sat up front, but Mrs. Grant led us past the bakery case with the mile-high pies, past the pay phone and the restrooms, to a booth way in back, far from any customers. Foley slid in first, across the bench seat. I put my phone on the table, in case Lisa texted, and slid in next. Mrs. Grant checked her phone, too, and then sat across from us.

"Wait," she said, scooting back out. "This has been a long day. Let me grab some coffee."

With every minute that passed, I felt what little courage I had evaporating. *I don't have to do this,* I thought. *Banana Man doesn't exist. The man from the woods is gone. I can walk out that door*—But Foley put his hand on my knee, squeezing. "She knows it's bad," he said. "She's stalling, but she needs to hear this."

Just when I was beginning to suspect Mrs. Grant of fleeing out the back, she returned with a tray and cups. "Sorry it took so long," she said. "I had to wait for a new pot."

As she slid back in, I caught a whiff of smoke. She'd gone out for a cigarette.

"If this is about Larry," she said, reaching for the sugar dispenser. "I know what happened. He told me everything."

I watched Mrs. Grant calmly stir her coffee and add another cream. I frowned. In the mirror behind her, Foley's eyes met mine. He shook his head ever so slightly. Mrs. Grant placed her spoon on the saucer and continued: "Larry said he slapped Lisa pretty hard. He feels terrible. He didn't mean to lose his temper with her, but you know how Lisa pushes his buttons." She sighed.

Foley raised his eyebrows insistently in the mirror.

"It's more than that," he said, squeezing my hand under the table.

I might've found a better way to say it. I don't know. I should've used stronger words than "think" and "suspect" because they created holes of doubt, holes big enough for Mrs. Grant to try and crawl through. I should've found softer words for "molest" and "rape." Mrs. Grant stared at me the same way the man in the woods had—pleading for me stop.

I was killing her.

"No-no-no-no-no," she cried quietly at first, and then louder, gasping for air as she put two and two together—and more. Things so horrible I hadn't even thought them yet: *Was the baby even Gabe's?*

Mrs. Grant's coffee cup fell to the floor, but it didn't break—those cups never do. But she did. Trying to stand, it was as if she'd forgotten that the seats don't move or that the tables are bolted to the floor. She hit her head on the pendant light above and went down and then tried standing again. I reached for her, but she was like a frightened animal caught in a chute, struggling to free herself. Foley pushed me out of the booth. He was going to help, but Val came rushing over and steered him out of the way. "What's going on?" she asked Foley, and then, "Sharon, are you okay?"

Collapsing against the seat back, her breathing hard and jagged, Mrs. Grant cried, "Val, it's Larry. He's been hurting . . ." Val lowered her ear to Mrs. Grant's lips and listened, her face curdling with disgust, until she collapsed, too, squeezing Mrs. Grant. My ring tone chimed. Val shot me a dirty look. But it was my brother. I couldn't not answer. I grabbed my phone and ran outside.

"Jesus, Scott. What took you so long? I left you a thousand messages!"

"Shut up and listen," he said. My anger swelled. I was about to hang up when he said, "Lisa and Katie are with me."

I stopped pacing the rectangles of light shining from the windows and stared down into a storm grate. "What are you talking about?" I said.

"That's why I didn't call. This morning I had all these messages from you *and* Lisa. Lisa said she and Katie were at the bus terminal, so I called her first. She needed to figure things out, so she asked me not to call you. She was afraid you'd go jumping on a bus, too."

"Did she tell you about Larry?" I asked hesitantly.

There was a long pause before he answered quietly: "Yeah. She did."

"Where are they now? What are they doing?"

"I just made them spaghetti. They're eating."

I pictured Lisa at the table, frowning at her plate. Not Lisa now. Lisa from sixth grade, back when Scott was working on his merit badge for cooking and used us as guinea pigs. I smiled at the two of us choking down dry eggs and burnt toast until a dark shape rose up and swallowed Lisa. Was that when it started for

her? I got a sick feeling as I realized how it was going to be—
now and forever—with my brain superimposing Larry's shadow
over every memory.

"Where are you?" Scott asked.

"I'm at the diner. I just told Mrs. Grant."

Scott paused, and then echoed my words to Lisa. I listened
for her reaction, but a tractor trailer shuddered past and I
missed it.

"Does she want to talk to me?" I asked.

"Not right now," Scott said. "Maybe later. She's calling her
mom. I'm gonna bring them home. There's a bus that leaves at
eleven something."

"I'll meet you at the station."

"No, Trace. Don't. Lisa doesn't . . . We'll talk when I get
there. Warn Mom that I'm coming."

Tears spilled from my eyes as I thumbed the power-save
button. I stood there forever just trying to breathe until Foley
grabbed me around the waist, startling me.

"Lisa just called her mom," he said. "They're okay."

"I know." I raised my phone. "That was my brother. They're
with him."

I turned toward the door, but Foley pulled me back. "Don't
go in there," he said, shaking his head. "Mrs. G asked us to
leave."

"What?" I said. "Why?"

Lacing his fingers through mine, Foley assured me I'd done
the right thing. If I'd done the right thing, then why was everyone treating me like I was radioactive? Walking in silence,
side by side, our strides perfectly matched, the distance from
the diner to my house had never seemed shorter. We stood
for a moment in the blue light filtering from my living room

window—my mother was home—and then went around back. Foley's bike was against the garage. I traced a crack in the driveway with my toe, and said, "You know what's crazy? This time last night we were hanging out at the coffee shop."

Foley whistled. "Wow," he said. "It *has* been a long day."

I glanced up at the stars. "It's been a long summer." Leaning on our car, I caught myself thinking about the night I'd slept in one. As Foley wiped chain grease from his ankle, I asked stupidly, thoughtlessly, "Adam's not back yet, is he?"

Climbing on his bike, Foley kissed the top of my head, and said, "I don't know, Trace."

Watching him coast down the driveway, my instinct was to follow, but my tires were flat and it was late. I wanted to catch my mother before she went to bed and tell her Scott was coming home. I used the front door expecting to find her curled up on the couch in her robe, but she was at the kitchen table, still dressed from her date, thumbing through a book in her hand. Katie's diary.

"I found this in the garage," she said. "What's going on in that house? What's all this stuff about Katie being stalked by some monster—Banana Man, or whatever you guys call him?"

I stared at my feet, trying to find the words to start. Some things never get any easier. How do you tell your mother that your best friend's stepfather is the worst kind of monster, the kind that devours little girls, devours his own daughters? I could almost feel his putrid breath on my shoulder as I whispered, shivering, "It's bad, Mommy. Really bad." I looked up. She knew. I didn't have to say it. She had this pained look on her face. I dropped down beside her chair and put my head in her lap. My mother stroking my hair was all it took. Something in me broke and everything tumbled out.

"Oh, Tracy," my mother said. "He never tried anything with you, did he? You'd tell me, right?"

My head on my mother's knee, I stared into the dark space beneath the kitchen table and asked, "Do you remember that kid from Troy?"

"Jerrod McKinney?" my mother said brightly.

I winced. "Jerrod McKinney raped me," I breathed.

I knew how it looked, how my mother would see it. It's not like I was walking down the street, minding my own business, when it happened.

Alone with a boy . . .

In an empty house . . .

My shirt unbuttoned . . .

I raised you better than that, Tracy Louise.

But sometimes my mom surprises me. Sometimes she knows just what to do. Like pulling me up onto her lap like an oversized doll and rocking me gently, whispering softly, "I'm sorry, Tracy. I didn't know. I didn't know." Like telling me it wasn't my fault and I could've told her, should've told her. *I'm your mother.* And then letting me stay like that—curled up against her—until my tears dried and my breathing calmed, and then saying she would get me help, whatever I needed, to work through it. That it was my decision.

"I used to be so normal," I said. "We all did. What happened?"

My mother didn't have an answer. "It'll be good to see your brother," she said.

"Yeah," I said. "I miss him. I miss Daddy."

For the first time she didn't get all weepy and say "Me, too." Instead, she kissed me on the head and said there was chocolate cake from her date with Jim. She brought over the container and a fork and then picked up the phone and dialed a number she knew by heart. Scott, I figured. He didn't answer, and a few seconds later she was leaving a message. But not for Scott. For my dad. She said she knew he was at work, but would he please come over in the morning.

"There's some stuff going on we need to talk about," she said, combing my hair with her fingers. "It's Tracy. She needs you."

twenty-six

Voices in the kitchen. Hushed and familiar but just out of reach, fragments from a lost dream. Mom. Dad. Scott. The three of them talked easily, back and forth, the rhythm of normal conversation. Scott said something and our parents laughed. Snuggled deeply in my bed, I savored the sounds of my broken family gathered together until the smell of pancakes drew me from my cocoon.

"If it isn't Sleeping Beauty," Scott said, standing over the griddle with a spatula, waiting for the batter bubbles to pop. He looked the same, except for the shaved head. I rubbed his stubble. My father had shaved, too. The stupid beard he had the last time I saw him was gone. "Come here, kiddo," he said, handing his coffee mug to my mom. "Give me a hug."

My dad's not always good with words, but he didn't need them. He wrapped me in his arms, and I pressed my cheek to his chest. He was still in his uniform, which meant he hadn't wasted time changing. He'd listened to my mom's message and come straight over. How many times after he'd left had I wished I could trade him for Larry? I cringed thinking about it. My dad would never hurt me. Not like that. His chin on my head, he squeezed me tighter and said, "Your mom told me everything."

I stiffened. Locking eyes with my mother, I questioned her silently. *Everything?*

"I thought it'd be easier if I explained about Lisa and Katie," she said, pulling a plate of bacon out of the microwave. I relaxed. My mom knowing about Jerrod McKinney was painful enough. The thought of my dad knowing was too much. I wasn't ready for that. Not now. Maybe not ever.

Scott plunked a stack of pancakes on the table and said, "I'm starving. Let's eat." But then we all just stood there, eyeing the four chairs awkwardly until my mother went to get the butter and my dad and I traded spots. For once I didn't mind sitting next to my brother. I had a million questions.

"No police yet," Scott started, drowning his breakfast in syrup. "Their mom was at the station with their grandmother. That's where they were going last night—their grandmother's."

The bacon went around the table and then the juice. I knew where their grandmother lived. I could get there by bus, but it would take an hour and a couple of transfers. I asked Scott to drive me.

"Don't go trying to see her just yet," he said.

My parents nodded in agreement.

Scott leaned sideways in his chair and pulled a folded piece of paper from his pocket. Tattered and yellowed, one side said MISSING with a photo of a cat. The other side was filled with Lisa's bubble print. I started to read, but my eyes got all blurry.

"Aren't you gonna eat your breakfast?" my mother called as I rushed down the hall to my room.

I closed my door and sat on the floor, trying to still the paper between my trembling hands.

Do you remember the first time we went to Hillhurst Park alone? Remember how we felt like big girls? For the first time it was just you and me without my mom or your mom or Scott. We were such dorks back then! We actually planned our outfits! I wore all pink—of course. And you wore your new sandals, the ones that stained your feet blue. Remember?

I did. We were in seventh grade. Too big for the swings and the slides, we'd hung out in the band shell, singing our hearts out, oblivious to everything except the echo of our voices.

I had strict orders from Larry to be home at five o'clock, on the dot, not one second later, but then that huge storm rolled in. Remember how we huddled in the band shell, waiting for it to pass but it just got worse and worse? There was thunder and lightning crashing all around and that insane wind that was blowing the leaves right off the trees. It was the worst storm in twenty years, or something crazy like that, and I was freaking out because I was afraid I'd be grounded if I didn't make it home on time. "I have to go," I kept saying. "I have to." I know you were terrified, but you linked your arm with mine and told me I

wasn't going anywhere without you. I loved you
for that. I still do. For sticking with me.

Do you remember the water? How deep it was at
the bottom of Bradley?

How could I forget? My mother freaked out when she saw
the flood marks around my knees. It's funny how at that age you
worry about the dumbest things. For me, it was ruining my sandals. For Lisa, it was losing her TV privileges. But it was my
mom who made me realize the real danger we'd risked. Drowning. Electrocution.

Someone knocked on my door, but I kept reading:

God, I was stupid. But we made it. We survived.
That memory has gotten me though a lot, Trace—
pretty much the last four years of my life.

Scott poked his head in and wrinkled his nose. "What smells
like feet in here?"

I shoved my Cons under the bed. It was time for a new pair,
even if they were just getting good.

"Have you read this?" I asked.

He nodded. "She wrote it on the bus." Plunking down beside
me, he hugged his knees to his chest. "She wanted to write more,
but she ran out of room."

Something in me flared. I'd always known Lisa had a not-so-
secret crush on my brother, but it never bothered me, until
then. "I'm her best friend. Why'd she go to you?"

Scott straightened his legs. "If you wanted to run away, where
would you go? A city of eight million people or two blocks from
home?"

He was right.

"Is she mad at me for telling her mother?" I asked.

"It's complicated," he said. "She's not angry. Actually, she is angry, but not with you. She's pretty messed up right now."

We sat there for a while—Scott and I—rocking sideways, knocking into each other, until my brother put me in a head-lock and rubbed his knuckles against my skull. I punched him in the leg and then winced. My hand still hurt. I flexed my fingers.

"Do you remember a story about a creepy guy who lived in the woods by the park?" I asked.

"Albert."

I made a face. "Albert? That's dumber than Banana Man."

He shrugged. "That's what I called him. I don't know his real name. That story's been going around forever. He's just some homeless guy. Built himself this weird tent-house out of tarps and stuff. It's pretty impressive. Why?"

"You've seen it?" I asked. "His house? When?"

"Last summer, when I had community service at Hillhurst. Some of the guys on my crew kept talking about him—this freak that lived in the woods. They dragged me with them once during lunch. They were all like 'fag' this and 'fag' that, and one of them was ready to tag his house until I reminded him why he was sentenced to community service in the first place—for tagging shit."

Scott rolled his eyes. He'd hated that summer. Not the community service part. He'd hated working with guys who, had they known he was gay, would've lumped him in the same category as Larry.

"You know me," Scott said. "I went and bought some supplies—peanut butter, bread, toothpaste, stuff like that—and left it outside his door. I guess he was offended or thought it was poisoned or something because the next day, when I opened my locker, there it was—the bag. Freaky, huh?" Scott wiggled his fingers in my face. "How'd he know it was me? How'd he know my locker?"

I glanced at my trunk, my stupid fears surging again. Those eyes, his eyes. *He's always watching.* But no. That was Katie. No one's watching. During your darkest moments, eyes always look in the other direction.

"Maybe it was one of the guys messing with you," I said.

Scott shrugged. "Who knows? Who cares? You ever notice how people project their worst fears onto anything different or strange? Maybe Albert lives like that for a reason. Maybe it's a choice."

Guilt gnawed my insides as I wondered where he'd gone. Another wooded area within the city? Another city altogether?

"C'mon," Scott said, pulling me up by my wrists. "Before Dad steals your bacon."

I followed my brother to the kitchen and picked at my soggy pancakes, but I wasn't hungry.

"You can't sit there staring at your phone all day," my mother said, clearing the table.

Yes, I can, I thought. *What else is there?*

My dad proposed we go do something. My mother agreed. Scott suggested mini golf.

"It's closed," I said. "The place with the storybook characters. It's pretty depressing."

I hoped that was the end of it, but Scott did a search on his phone. "This one looks awesome," he said, showing me the place I'd gone with Adam and Chris. There were pictures of the moated castle and the giant octopus and the ice cream stand. I'd wanted so badly to take Scott, but not now.

"There's a dinosaur exhibit at the museum," my father said tentatively. Scott and I just looked at each other, and then Scott clapped his hands on my shoulders, smiled winningly, and proposed, "Let's go fly kites!"

"You're joking," I said. "That's the lamest idea ever." But my dad didn't think so. Scott prodded me out of my chair and toward my bedroom to change. I assumed my mom was coming, too, but she begged off at the last minute. "You guys go," she said, shooing us out the front door, and then to me, through the screen: "Try to have fun. Okay?"

Squashed together in my dad's noisy old pickup, it felt like old times, but the part of me that was worried about Lisa kept chipping away at the part that was happy to be with Dad and Scott.

"There's a toy store in that new plaza out past the traffic circle," my dad said.

How would you know? Had he taken the troll's offspring? My mood sunk even lower. It was a long way to go for some stupid kites, but my dad insisted. I stared out the windshield at the kids making faces at us from the car ahead and asked if I was ever that obnoxious.

"More," Scott said. "Remember how we used to try to get truckers to blow their horns?"

When did we stop? When did we grow up? When I was little, every Sunday night I'd lie awake afraid of just that— growing up. I'd wanted us to stay just the way we were forever. I don't know why Sundays. Maybe because I'd had two whole days to be with my family and we were happy. All of us. Once. Braiding the frayed edges of my cutoffs, I cried quietly, Scott and Dad filling my sorrow with small talk until we pulled into a lot where a man in a bear costume was twisting balloons into animals.

"I'll wait here," I said, clutching my phone.

"Don't you want to pick your kite?" Scott asked.

"You pick for me," I said. "Don't get anything stupid."

Scott shrugged. My dad unrolled his window. I turned on the radio and waited for the sliding glass doors to close behind them before sending a text to Lisa. One word, no pressure. Just *hi*. The crackly speakers pumped out one oldie after another while I counted the number of parking lot seagulls and then rummaged in the glove box for mints. I hadn't brushed my teeth or showered. I found what I was looking for—the familiar red-and-white tin—but dropped it on the floor like a spaz. Mints flew everywhere. I popped one in my mouth and quickly put the rest back, only to spill the tin again when Scott poked his head in the window and shouted, "I got you one with princesses!"

"I hate you," I said, chucking a mint at his chest.

"Don't be silly," he said. "I didn't get you princesses. That's for me. I got you a big yellow smiley face to match that sunny disposition of yours."

"Don't even think about taking the alien head," my dad said, climbing in. "That one's mine."

Scott tossed the bag in my lap and then tore open a package of strawberry licorice twists.

"Where are we going to fly them?" I asked.

My dad said he knew the perfect place, but he wouldn't tell us where. We drove and drove, the city slowly shrinking in the rearview mirror, the strawberry licorice twists dwindling, until Scott turned to our dad and said, "You know I've got a bus to catch tonight, right?"

"Tonight?" I said. "You just got here!"

"I've got a job. Oh, right, you've never had one." Scott poked me in the ribs. "Seriously, where are we going? You're not kidnapping us, are you? We're a little old for that."

"We're almost there," my dad lied. It was another fifteen minutes before he turned onto a narrow road that turned to dirt, the trees edging closer and closer. It was dusk dark and cooler there. We bumped along slowly, the truck squeaking and squealing, the tires kicking up dust and rocks. Just when I thought we were lost, the trees parted and the sun broke through, shining on a gently rippling lake spread before us.

My dad parked on the shore and got out, shading his eyes. "Reservoir's low," he said.

"I remember this place," Scott said quietly.

"Your mom and I used to bring you guys here for picnics when you were little," my dad said.

I didn't remember.

"Is this the place where we found that arrowhead?" Scott asked.

My dad nodded.

I still didn't remember, but something about the place instantly calmed me. It was magical—spooky, almost—as if we were the last people on the planet. Or the first. Except for us, and my dad's ancient pickup, there wasn't a single sign of life. No houses. No docks. No power lines. No trash. You can't go anywhere without finding wrappers or cigarette butts, but the shore was immaculate, untouched. I felt my mood lifting, even after Scott made me leave my phone in the truck. I kicked off my sneakers and waded up to my knees, watching the sun bronze across the water. We were less than forty miles from home but it felt like another country. Maybe the man from the woods would find a better place, a place like this.

"Hey!" Scott called. "You want your kite?"

They weren't anything special, just cheap plastic and a spool of string. I flattened the yellow diamond on the grass and walked with my back to the wind, letting out the line as I went. Scott did the same, farther down the shore. His kite lifted instantly, but mine cartwheeled, skipping along until my father came jogging over. Grabbing the points, he told me to reel it in a little and then tossed the kite in the air. The wind caught. The line went taut. "Now let it out a little," he said, helping me work the spool. The smiley face rose higher and higher. As I raced along the shore toward Scott, my dad cheered, "That's it! You got it!"

"What made you think of this?" I called to my brother.

"Think of what?"

"This!"

Scott shrugged. "It seemed mindless. You needed mindless."

My dad kicked off his work shoes and rolled up his uniform pants. After he got his green alien head launched, the three of us stood at the water's edge, our kites staggered gracefully above. Wheeling, tumbling, mine took a nosedive until another current lifted it straight up toward the ragged strips of clouds parked over the reservoir. Sometimes it feels like the world is filled only with ugliness and pain, but there's beauty, too, in the simple act of flying a piece of plastic tied to string, with cool mud squishing between your toes and the bright sun warming your face. I let out my line and my kite soared higher. I was soaring, too, up there with the clouds, looking down on myself, a girl with messy hair and dirty feet, wrestling her brother for the last strawberry licorice twist until their father broke them apart.

"Do you remember when I used to take you guys sledding?" he asked, tearing the candy rope in two.

I did. Back before he left, before Scott left. Back before Scott and I were old enough to choose our friends over our family. Back when doing stuff with my parents felt like a reward instead of a penalty. Swimming. Ice-skating. Saturday matinees. We tripped along the shore, pulling our strings, our dad pulling us back in time. "How about the ball games I used to take you to?"

"I just remember the nachos," I said.

"I don't remember nachos," Scott said. He smiled up at the princesses dancing and twirling. "Oh right, that's because I never got any. You'd have them all eaten before we got back to the bleachers."

I sucked my finger and aimed for Scott's ear, but my brother was fast. I chased him down the beach and around a log. Round and round we went, slipping, screeching, getting dizzier and dizzier, the world spinning. With my laughing and Scott's howling, neither of us heard our father's warnings. "Hey guys!" he shouted, pointing out over the water. "Stop!" I skidded to a halt and gazed up. Our kites spun, tangling together, falling. I tossed my spool to Scott, but it was too late. The pink and yellow diamonds dropped from the sky. Scott pulled them in and fished them out of the water and then stood there giving me the evil eye while our dad examined the snarl of wet string. Teasing them apart was impossible. One of the lines had to be cut. Our dad sacrificed the princesses.

"You suck," Scott said, driving his knuckle into my arm. "You always ruin everything."

I stuck out my tongue.

"Knock it off, you two," our dad said, giving Scott his spool and kite. Chuckling to himself, he went to the truck and came back with a blanket and stretched out on the grass. He looked so happy with his fingers laced behind his head, soaking up the sun, offering his advice to Scott and me as we tried to get the alien and the smiley face airborne again.

"You think maybe next time we could get the kind with two strings?" I glanced back at my dad but his eyes were closed. He'd been up all night. "You must be tired, too," I said to Scott.

"I slept on the bus."

"What time did you get in?"

"Four something." Scott pointed out a hawk cruising the tree line. It soared out over the reservoir and shadowed our kites. "Mom made coffee and we talked until Dad showed up."

"Was it a good talk?" I asked. "Did she tell you she's not angry about you being gay? She loves you, Scott. She was shocked, is all."

"And disappointed." Scott skipped a rock across the water. "You can't tell me she wasn't."

Disappointed with herself maybe, for not knowing, but not with Scott. It was like our mom went Scott's whole life assuming he had brown eyes, just like hers, until he pointed out that, no, his eyes were blue.

Scott shrugged. "Dad took it better. I think he knew."

My eyes drifted from my kite to my brother. "You shouldn't have left the way you did," I said.

Scott collapsed to a squat. "Can I be honest?" he said. His spool between his knees, he cast off more line. "I needed to go, but leaving's hard. It was easier to pretend Mom wanted me gone. You're right, though, I should've found a better way. I couldn't find my old duffel bag. I couldn't find any bags. I looked ridiculous, with all my stuff tied up in a bedsheet."

I laughed, and Scott laughed, too, the alien kite sailing away, shrinking into the blue. Racing to catch up, I let my spool spin. "How high do these things go?" I asked.

"Let's find out," he said. Dragging his kite back to earth, he severed the knot at the bridle and tied his string to mine, doubling the line. Up it went, higher and higher, the diamond tugging at the spool, greedy for more freedom, until it was just a yellow fleck against the neon clouds. It's a strange sensation controlling something so far away. Powerful. I knew it was only an illusion—if the wind died suddenly, my kite would plummet—

but that didn't stop my heart from believing it was all me, radiating some invisible force that sent it climbing toward the sun.

"We couldn't have asked for a better day," Scott said to the sky.

It was true. I would've stayed there forever—with the birds and gray stones, surrounded by trees and sun-dazzled water . . . forgetting—but Scott had a bus to catch. I started reeling in the kite—slowly, gently—but then the wind gusted. The spool jumped from my hand. Snatching at the line, my calm evaporated. As I scrambled for the spool bouncing down the shore, my father called, "Don't sweat it! It's only a kite!" But I kept going, my panic spinning out with the line until I reached out and hooked the white vein drifting toward the water. The string raced across my palm, burning my skin, but I couldn't let go. Wincing, I dragged the line, hand over hand, the slack pooling at my feet until Scott ran out and retrieved the spool. The diamond grew bigger and bigger, the plastic snapping loudly in the wind, but then the current shifted and a great *whoosh* flung the kite behind us, out over the trees fencing the shore, where clawing branches threatened to shred the face to pieces.

Angry and sweating, my palms stinging, I surrendered. I opened my fists, but I couldn't watch. Head lowered, I stalked toward Scott, still on his knees, winding the slack around the spool. My dad shook out his blanket and stepped into his shoes. I was about to slip on my sneakers when a powerful flapping drew my eyes skyward. I squeaked like an idiot as the line arching over the shore rose straight up. The yellow diamond smiled down. I smiled back. Scott passed me the spool. After I'd reeled it in, my dad inspected the angry welts bisecting my palms. "You know those kites only cost a couple of bucks?" he asked.

"I have attachment issues," I said.

Scott flicked the back of my head. "Ya think?"

My dad cleaned my burns with an antiseptic wipe from the glove box and then checked his watch. He needed to eat before work, so we headed back to the city, to the drive-in down by the river, the one with the grinning jester and every surface colored in neon yellow. I'd expected an explosion of notifications when we reached civilization, but my phone sat silent. As my dad trolled the lot for a place to park, Scott shook his head at the lines. I didn't mind. I wasn't in any hurry to return to my life.

"One of you go snag a table," my dad said, locking the truck.

I told Scott what I wanted—vanilla soft serve, rainbow sprinkles—and then we split up, our dad making a beeline for the burger stand, Scott charging toward the ice cream window. I grabbed a pile of napkins from the condiment station and wound my way through a Little League team, seeking something that didn't exist: a clean picnic table with an umbrella. Settling for a spot in the shade of the bridge, I waved to my dad. He gave me a thumbs-up. It was better than nothing, even if the benches were sticky with ketchup. I spread out a couple of napkins and plunked down, then put my elbow on the rest of the stack to keep them from blowing away. Squinting against the wind, I stared out at the crowd.

My breath caught.

I gulped.

His hair was a little longer. Still pale. Same white oxford. Same faded jeans. My pulse quickened. Two more faces followed his gaze. Trent and Rachel. My hand shot up before my brain could stop it. Rachel's face brightened until she realized her mistake. Trent flashed me a hard look, dismissing me with his middle finger. I didn't expect Adam to run over and give me a hug, but it stung when he looked through me and turned away. Maybe I never loved him, not like that, but I did miss him, I did care.

"What are you looking at?" Scott asked, thrusting a melting cone in my face.

"Nothing," I said. "I thought it was somebody, but it's not."

I licked around the edge and tried not to watch the three of them horsing around on the riverbank, laughing at something—me, probably—all their gestures a wildly exaggerated pantomime of fun. I knew they were doing it on purpose, but it still hurt. Loneliness tugged at my insides. I turned to Scott. "You're not coming back, are you?" I asked.

My brother gave me a lopsided grin. "To visit? Yes. To live?" He frowned. "Probably not."

I licked faster, round and round, trying to stem the vanilla dripping down my knuckles. The wind blew my hair into my ice cream. My eyes flicked to the riverbank. No one was watching. As Scott was cleaning me up with a napkin, my dad came marching over with a red tray piled with burgers and fries and a giant coffee to keep him awake. He shooed a pigeon strutting beneath the bench and asked, "What's with the long face?"

My eyes drifted to the bank again. It was a mistake. A pixie-cute blonde in big black sunglasses collapsed in Adam's lap. I knew her from school, but only the halls. She's wasn't anybody. I guessed it was better to get it over with—the shock of seeing him with someone else—than have it play out at the lockers on the first day of school. But then Adam caught me staring and stole her sunglasses. He looked so good my face flushed. My dad said something I didn't catch and touched my wrist.

"Are you okay?" he asked. "You're a million miles away."

"I'm fine," I lied, my heart aching fiercely. I focused on my dad devouring his burger and raised what was left of my cone. "Thanks for the ice cream," I said. "And for the kites."

It's absurd to think about snow days when it's eighty degrees and muggy as hell, but the whole afternoon felt like one—a sweet surprise that blasted me out of my ordinary life. I love them—snow days—but I hate them, too, right after dinner, when the slow sadness of reality kicks in. Because tomorrow will come—it always does—and you'll be right back where you started.

That's what I was thinking as I suffered through Adam kissing a girl who wasn't me, and when Scott asked me to keep him posted on Lisa and Katie, and again when my dad pulled up in front of our house. He shifted to park, but he didn't turn off the engine. He wasn't coming in. Scott and I collected our kites and started up the walk, but then my dad called me back to the truck. Leaning in the passenger window, the knocking motor vibrating my insides, I asked, "What's up?"

"Just so you know, I told your mom I'm not going to the reunion." My dad rubbed his eyes, red and tired from being up all night. "I thought about what you said and you're right: she needs her space. I don't know if she'll go, but it won't be me stopping her."

I picked at the rubber window seal, stiff and cracked with age. "Cool," I said. "Thanks." While my dad exchanged waves with our across-the-street neighbors, I stared down at the floor. I'd missed a couple of mints. I popped the door and brushed them into the grass.

"Did you ever get your permit?" my dad asked.

I shrugged. "Yeah. But I've only been out once. Mom says I'm a road hog."

"I'll teach you."

"Really?"

"Yeah, really. Give me a call."

"When?"

"Whenever. Soon." My dad patted the door of the truck like it was a loyal old dog. "I'm thinking of getting something newer. I won't trade this in if you want it."

I looked at him, smiling, and said, "Wait here."

I ran inside to my room and raised the lid on the trunk. Beneath my sweaters and Adam's oxford was the picture I'd sketched, still wrapped from last Christmas. I tore off the paper and unrolled the tube, slumping with disappointment. It wasn't nearly as good as I remembered. Except for the eyes. They were definitely his. Soft and gentle, laugh lines forking from the corners. Rolling it up, I tucked it under my arm and ran back out.

"Happy birthday," I said, passing the tube through the window. "Sorry it's late. I wasn't done. And sorry it's not . . . better."

My dad flattened the stiff paper against the steering wheel and leaned his head back for a better look. "You drew this?" he asked, sounding impressed. He leaned out the window and kissed my nose and then reluctantly checked his watch. If he didn't leave soon, he'd be late for work. Climbing the front stairs, I expected to see my mom peeking around the curtains, staring longingly at my father, but she was in the kitchen with Scott, the two of them laughing about something.

Sometimes things are broken beyond repair. But that doesn't mean you can't make something new out of the pieces.

twenty-seven

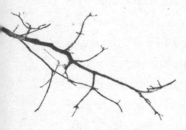

his lawn was the first thing to go, the bright green grass fading to a sickly yellow. My mother thought I was on a health kick—all the walks I was taking—but really it was a sickness that drew me to Larry's house. Two, three, four times a day. I would go there at night, too. I'd see his shambling silhouette moving from room to room, hunched against the cold blue light of the TV. The same sour wish kept pulling me back: to see the police shoving him into a cruiser.

I wanted so badly to text Lisa. *He's gone. Come home.* But that never happened. I texted her when I got my class schedule, but she never responded. She missed the audition, too. She even avoided me in my dreams.

It's weird how quickly a place can look abandoned. All it takes is a week's worth of newspapers piled on the welcome mat, a few cans and wrappers cowering against the fence. Their house no longer stuck out as the nicest on the block. It was an illusion, what Larry had created, like putting makeup on a corpse. Now it looked the part: just one more soulless husk in a stretch devoid of life.

twenty-eight

listening to my mom clunk around the bathroom in her new heels, I tried to imagine my life in thirty years, but I could barely visualize next week. Was Lisa going to contact me before school started, or just show up at the corner like always? Odds were against us walking together. Earlier, while Larry was at work, I'd crept down the driveway and peered in Lisa's window, hoping to find nothing changed. But my hope of everything being the same this next year faded when I saw the blank walls, the bare floor, everything gone except her blue striped mattress sagging against the closet door.

"How do I look?" my mom asked, twirling in the doorway. "Be honest."

I touched my finger to my tongue, then touched the pocket of my shorts and hissed.

"Really? I'm feeling dumpy." She plucked at the arms of her dress and then loosened the belt. "Believe it or not, I used to be skinny. Skinnier than *you*. This is what you have to look forward to."

I'd never really given much thought to Future Me, but a vision of myself as fat and gray, with a husband and a house, doing community theater on the weekends, made me shudder. No point in thinking beyond the present anyway. I'm sure my mom never predicted she'd be going to her reunion with someone other than my dad. And yet there she was, peeking around the curtain every five seconds, waiting for Jim. It was strange seeing her so happy again. She actually giggled when she spotted his car coming down the street. Checking her makeup one last time, she grabbed her clutch and tottered out the door, calling, "Make sure you eat dinner!" and "Don't wait up!"

I don't think it's ever easy seeing your parents with anyone but each other. Watching from the window, I thought it was sweet when Jim jogged around the car and opened her door. I thought it was sweet the way he touched my mother's shoulder and she straightened his tie. I thought it was sweet when his hand trailed down her arm and made the leap to her waist. But my mother leaning forward, eyes closed, lips divided, was a shock. They kissed. The curtain fell. *I* fell, my insides tumbling in gray confusion.

After they drove off, I picked myself up and trudged to the kitchen for something to fill the hollow gnawing. I'd been doing it with Lisa, too. Blaming myself. For her silence. For things that had nothing to do with me. Why wouldn't she respond? Scott had said she needed time. But how much? I sat on my bed and reread the note she'd written me, trying to understand. It wasn't true, the part about me refusing to let her face that storm alone. I wish I'd been that kind of friend. I had followed out of fear. The selfish fear of being left behind.

Wandering the house with a can of chocolate frosting and a

spoon, I kicked myself for ever listening to my brother. Lisa didn't need space. She needed me. Her silence was her message. She expected more from me than a bunch of lame texts.

I was studying the bus schedules—getting to her grandmother's was more complicated than I'd thought—when the doorbell rang. *Lisa.* There I was, trying to figure out how to get to her and she had come to me—our hearts were that perfectly synched—but the hazy shape behind the front door curtain crushed that sentiment. My insides caught fire at the sight of Foley leaning against the porch post. I opened the door but kept the screen between us.

"I hadn't heard from you in a while," he said through the mesh. "I wanted to see how you're holding up."

I shrugged. "I'm okay, I guess."

"How's Lisa? Have you heard anything?"

I shook my head.

Foley frowned. "You probably don't need any more shit to deal with," he said, his face foreshadowing the bad news he was about to deliver. "But Adam's back. I ran into him at a party."

"I know," I said flatly. "I saw him."

Foley shoved his hands in his pockets and hunched his shoulders. More bad news. "He's seeing someone," he said.

When I told him I knew that, too, he looked mildly surprised. I guess my calm threw him. He aimed his thumb over his shoulder and backed down the steps. "If you're fine, then . . . you know . . . I'm around if you need me."

"I don't need you," I said coldly, my heart shutting down. "That must've been somebody else's distress call you heard." I unlocked the screen door and stepped out onto the porch. "Go if you want." I plunked down on the step with my frosting and sighed. "Or stay."

Foley stopped.

"On one condition," I said, leveling the spoon at him. "We're only allowed to talk about stupid stuff. If I catch you trying to dredge my soul, you're leaving. Got it?"

Foley stepped forward. "Can we talk about us?"

"Is it stupid?"

Foley shook his head.

"Then no."

I offered him a mouthful of chocolate. His teeth against the spoon made me shiver.

"So what do you want to talk about?" he asked.

"I don't know." I flicked his earring. "Tell me something you've never told anyone else."

Foley tapped his chin and then tipped his head back, thinking.

"Remember when someone plastered pickle slices all over Trent's car?" he asked.

I did. Bumper to bumper. All those green scabs made it look diseased. It wouldn't have been a big deal except it was winter and the pickles froze.

"That was me."

"No way!" I shoved him and he fell sideways. "You did not! Why?"

"Because he's an asshole."

I rewarded him with more frosting. I even let him hold the spoon. "Tell me something else," I said.

"I don't like to brag, but I once did two hundred push-ups," he said. "Not in a row. In a year."

"Keep going."

Scraping the bottom of the can, he said, "I'm adopted." I rolled my eyes at him. "It's true," he said. "When I was a baby my real mother tried to drown me in a bathtub."

I took the spoon from his hand and put it on the step, then took his hands and held them under my chin. "That's sad," I whispered. "I'm sorry."

"I'm sorry," he said. "That one's a downer. Here's something everybody knows but you—"

A burst of gunfire sent us scrambling for the door. Inside, on the floor, Foley pressed my head to the carpet. "Stay down," he breathed. Maybe it was all the sugar, or Foley's curls tickling my neck, but I started laughing. Another round of explosions sounded out front. Foley gripped me tighter, and then the bitter stink of sulfur hit us. I crawled to the storm door and watched our neighbor's kid kick a smoldering string of firecrackers. I wanted to march across the street and yell at him, but I punched Foley instead. "C'mon," I said. "Let's get out of here."

I think we spend the majority of our days experiencing life through a pinhole, but every once in a while the aperture widens, flooding our senses with electric clarity. There's a shifting—you can feel it—as every cell in your body awakens and you realize you're perfectly present in the moment. I was having one of those moments as Foley and I drifted through shadowy lots, in and out of alleys, aimlessly wandering until Foley pointed to a soda machine glowing brightly beside a vacant building and shouted, "Race you!" and "Loser buys!" Sprinting down the deserted street, I pushed hard to beat him. Maybe he let me win. I don't know. Raising my arms in victory, I spun around, marveling at the rarity of everything: the light. The air. The sidewalk beneath my feet. As Foley fed a dollar into the slot, I gently removed the hoop from his ear and threaded it through my own.

"So what were you about to tell me?" I asked. "Before the little pyro next door scared the crap out of us." I pushed the button for orange, but nothing came out.

"I was going to declare my undying love for you."

"No, really," I said, pushing the button again. I pushed the next button, and the next, every single one. Foley tried, too, and then kicked the machine for stealing his money.

"Do you think we'll ever be more than whatever this is?" he asked, touching the hoop in my ear. His finger trailed down my neck. There it was again—that connection. Like we'd always been together. Like we'd be together always. There was no escaping it. Was it something we created—the two of us together—or was it just Foley? I can't explain it, the power he has to make you believe you're the most important person in his life. Ask anybody. It's not just me.

"It's not complicated," he said softly. "It's either yes or no."

My heart swung back and forth, strangling in its own noose. I stared blankly over his shoulder until he lifted my chin and reached inside me with those eyes, shaking loose whatever was stuck.

"Do you remember the first time we kissed?" I asked.

Foley leaned against the soda machine and pulled me to him. "I was about to ask you out," he said. "But you ran away."

"You were not," I said, wriggling out of his arms. "And I didn't run away."

"You did," he said. "You're always running away."

I reached around his hip and tried all six buttons again. "We're supposed to be keeping it light," I said. "There's still a ban on deep conversation." The guts of the machine clanked loudly, startling us both. A can of something dropped into the black tray. Grape, which wasn't even a selection. I popped the top and offered Foley the first sip, but he shook his head. "I should probably head home," he said. He stepped back unsteadily, as if an invisible hand had him by the collar. "Long story, but I'm grounded. I'm not supposed to be out. I escaped."

"Will I see you before school starts?" I asked.

Foley frowned. "Probably not." Eyes locked on mine, he walked backward, one foot directly behind the other, like he was measuring the distance between us.

"Wait," I called, pulling his earring free. Foley squinted. "You don't want your hole to close," I explained, but he just turned and jogged off, waving as he went.

Foley was right about me running away. I'd forgotten that part. Freezing and giddy, my heart so full of strangeness, I'd *had* to tell Lisa. So I had run off.

I folded my fingers over the silver hoop and followed a restless current toward home, longing for what might be. But nobody can know the future. It's a trick the heart plays to get its own way. It was safe what we had—Foley and I. What I felt was singular and terrifying. Something so deep I could lose myself. Or him. Forever.

It seemed crazy to risk it.

It was dark when I stopped and unclenched my fist. Fastening the hoop through my earlobe, I thought, *One more thing to end up in the bottom of my trunk,* and then froze. That back-of-the-neck tingle like someone was behind me, watching, waiting, but I shook it off. There was nothing to fear. The real monster was in his recliner, watching a baseball game. I knew because he had the volume turned way up, loud enough for me to hear the play-by-play from across the street.

twenty-nine

t was stupid and reckless, but I did it anyway, shrugging off the sinking in my gut as I climbed through Katie's window. My landing was shockingly ungraceful and loud. Not that it mattered. Larry was at work. The ghost of his lunch—hot dogs and coffee—still hung in the air, overpowering any trace of Katie that might've lingered. There was nothing left of her or Lisa. The house was all Larry now. The phone rang and I tripped over Larry's boots. I kicked them under the table and then froze, waiting for the answering machine to pick up. It was still Katie's voice on the message, but it clicked off when whoever was calling hung up. Tiptoeing down the hall toward Lisa's room, I wondered what the hell I was doing. What did I hope to find besides a lumpy mattress and some bobby pins, dust perimeters marking the voids like crime scene chalk? It *was* a crime scene—her room. The sun was shining through the window, but something dark loomed. In a twisted way, I'm one of the lucky ones, I guess. I didn't have to live with Jerrod McKinney. I never worried he was lurking in the shadows, waiting to strike again. After I left Troy, it was over.

The phone rang again—once, twice—but that's not what sent a rush of adrenaline to my arms and legs. In the heightened silence that followed, the unmistakable clicking of key probing lock. Larry. He'd forgotten something. I raced for the upended mattress leaning against the closet and fit myself into the wedge of space. Cowering, my nerves crackled as he stalked around the kitchen. *Stay calm,* I reasoned. *He'll be gone soon.* But then his pace changed. The stalking turned to creeping, like he'd sensed something off. A rippling dread seized my stomach and seeped lower. As he moved from room to room, slowly, methodically— the giant sniffing out the intruder—I choked back a whimper. But then the footfalls ceased. At Lisa's door. A pressure in my bladder swelled. I pinched my eyes shut, bracing for the booming voice.

"Please don't hurt me," I blurted.

It was the same full-body scream from that night at Trent's, only amplified by the echoey room. The softball bat in her grip dropped to the carpet and rolled. Clutching her heart, Lisa let loose a string of curses. "You are so dead, Kolcun!" she shouted, snatching up the bat and advancing.

"Hold that thought," I said, scrabbling out from under the mattress. Unbuttoning my shorts, I ran for the bathroom and slammed the door. Elbows on knees, I sighed heavily, the release deflating me until my phone vibrated. A text bubble from Lisa: *Prepare 2 die.* Out in the hall, her phone chipped with my response: *Drop ur weapon. I surrender.* And then: *Hand sanitizer?* All the nice soap was gone. In its place was that rough stuff

Larry used. I dried my hands on my shorts rather than use his towel.

"What are you doing here?" I asked, swinging the door wide.

"What are *you* doing here?" Lisa countered.

I shrugged. Lisa slit her eyes like she suspected I was keeping something from her. "I swear," I said. "I was wondering the same thing myself."

Bat in hand, Lisa marched toward the kitchen.

"How'd the audition go?" she asked, poking through the snack cupboard.

"I'm pretty sure I bombed," I said. "Why have you been ignoring me?"

Lisa pulled a chip clip from a red-and-yellow bag. "You always think you bombed," she said, crunching a triangle. "And I wasn't ignoring *you*, per se. I haven't talked to anyone. You got D'Angelo for English?"

"Yeah," I said. "You?"

Lisa made a yuck face and spit the chip in the sink. "Don't eat these," she said. "They're stale." And then, like it was no big deal: "I'm supposed to have Richardson, but I'm not going back. I'm transferring to East Glendale."

Maybe it was shock, but my first reaction was anger. She was ruining everything. The kitchen went all blurry and I dropped to the floor, gritting my teeth. "Temporarily, right?" I asked, but I already knew the answer. Lisa stretched above me and swatted at something on the top shelf. A can of mixed nuts fell in my lap. Dropping down beside me, she shrugged and combed through the peanuts for a cashew. "We'll still see each other," she said.

"This sucks," I said. "You know that, right? What about Gabe?"

Lisa touched the heart pendant he'd bought to replace the one she'd lost in the woods. "We broke up," she said. "I broke up with him."

"Why?"

"It was easier than explaining what happened." Lisa dropped her head. "Promise you won't tell anyone," she whispered. "Ever. If anyone asks, just say my mom and Larry split up and we moved. Understand?"

I did. Everyone would think differently about her if they knew. Tragedy does that. It becomes your identity. Like a sign around your neck: I TRIED SUICIDE. I HAVE CANCER. MY FAMILY LIVES IN A VAN. MY STEPFATHER MOLESTED ME.

"This is bullshit," I said. "Why is he still walking around? Why isn't he in jail?"

"It's complicated," she said, picking at her nails. "My grandmother thinks it'll be easier on everyone if I just forget everything that ever happened. Move on. Start over."

"What about your mom?"

Lisa snorted. "My mom doesn't know what to do. She says it's up to me." She grabbed the bat and used it to stand, then stepped over my legs and opened the fridge. "Adult beverage?" she asked.

I raised my eyebrows. We never touched Larry's beer. Ever. Lisa was sure he kept count.

"What's he gonna do?" she said as she tossed the drawer for a bottle opener. "Ground me?"

I wrinkled my nose at the skunky fumes but took a sip anyway. "You're gonna report him, right?" I said. "Your grandmother's wrong. He deserves to rot in jail."

"He deserves worse than jail." Lisa chugged her bottle and opened another. "You must think I'm an idiot," she said. "For believing in him—Banana Man. What happened in the woods . . ." She shook her head sadly. "I wish I could do something." Lisa blew across the top of the bottle, making it whistle. "Part of me knew," she said. "That's why I didn't trust Larry to protect Katie. But then another part of me kept thinking how she's just a kid." She shrugged. "Why would he want her when he had me?"

My stomach curdled at the wrongness of her question. *She* was just a kid.

Lisa checked her phone. "My mom thinks I'm at the mall."

I put down my beer and scooted closer. "Why are you here?"

Lisa's jaw tightened. Her eyes floated toward the ceiling, trying to stanch the tears. I drew my best friend to me and squeezed her tight, but she stiffened. Is it possible to hold someone too close? I knew the rhythm of her heart, her breath, the way her bones felt pressed against mine, but when she pulled away, I realized the person I thought I'd been holding was someone else. We'd never again be as close as we once were. His shadow loomed between us. I don't think I'll ever know what compelled me to break into their house that day, but I knew why Lisa was there. If I'd asked her, she would've denied it. But I knew.

While Lisa dried her eyes, I helped myself to another beer and then hefted the bat, testing its weight. Can two wrongs ever make a right? Maybe. But I doubt it. The thought of protecting Larry felt like a betrayal, but really I was saving Lisa. From herself. From making the biggest mistake of her life. I raised the bat over my shoulder and swung.

The bottle on the counter exploded, raining beer and glass across the kitchen. Lisa yelped, "What the hell!? What the—" But I swung again, aiming for the dishes in the drainer. The tumblers were plastic, but the plates shattered nicely—flowered shards skittered across the tiles. I went after the microwave next, bashing a hole in the door. Woozy but clearheaded, I turned and offered Lisa the bat. A wicked grin split her face. She wanted to start with the fridge.

Orange juice. Milk. Salsa. Larry's special pickles. Everything except the last two beers ended up on the floor and walls. Dripping with back spatter, we sidestepped the broken glass and exploded cartons, and moved on to demolish the rest of the house, shattering mirrors, breaking lamps, overturning everything in sight. Coffee table. Entertainment center. Larry's recliner. I knew someone would call the cops eventually, but I hurried things up by putting a speaker through the front window.

Sitting in the police cruiser, waiting for my mom to come get me, I wondered if Larry would regret not pressing charges, later, when the reality of what he'd narrowly avoided had sunk in. Or would he just be grateful? Grateful that the broken shards weren't his bones or that the sticky mess coating the floor wasn't his blood. Grateful again a few days later that it was the cops hauling him away in cuffs and not a coroner hauling him away in a bag.

thirty

*t*he shack was calling. Lisa was calling. But it was dark and I couldn't see my way. I ran and ran until suddenly the sensor lights blazed, and there it was, with its black tarp roof and carpeted lawn, Lisa beckoning from the doorway. *Where have you been?* The inside was bigger than I remembered. I followed Lisa through a maze of halls to a room with a bricked-up fireplace and a bed and a chair. Katie's and Ryan's cheeks glowed from the cold, but something else made them shiver: a dark cocoon oozing from the shadows. Long gray teeth. Pits for eyes. My knees quaked as he rose up, towering above us, but then Lisa sang softly, gently, and he slumped over, scaly hands reaching blindly for his chair. The yawning holes in his face searched for something. Katie knew. She fetched two blues from the box on the mantel. They shone brightly beneath his waxy lids. But he wanted something else, too. His eyes skimmed the room, landing on a book, thick and ancient and heavier than anything I've ever lifted. I swallowed my fear, and knelt before him, and settled it on his lap. Lisa brought over a lamp. Cross-legged on the bed, Katie and Ryan exchanged nervous glances and squeezed hands. His jagged fingernail lifted the cover. The pages were blank, but he read the white space, his voice rasping gently.

Once upon a time, two girls were lost in the woods . . .

The happy face above my bed fluttered in the dark, waking me. The curtains billowed with an end-of-summer chill. Slipping out of bed to close the window, something cold knocked against my chest. My hands shook as I switched on the light and unfastened the clasp at my neck. The room started spinning. I knew what it was before I saw it: Lisa's gold heart, caked with dirt, the thin chain kinked and rusty. I rushed to the window, but the light behind me made it impossible to see anything except the pink sliver of sky above our neighbor's roof. I clutched the heart tighter, its point piercing my palm. Someone had been in my room. Not the man from the woods. Someone else. Something else. Something bent on perpetuating its existence. I fought the urge to hide the necklace—just crawl back in bed and pretend it was all a dream—because I had to know. I examined my room, searching for signs. My eyes stopped on the black trunk.

Heart thumping, I lifted the lid and dug through layers of old jeans and ugly sweaters, feeling for the cold, hard glass, but my fingers came up empty.

My mom knocked gently. "Hey, Trace," she whispered, poking her towel-wrapped head in the door. "I'm done in the shower if you want to get in there."

The first day of school always fills me with a mix of hope and dread, but that morning something else gripped me as I forced down breakfast and headed out the door, my mother's voice following me down the steps, reminding me to come straight home. It was a half day, but I was grounded. Not so much for trashing the house, but for drinking. My mom doesn't blame me for what I did to Larry's. It got Mrs. Grant's attention. I think Mrs. Grant was thinking like Lisa's grandma: if she closed her eyes, it might all go away. But it doesn't go away. I hate comparing what happened to me to what Lisa went through. But rape is rape. That's what the counselor said during our first meeting.

My phone chirped. Lisa wanted to know if I'd found my way to school without her. *Not yet,* I responded. My head was somewhere else, but my legs crossed the street out of habit. Skirting the shadow of Hillhurst Middle, I watched a pack of girls drag their friend to the curb and point to the woods across the way. There wasn't enough concealer in the world to hide the distress darkening the chosen girl's face. It wasn't just the itchy sweater and stiff jeans, the tender blisters throbbing inside her new shoes. It was the look of not wanting to chicken out on a dare.

"Don't go in there," I said. "He's real. Trust me."

The leader whispered something and everyone laughed. They looked so small, so fragile, but tough, too. They'd survive. We all do. As the girls strutted toward the playground, the spared one, bluffing for her friends, turned and rolled her eyes at me. I didn't care. Fear is good. It keeps us safe. Not always, but it keeps your eyes wide, alert. But sometimes it keeps you from living. It's hard to know which is which. You have to trust your instincts.

Trusting mine, I sprinted across the street and into the tangle of brush. Branches snatched at my face, my arms, my legs, but I pushed on, moving swiftly. I was running late. *Please wait for me,* I thought. At the top of the stairs, I stopped to catch my breath. The back of my knees tingled. It was a long way down, with no one to catch me. The shelter was gone. No ropes cinched the trees. No black tarps sucked up sun. Just a mountain of garbage. Tires and barrels and broken furniture. For the first time in a long time I didn't feel like I was being watched. It was just me, alone.

Clutching the heart at my collar, I plunged forward, down the stairs, through the trees, pulled by something more powerful than fear. My head and heart had called a truce. Fighting my way through the prickly scrub edging the woods, he was right where he'd said he would be, waiting on the other side. I kissed Foley and he kissed me back. We needed to start from the beginning. The beginning beginning.

If I can do this, I thought, *I can do anything.*

FICTION STEWART

Stewart, Barbara.
What we knew

SEAST

R4001649695

SOUTHEAST
Atlanta-Fulton Public Library